With Coffee Spoons

Tabitha Ormiston-Smith

First Printing: 2020

ISBN: 978-0-6485519-7-3

DEDICATION

For Marcus Mellick.

For I have known them all already,
known them all:
Have known the evenings, mornings,
afternoons,
I have measured out my life with coffee
spoons...

The Love Song of J. Alfred
Prufrock

CONTENTS

❧ACKNOWLEDGMENTS☙

First of all, I'd like to thank Garry Day, who gave generously of his time and his experience as a social worker working with the homeless, when I was writing Nowhere But Up.

I'd also like to thank Melissa Herman, who recounted to me the old stories, traditional in her family, on which Norwegian Blue and Uncle Zan's Dog are based.

Jenny and Tamara both contributed a number of true-life anecdotes when I was writing Sophie and the Frog. Due to the nature of the material, I mention only their given names.

Adriano Mantarro added a certain *je ne sais quoi* when he volunteered to be a character in Danse Macabre. I gave him a fictional name, but Adriano also appears under his own name in my novella, Dancing Feet.

Emily and Ferret deserve a mention, of course. They stop me from working too hard or taking myself too seriously. And my wonderful husband. Where would I even start? The love, the support, the encouragement, the belief in me... I am so blessed.

And finally, of course, you, my readers. It is for you that I write.

There comes a time in the life of every married woman when she realises she is completely on her own. For Jenny McCallum, this occurred on a Thursday morning, at three minutes past eleven.

'Bloody, bloody hell,' she fumed, slamming the phone into its rest with excessive force, so that it bounced out again, making that smart-alec beeping sound. She slammed open the refrigerator door and threw in the meat and milk at random, knocking over the milk jug, which gushed forth its creamy treasure in silent protest, all over the freshly-mopped floor and, on the way, all over the inside of the fridge, which would now have to be cleaned out, or it would stink. Jenny knew this from bitter experience. It wasn't the first time she'd knocked over the milk jug. Leave it in the bottle, Greg always said. But the big two-litre containers, once the level got down a bit, were too chancy. The centre of balance shifted too quickly, and instead of delivering a precisely controlled amount of milk into her tea, she'd get a sudden flood, which made it undrinkable. The one-litre cartons, being narrower, were even worse.

Anyway, she fumed. Screw bloody Greg and his bloody logical ways to do everything and above all, screw his bloody, toxic, stuck-up, arrogant, controlling, shitty mother. 'FUCK HER!' she screamed, kicking a box of cornflakes clear across the room, where it came to rest in the washing basket with its cargo of unfolded washing. It was just one of the many things she'd been planning to do on this, her Day Off, the first day off she'd had in weeks. So you'll still be doing it, she tried to comfort herself. But the frantic cleaning marathon now looming was a far cry from the slow, reflective, pottering sort of day she'd been looking forward to. Jenny sank into a chair, put her head down among the toast crumbs and unsorted groceries, and burst into tears.

Outside, on the windowsill, Toadflax flattened his ears and jumped down.

***

There had never been a time, Jenny thought, when there had existed even a tiny possibility that she and Audrey would get on. Right from the first time Greg had taken her to dinner at his parents' house, Audrey had set herself against Jenny in implacable enmity, or that, at any rate, was what it had looked like from the receiving end. Even before they'd got inside the house she'd looked Jenny up and down and sniffed, yes actually sniffed, as if she smelled something bad. 'I suppose you had to come straight from work,' she'd said, ignoring Jenny's outstretched hand, her tone dripping distaste. 'An orderly or something, aren't you?' Jenny, who had been doing her surgical residence at the Alfred Hospital, and who had taken an uncharacteristic two hours getting ready, just to make sure everything was perfect, had shrivelled inside.

And then there had been the thing with the fish. They'd been engaged by that time, although it was only the second time Jenny had seen Greg's parents, having angrily refused every other time Greg had tried to take her to visit them.

They'd been bidden to dinner at eight, and had arrived exactly on time, Greg clutching a large bunch of white carnations. Jenny had dressed with the utmost care, and had had her hair and nails specially done at a salon that day. She wasn't going to be made to feel like gutter trash again.

Inside, they'd sat nervously on the edges of hard, uncomfortable chairs. Everything looked brand new; there were no worn patches on the arms of favourite chairs, no dog-eared paperbacks or incongruous treasures. The whole room might have been taken, all of a piece, from Better Homes and Gardens, and probably had been, Jenny had thought, noticing with interest that Greg wasn't any more relaxed than she was. He'd been all tense the other time they'd come, too, but she'd put that down to nervousness about introducing her to his family.

She'd thought the lasagne smelled off when it was brought in, but, distracted by the cringeworthy Grace Audrey's creepy minister husband insisted on pronouncing, where they all had to hold hands around the table, gamely ploughed into it. Concentrating hard on not reacting to the pointed way Audrey kept asking about the wedding date and staring at her stomach, she had eaten half of it before she identified the strange undertaste. And then it had been too late, because the attack had hit. Full-on anaphylaxis. Luckily she'd had her epi-pen with her.

Greg thought she was paranoid, of course, but Jenny knew what she knew. At the end of the disastrous meal, she'd seized a couple of plates and barged into the kitchen over Audrey's protests, and she'd seen it in the kitchen tidy. An empty can of salmon. It was right on top. Audrey must have added it after Jenny's polite call to make sure she knew about her violent fish allergy. That night, Jenny and Greg had had their first fight.

***

Jenny was recalled to the present by a gentle tapping at the door. Through the screen she could see her next door neighbour, holding a plate of something.

'Hello! I made gingerbread, so I brought you some over. Good for what ails you!'

'Oh, Sophie, thank God. Come in. I really need to vent.'

Handing her the plate, Sophie drifted in and settled in the kitchen, Toadflax, her battered old tomcat, winding round her ankles. 'What's up?' she asked. 'You look stressed.'

Just thinking about it again caused Jenny to bang down the teapot with rather more force than was advisable. 'It's Bloody Audrey. Mangy cow,' she muttered, slamming two mugs onto the table.

'Steady on there, you'll break something. Look, why don't you sit down and relax a bit, and I'll get the tea.' Sophie had risen to her feet and was already moving smoothly about the kitchen, seeming to drift aimlessly but actually getting everything done with remarkable speed. She was always like that, Jenny mused; slow-moving and calm, and yet everything just seemed to fall into place. Kind of the opposite of her, Jenny, on a bad day, when she felt like she was rushing around full bore but somehow not achieving much.

Sophie sat down and poured. 'Milk? Here you go. Yes, Toadflax, I hadn't forgotten you. Here's yours. Alright, now who exactly is Audrey?'

'My mother-in-law.' Jenny stuffed a piece of gingerbread into her mouth and chomped down on it as if it was Audrey's head. 'Mmmm, this is GOOD.' She took another bite, not really wanting, now that she had the opportunity, to dredge it up. Audrey somehow managed to make her feel vaguely ashamed, as if she really were a badly-dressed, incompetent, gold-digging failure that anyone would be ashamed to have in their family.

Sophie sat, poised, confident, a little smile of polite enquiry on her face. You could just tell she'd never had to deal with a mother-in-law, or anything else toxic.

'She's just rung up and invited herself for dinner. Tonight. No notice or anything, just, oh I want to see my son. She acts like I'm some kind of servant. And now I'll have to spend the whole afternoon cleaning, and it's the first day off I've had in three weeks.'

'Cleaning? Why, it looks alright? Ten minutes to straighten up, that's all you need, the house looks lovely.'

'Not for Audrey. She's got this way of sniffing out the one thing that isn't immaculate. Honest to God, she runs her finger along surfaces and sort of looks at it with her eyebrows up. And it always happens to be the one place I forgot to dust. And her god-awful creepy husband, I swear he gives me the total heebie-jeebies, he's like a zombie or something with his eyes that never focus. And they make you hold hands and pray.'

Sophie looked sympathetic and pushed the plate of gingerbread a little closer. 'Well, that's rather rude, but surely it's not the end of the world?'

'And the worst of it is, Greg and I always fight after she's gone. Always. Every single time. It's like she's got some kind of poison that she sprinkles, and it infects him.'

'Are you sure that's not just because you're both getting so tense about her visit?'

'Yes, I bloody am sure. Honestly, Sophie, you can't imagine. Like, she'll make some subtle poisonous remark about my outfit, and then hours later he'll echo it, or the thought behind it, it's like she put some kind of spell on him. Last time she came to dinner I had a red dress on, and she said it reminded her of the one Liza Minelli wore in that movie, and then after they went home Greg said he wished I wouldn't dress like a tart when his mum was coming. I swear. And he loves that dress, he always has. But the minute bloody Audrey gets her hooks into anything, he's like a little puppet boy. And she'll ferret out the one thing in the house that isn't immaculate and make some little remark, and next day he'll be on at me about the state of the house and why I can't keep it nice.'

'But you work longer hours than he does, surely it's his responsibility just as much as yours?'

'Of course it is, and he knows that, and he does do his share, but that all goes by the board the minute bloody Audrey makes one of her remarks. It's like she knows how to push all his buttons, well I suppose she does, but it's like she's trying to split us up.'

'Have you talked to Greg about this?'

'Oh, I've tried, but the minute her name comes up we're back on the same old treadmill. Greg thinks I'm not rational about her, and I'm probably not by now, after everything that's gone on.'

Sophie shook her head in a sympathetic way. Toadflax leapt onto the table and started to drink from the milk jug.

'I don't think I can make you understand what she's like. Honestly, Sophie, she's the bitter end. You know how I had that miscarriage last year? Well she came to see us the week after, and when Greg was out of the room, she said I shouldn't worry about it so much because it had probably been for the best, and that miscarriages were God's way of getting rid of rubbish.'

A little frown had developed between Sophie's eyebrows. 'She doesn't sound very... nice, somehow.' She appeared to reach a decision, and her expression cleared. 'Look, I'll tell you what. I'll help you fix up the house, and I'll come to dinner too. Give you some moral support, kind of thing. She might not be so nasty with a stranger there.'

***

The cleaning marathon, with Sophie's help, didn't take nearly as long as Jenny had expected. In fact, by the time Jenny had finished folding the washing, ironed Greg's shirts and put everything away, there didn't seem to be much to do at all. Sophie was in the living room, plumping up the sofa cushions. Every surface gleamed richly, and the air was redolent with the scent of lavender polish. A huge bunch of chrysanthemums in a cut glass vase adorned the coffee table, nicely positioned towards one end, their lavish disarray giving a sophisticated, painterly touch to the room. The carpet appeared to have been shampooed.

In their bedroom, everything was similarly immaculate, except for Toadflax, who was curled on one pillow, and roused slightly to fix her with a slitted yellow glare. Right then, just the bathroom and kitchen left to do. But in the bathroom, it seemed once again that she'd been pre-empted. All of the porcelain seemed brand new, and the reflections from the chrome fittings were blinding. Matched grass-green towels reflected the colour of a series of maidenhair ferns in graduated sizes which now adorned the windowsill. In a state of shock, Jenny wandered back to the kitchen, where Sophie was humming to herself and wiping down the draining board.

In the few minutes since she'd left the kitchen, it, too, seemed to have undergone a sea change. Surely the floor hadn't been that white before? And she was quite certain the curtains had been more faded than that.

Of all the questions whirling in her head, Jenny gave voice to that which was uppermost.

'Where did those towels come from?'

'Oh, I found them in the back of the linen cupboard. They must have been a wedding present, they were still tied up in a ribbon.'

Jenny decided to go with the flow. She didn't remember receiving any green towels in their wedding presents, but there were more important things to worry about. Like what to make for dinner, for instance.

'Right,' said Sophie, pulling out a chair, which seemed to have been freshly painted. 'What were you going to make for dinner? Actually, why don't you let me cook dinner? You could get out for a nice walk in the sunshine, and then go and have a lie down and a good soak in the bath.'

Jenny shook her head, feeling dizzy. 'I hadn't even thought. Roast lamb, perhaps? Whatever it is, she's bound to criticise it anyway.'

'I tell you what. You just leave it to me.'

'But the shopping...'

'Never you mind all that. Leave me the key and you get out for that walk. It'll do you good to get out in the sunshine.'

***

Some hours later, home from a long, relaxing walk along the Esplanade, Jenny soaked in a steaming, lavender-scented bath (where had that bath oil come from? She didn't remember buying it) and watched Toadflax pick his way between the ferns. Sounds of activity could be heard from the kitchen, but it was calm, quiet, soothing activity, rather than the frenetic scramble she'd expected to be doing at this hour. She had apparently ceded the running of her household to Sophie, and rather than the faint panic she usually felt when anything was taken out of her hands, it was nothing but a blissful relief. Even Audrey seemed very wee and far away just now.

***

Audrey and her husband arrived twenty minutes early, of course. Jenny had expected that. She had known the old bat wouldn't miss an opportunity to catch her half-dressed and hunting for her other shoe. But this time, Jenny opened the door with more confidence than ever before, comfortably aware of Sophie in the kitchen putting the finishing touches to a platter of raw vegetables cut into fantastic shapes and a selection of gourmet cheeses, of Greg relaxing over a cold beer and telling a funny story about his office, of the rich smell of roast duck wafting through the air in a lovely counterpoint to the lavender furniture polish. It was just like a house in a magazine, she thought hazily as she opened the door to reveal Audrey and The Creep. Really, she thought in amusement, could Audrey purse up her lips any more?

Her mouth looked just like a cat's arsehole.

Alerted by the sound of the doorbell, Greg emerged from the kitchen, followed by Sophie, who at some point had managed to nick home, change into a slinky black dress and put up her hair in an elegant French pleat. Audrey's pencilled eyebrows disappeared into her blue-rinsed hair as she registered the extra person. A look of amazed disgust spread over her face, and she swept her gaze up and down Sophie, continuing to stare pointedly at her while greetings were going on. Jenny took this as an opportunity to omit the normally-required cheek kiss.

'And this is our friend, Sophie Green,' Greg went on, as usual oblivious to the undercurrents of scorn and hostility. 'Sophie, my parents, Audrey and Phil.'

'Oh, a friend,' sneered Audrey. 'I thought you must have hired a cleaner. God knows you need one.'

Jenny cringed, but Sophie, fortunately, appeared not to take offence. A happy little smile settled over her face, and she nodded slightly to herself, as if confirming something long suspected.

As they settled in the living room ('Hmmph! I see you haven't got any better at flower arranging. Just shove it in a jar like a two-year-old, that's our Jenny'), for pre-dinner sherry ('Really, Jenny, you don't honestly think decanting that cask muck into a Tio Pepe bottle actually fools anyone, do you?'), Jenny could feel all the happiness draining out of her, all the tension she'd shed during the long, beautiful, let-off-the-hook afternoon swarming back up her spine and settling in the base of her skull. For a few wonderful hours, she had dared to dream that in some way Sophie might be, somehow, a match for Audrey, that Audrey might even in some mysterious way Get Her Come-Uppance. But as the stilted, painful conversation limped on, she realised that had been silly. No one was a match for Audrey. Her vileness was greater than the sum of anything that could be marshalled against her. Sophie didn't, as Jenny had dared to hope, engage with Audrey and send her defeated to her corner. She just sat, smiling quietly, murmuring pleasant nothings, her hands quiet in her lap, watching Audrey with apparent pleasure, as if re-reading a favourite book.

Things didn't get any better over dinner. Most uncharacteristically for her, Sophie, who had insisted on serving the meal, caught her bracelet in Audrey's hair when she was bringing in the vegetables, and yanked out several strands. Audrey spent the rest of the evening pointedly rubbing at her head, to the detriment of her lacquered purple helmet. On hearing that Sophie had cooked the meal ('I might have known you didn't cook it, Jenny. It's not all dried out. When are you going to stop playing at nursing and look after your husband properly? All that rushing about and those strange hours, it's hardly any wonder you can't get pregnant. Although it's probably just as well at your age'), she pointedly shoved her food about on her plate and ate almost nothing. Starve, you bitch, thought Jenny, who was now an emergency surgeon, and who had been longing for a baby ever since she and Greg had got married.

This, however, was as nothing to the performance she put on when she caught sight of Toadflax, who had been quietly resting under the table, and emerged halfway through dinner, frisking about and playing with some small object. 'Eeeek!' she screeched. 'What is that thing?'

Sophie looked mildly surprised. 'It's only Toadflax,' she said.

Audrey had buried her face in her table napkin and was snuffling repulsively. 'Get it away from me,' she moaned through the fabric. 'I'm allergic to cats. Terribly allergic.'

Serve you right, thought Jenny, remembering the salmon, and the very real threat that attack had posed to her life. Suffer, you bitch. The doctor in her noticed, almost without conscious thought, that there seemed to be no reddening of the sclera, as might have been expected with a cat allergy, and also that onset of symptoms had only occurred once Audrey had become aware of Toadflax.

Toadflax was rushing about in little circles, batting at his found object. Sophie stooped and picked him up, along with whatever it was he'd been playing with. 'I'll just take him home, then,' she said. 'I'm so sorry, Audrey, I had no idea you were allergic.' She shifted Toadflax to her shoulder. 'Goodnight, everyone, it was lovely to meet you, Audrey and Phil. I'll see you tomorrow, Jenny. You're on nights this week, right? I'll come over about two.' With that, she was out the door, so smoothly that Jenny hardly registered her departure.

After that, the evening went from bad to worse. Following the departure of Audrey and Phil at eleven thirty, Jenny and Greg rowed far into the night, collapsing into bed for tearful, unsatisfactory make-up sex at four o'clock in the morning.

***

When the doorbell rang at nine, Jenny tumbled out of bed and rushed to open the door without grabbing her dressing gown or even stopping to look at the clock and think how very unlike Sophie it was to be inconsiderate about anyone's schedule. But it wasn't Sophie at the door. It was Audrey, in full battle cry.

***

By the time Sophie arrived as expected, precisely at two o'clock, Jenny was in what her own mother would have called a Right Old State. The beautifully arranged sitting room was no more, having been succeeded by a scene of destruction and mayhem. All the cushions had been pulled off the furniture and tossed anyhow about the room. Books from the now-empty bookshelf were messily piled in one corner. In the dining alcove, dishes from dinner still littered the table, although the cloth hung drunkenly off one end and trailed on the floor. Jenny herself, wearing a tatty bathrobe with her hair standing on end, was on her hands and knees, feeling about under the sofa and crying.

Sophie, who on receiving no answer to the doorbell had simply walked in, sank gracefully onto the carpet and pulled Jenny, gently but firmly, out from under the sofa.

'Now whatever is the matter? Have you lost something?'

Checked in her panic, Jenny burst into a storm of weeping.

Some minutes later, as they sat over a pot of tea in the kitchen, the story emerged.

'It was Audrey. She came over this morning.' Jenny, now completely cried out, spoke in a flat, hopeless monotone.

'Well, that was a bit inconsiderate when she knows you're on night shift, but surely...'

'No, Sophie, she lost her earring. She says she lost it here. And I can't find it...'

'Now come on, don't start crying again. Here, take this.' 'This' was a linen handkerchief, immaculately pressed and smelling faintly of lavender. Jenny clutched it and hunched her shoulders, staring hard at the teapot to hold back her tears. She sniffed, and took a deep breath.

'Apparently it's a one and a half carat diamond, worth an absolute fortune, and, oh, Sophie, she thinks I've stolen it. She said if I don't give it to her when she comes back this afternoon she'll go to the police. Oh God.' She started to cry again.

'But surely... the police won't think you took it.'

'They might when she gets through with them. And Sophie, I'm a doctor, I could be struck off...'

'Don't be ridiculous. No one is getting struck off.'

'She said, she said she'd make sure I was... for dishonesty... she said I was a thieving, gold-digging tramp...'

'Fiddlesticks. Honestly, I really don't see why you're so upset. Anyway, it doesn't matter, this must be it.' She slipped her hand into her pocket and produced a large and flashy diamond stud. 'Toadflax had it on the floor last night, and I picked it up without looking at it. I'm so sorry you've been worried. I'd have brought it over first thing if I'd realised it was valuable. It just looked like cheap costume jewellery to me.'

Jenny took the earring, turning it over wonderingly. It did have rather a Klein's look about it, she thought. Not heavy enough for its size.

'Now, you go and have a nice hot bath and get dressed and I'll tidy up a bit, so she hasn't anything to complain about when she comes back. Did she say what time she was coming?'

'She said three...'

'Yes, well she'll probably be earlier just to catch you in a mess, but we're up to her tricks, aren't we, Toadflax? Go on, off you go.'

***

Emerging forty minutes later, Jenny found the house once more pristine, and

Sophie and Toadflax in possession of the kitchen. Toadflax was drinking a bowl of milk on the kitchen table, and Sophie was taking a tray of scones out of the oven. The rich, warm smell of baking caught in her throat, calling up a memory of her mother. The doorbell chimed, and once again she felt her calm happiness draining away, swirling down and out like used bathwater.

'Now, chin up,' said Sophie. 'Here's the earring. Just give it to her, you don't need to invite her in.'

'Oh, I have to...'

'No,' said Sophie firmly, 'you really don't. Not after the way she behaved this morning. I'm serious, Jenny, this is important. Just give her the earring and close the door. Do not let her cross the threshold.' She took hold of Jenny's shoulders and gave her a little shake, staring into her eyes. 'I'm serious, Jenny. You must not invite her into this house; not today, alright? Promise me you won't. Besides,' she went on, 'Toadflax is here, and she's allergic.'

'Alright.' Jenny squared her shoulders. The doorbell rang again, chiming on and on as the button was held down. Why can't she just press it like a normal person, Jenny wondered. She lifted her chin, marched to the door and flung it open.

Audrey stood, her finger still on the doorbell. Her pursed-up mouth started to open, but Jenny was faster. She shoved the earring at Audrey, forcing her to take a surprised step back.

'Here's your earring, now bugger off, you old bag.'

The last she saw of Audrey, just before the door slammed with a satisfying bang, was her mouth opening and closing in shock, her hands automatically raised to insert the earring.

***

There were currants in the scones, just like Jenny's mother had always made, and as the afternoon drew towards evening and a second pot of tea was made, Jenny felt a lightness that, she realised, had been absent from her for a long time. She'd finally stood up to the old cow. Flushed with happiness, she described Audrey's stunned expression at length to Sophie and Toadflax.

'And the best of it is,' she said, 'I

feel like I've broken her power. I just said, bugger off you old bag, and she was just standing there with her mouth open. It was wonderful! I should have done it ages ago. I honestly feel like I'll never be bothered by her again.'

'No,' said Sophie, smiling her little, calm smile. 'I really don't think you will.'

The front door banged and Greg came in, flushed and cheerful, bearing a huge bunch of yellow roses. He kissed his wife with enthusiasm.

'Here, love, sorry about last night. Oh, hello, Sophie. Dinner was fabulous, thank you so much. You left so quickly I didn't get a chance to say anything. Hey, you like wildlife, don't you, you've got to come and see this, it's the biggest one I've ever seen, just sitting on the doorstep.' He turned back and headed for the front door. 'Come on, come and have a look at him before he moves. I've never seen one this size, have you?'

Jenny froze on his heels as they reached the door. 'Oh, yuk! A huge frog, right up on the porch. I can't stand frogs. I'll get the broom.'

'Oh, don't worry,' said Sophie. 'She's just lost.' She bent and lifted the frog gently in her two hands. The frog let out a loud croak. 'Gregggggg, Greggggg,' it seemed to say. Sophie smiled gently. 'Poor old thing. I'll just put her over here in the grass. She'll soon adjust.'

❧AUTHORISED STAFF ONLY☙

The weather was fine and sunny. But then it always was, under the Show Dome. Corporate interests decreed that no rainy days or sharp winds could be allowed to interfere with showgoers' pleasure.

Barry, Tommo and Russ wandered happily through the crowd. They'd won their tickets by being the top performing shelf-stacking team on the Safeway night shift for three consecutive months. Now, on this, their special day, they were at peace with the world and each other.

'Oy,' said Tommo. 'Lookit that wheel!'

They looked. The Wheel of Death whizzed horridly at a forty-five degree angle, its screaming victims trailing a fringe of waving arms and legs. It was impossible at this distance to tell if the screams were of terror or delight. Perhaps a little of both for most people, Barry thought. A lot of stuff that everyone accepted as being fun, when you boiled it down, wasn't actually that pleasant. Like getting drunk, for example. Where was the fun in puking your guts up in some smelly toilet, he'd like to know.

'Tell you what,' said Russ. 'I wouldn't mind getting into the Premium Enclosure. I heard they've got every pleasure known to man in there. Some that aren't even legal, I heard.'

'Yeah, like what?' asked Tommo, distracted from his fascinated contemplation of the Wheel of Death.

'Oh, I dunno... drugs, underage whores... and weird stuff, stuff that you've never even heard of. That's what I heard.'

'That doesn't seem right,' objected Barry. 'If whoever found that out knew enough to know they had stuff you'd never heard of, then he'd know what it was, and then you'd know, wouldn't you?'

'Ahhh, shut up, clever bastard.' Russ gave him a shove, only half joking. Cleverness wasn't appreciated in working-class Australia. Being a feature of the Boss class, it was generally resented. 'Anyway, the likes of us will never see inside there. Strictly for Bosses only, that be.'

'Tell you what,' said Tommo. 'Let's go in the Sex Tunnel.'

'Later, mate. I want to get some show bags for the missus and the kids.'

'Naah, don't get that now,' Barry objected. 'Get the showbags last thing, before we leave, then you don't have to lug them round all day.'

'Wonder what kind of showbags they've got in the Premium Enclosure? I heard they've got ones with real pearls and diamonds in for the ladies.'

'I bet it's the same overpriced crap as out here.'

'Jeez, Barry, lighten up, willya? This is our special day. Don't be a fuckin misery-guts.'

'Sorry, mate.' Barry rolled his shoulders and resolved to do his best to make it a good day for everyone. 'Hey, did you know the Show used to be all about farm animals?'

'Bullshit.'

''S true. It used to be called the Royal Melbourne Agricultural Show. Back then it was run by the Agricultural Society.'

'The what?'

'It was sort of like a club, for farmers. The exhibits were all cows and sheep and stuff. And exhibitions of cooking and handcrafts and that by the ladies. And then there was contests, anyone could enter. Wood chopping, and they had events on horseback, show jumping, sheep herding, all kinds of stuff. Course, that's back in the days when there was lots of little farms, all owned by families.'

'Crap, how could a family own a farm? That's a multi-million dollar enterprise, that is. Only companies could own a farm.'

'They weren't like farms now. They were smaller and there was lots of them. Farmers used to have cooperatives to sell their produce. It was a different time.'

'How d'you know all this, then?'

'Read it on Wiki. Anyway, after a bit the companies started getting in the game and you got these rides starting, and all the concessions and sideshows and stuff, and gradually it became less about the farm stuff and more about the money, and then of course in 2016, when Abbott the First dissolved the last Parliament, the Agricultural Society was made a proscribed organisation for having subversive aims, and the government took over the show and made it what it is now.'

'Well, that's good.'

'Good?' Barry was appalled. 'What's good about it?'

'Well, like you said, now it's for everyone.'

'It was always for everyone, Tommo. Anyone could just buy a ticket and go. Not like now where you have to win tickets off your Boss. You could just buy a ticket, whenever you felt like it. And nobody could stop you, as long as you had a day off work you just went.'

'No shit?'

'I kid you not, mate. And there wasn't any Premium Enclosure, either. Everything back then was for everybody.'

'Nah, bullshit. I don't believe that.'

'I'm busting for a piss,' Tommo put

in. 'Shouldn't'a had that last tinnie. Where's the bog? Prob'ly in here.' He darted into a plain, unmarked door on the heels of a uniformed worker.

'Aw, shit,' Russ moaned. He'll get lost in there. I don't reckon that's a toilet, look, there's no sign or anything.'

'No worries, Russ. I'll go after him.' Barry shot after Tommo, just managing to catch the door before it swung shut. Tommo was a constant worry with his combination of enthusiastic optimism and subnormal i.q. Barry and Russ were used to having to take care of him everywhere they went.

Inside the door, it was cool, and suddenly quiet as the heavy steel door swung shut, abruptly cutting off all sound from the outside. Barry found himself in a wide, unpainted concrete corridor, stretching off on both sides. There was no sign of Tommo.

He couldn't have gone far in a few seconds, Barry thought, irritated. He raised his voice and called out. 'Tommo! It's not a dunny, mate. Come on back, we'll find you one.' Echoes died slowly away down the concrete tunnels, until silence reigned again. Damn. Which way had he gone?

There was a large blue-painted double door set into the inside wall a short distance down the left-hand corridor. AUTHORISED STAFF ONLY, it said, in large white letters. MAINTENANCE. There were no handles on the door, just a thumbprint sensor on one side. Barry decided to try in the other direction.

Fifty metres or so along the other side of the door he'd come in, there was another set of big doors. These were painted a darker blue. AUTHORISED STAFF ONLY, they said. SECURITY. As well as the thumbprint sensor, a camera jutted out above the door. Ahead, the corridor curved round to the left. It must go all around the building, Barry thought, trying to remember what the building had looked like. He had a vague impression of it being roundish, but that was all – unlike most buildings in the Show Dome, it hadn't been plastered with neon signs and come-here gear, at least not on the side they'd been. He hurried along to be out of sight of the camera. You didn't want to draw the attention of cops. They were just as likely to beat you into a paste for the sheer hell of it. Ever since the police had been exempted from the operation of the Crimes Act, it had been unsafe to draw their notice. And if they hadn't met their terrorist quota that week, well... best not even to think about that. Once, Barry knew from his historical reading, people had asked a policeman if they were lost, but those days were long gone, lost in the unimaginable past, along with things like 'one man one vote' and free public education.

Barry passed a couple more sets of doors, painted green (AUTHORISED STAFF ONLY, ENVIRONMENT) and yellow (AUTHORISED STAFF ONLY, ELECTRICAL), before he finally came to a set that weren't forbiddingly labelled. These doors had glass panels set into them, and a standard handswipe opener. It looked like anyone could go in here. He looked through the glass, and froze in astonishment.

It had to be the Premium Enclosure. Just had to be. The people inside were completely different – jewelled, dressed in exotic fabrics, tall, blond, and with that, Barry didn't know quite what it was, but just that Boss look about them.

Something about the way they moved, it might have been, or the calm way they looked around, as if they'd never had to worry about a police beating or a bad performance report in their lives.

Barry stood staring through the glass for a long time, just looking at everything. A rumble from his stomach finally reminded him of the passage of time, and with a start he remembered that he was supposed to be looking for Tommo. Well, Tommo wouldn't have been able to resist this, he argued with himself. He'd have gone in here for sure. And in his denim jumpsuit he'd stick out like dogs' balls among this mob. He'd have to go in after him, he managed to convince himself, against a sick awareness that he had no business in the Premium Enclosure and if caught would be subject to God knew what penalty. But there was Tommo, poor silly retarded Tommo, wandering around no doubt with his mouth open, and more likely to get himself into strife with every passing moment.

Sucking in a deep breath and squaring his shoulders, Barry swiped the handswipe and passed through the doors.

The first thing he noticed was the

smell. Gone were the traces of sweat, fried foods and popcorn that permeated the outside. Here the air was redolent with some kind of exotic, flowery perfume. As he breathed it in, shivering with pleasure, he felt his heart speed up and his skin tingle with anticipation. He had to, had to... had to discover everything, that was what. He scanned the crowd for Tommo, much easier done here where it was far less crowded, without success. Well, that was that, he'd just have to keep looking until he found him. He drifted to the left, moving with the flow of traffic and trying to stay unobtrusive, although in his plaid shirt, khaki shorts and runners he felt like a janitor in the boardroom. No one seemed to take any notice of him, though, any more than they did outside. People like him, workers, were generally almost invisible to Bosses, unless they wanted something, and that didn't seem to be any different in here.

Over on the other side of the huge enclosure there seemed to be a collection of stalls selling food. Snatches of exotic smells drifted over through gaps in the shifting crowd. Barry moved a bit closer to read the legends above each stall. Lark pies, one said. Premium meat, said another. That was odd, Barry thought. What kind of premium meat? You'd think they'd say, beef, lamb, pork or whatever. It smelled rather like pork, he thought, drifting closer to the big spits. His mouth watered. But he was quite sure he wouldn't be able to afford anything that was on sale in here.

As Barry moved closer to the food stalls, the scent in the air changed to a sharper, tangier scent, and Barry felt a rush of saliva in his mouth and a wave of almost overwhelming hunger. He paused, intrigued. Where did that come from, he wondered. He'd had a pie and some chips not two hours before. Looking up, he noticed a small vent in the ceiling.

Further along was a section full of tables where strange games were being played. It looked like gambling to Barry. A bit like Crown Casino, although without the sad, tired air of despair that people in there always seemed to have. Barry didn't like the Casino, and only went there under protest when dragged by his mates. It was hard enough to make ends meet without gambling, and Barry didn't believe in the big win. He walked briskly past the gaming area, slowing just enough to check that Tommo wasn't there. Big sigh of relief there. Tommo would probably have lost his shirt, and then he and Russ would have had to share their food coupons with him till next payday. It had happened before.

Past the gaming area, the scent in the air changed yet again; now it was heavier, musky. Barry felt his pulse quicken again. It made him think of... he flushed uneasily. There was another little vent in the ceiling, and now he realised. These were mood-altering scents being pumped into the room, each one selected to increase the attraction of whatever items were nearby.

He was now entering an area seemingly dedicated to the pleasures of the flesh. Dotted about were cage dancers, both male and female, mostly in an extreme state of undress. Various curtained entrances advertised forbidden pleasures. Barry didn't know what most of them meant, but could guess; one had pictures of naked children. He shuddered. Were they really... no, couldn't be, he told himself. Young-looking prossies, that was all, depilated and made up to look like kids in a dim light, it must be. Sick, all the same. He dodged to the side as a laughing group of men exited one of the booths, not wanting even to brush against them.

Another booth had a picture of a toilet. What? Shit, he'd bet that was where Tommo had gone, he'd been looking for the dunny. Then he read the printing. Your choice of man, woman, boy or girl would... aw, no. Barry recoiled, almost retching. That was beyond sick.

Barry staggered away, reeling, wanting nothing more than a long, hot shower and a good scrub. He felt dirty just from knowing about stuff like that. He'd settle for a sit down, though, and a good strong cup of tea. He wondered if the Premium Enclosure had anything as plain as tea.

A flock of people in furry animal suits surrounded him. Completely covered in the baggy suits, looking out of their animal masks, they were unrecognisable as to gender. They gambolled and danced around Barry, getting in his way whichever way he turned, linking hands and dancing round and round him, gesturing him towards a section in the far corner which seemed to be sectioned off with ropes and covered with squashy mats. Whatever it was, Barry decided, he didn't want to play. He was here on a mission, and he had to find Tommo and get out, he'd seen enough of how the Bosses amused themselves, enough for a lifetime.

Shoving through the capering fursuits, Barry encountered a solid wall of backs. Boy, there must be something interesting in the next exhibit. By dint of very careful pressing and a lot of patience, he made it through to the front row in just a few minutes. The exhibit was a large one, decorated in sombre shades of brown, and headed with the legend 'CRIME AND PUNISHMENT – CONFESS YOUR SINS'. It was presided over by two nuns, the old-fashioned kind in the black floor-length habits, with no hair showing under their long veils. On one side was what looked like a confessional booth. On the other, a low opening shrouded in black curtains. As Barry watched, a middle-aged man in a conservative suit took his ticket from the booth and mounted a short flight of steps up to the platform. He was taken into the 'confessional' by one of the nuns.

Barry was Catholic, of course – the Religious Freedom Act of 2024 made it a criminal offence not to be – but somehow, he felt, this didn't seem right. Surely this couldn't be real? Apart from anything else, women had been barred from ordination, and from holding any public office, by the Gender Equality Act of 2039. How could they be hearing confessions?

Another 'penitent' mounted the steps and stood waiting. Presently, the first pair emerged and he entered the confessional with the second nun. The first nun led her charge to a tall steel frame on the platform, and waited while he shed his coat and shirt. Fastening his wrists to the upper corners of the frame, she chose a whip from the adjacent rack.

Barry felt a little sick. She was flogging him. It wasn't just play, either; he could see the red lines rising on the man's back with every stroke. Where two lines crossed, a thin trickle of blood started. Meanwhile, the other penitent emerged from the confessional and was conducted to the black curtains. The opening was not high enough to walk in, and he was forced to enter it on hands and knees. As the black curtains gaped open, the interior showed, lit in flickering red. The nun passed through behind him, flashing a glimpse of scarlet garter belt as she hiked up her habit to crawl through. No way could they be real nuns, Barry thought, but still. But still. Then, from beneath the platform, the screams started.

Barry had had enough. He turned away, blindly shoving against the press of humanity, desperate for a breath of air. Once clear, he turned back for a last look. The exit from the thing was behind it, he realised, watching a woman emerge from it. Whatever went on inside there, Barry thought, it couldn't be much fun. She was staggering blindly, caroming off people in her path, her face white and greasy with sweat, her expression a ghastly, fixed stare. As he dithered, torn between offering help and keeping a low profile, she went to her knees, then flopped onto her face and lay still, twitching slightly.

Before Barry could make up his mind to go to her assistance, a team of white-uniformed staff jogged up, carrying a stretcher. Paramedics, Barry saw with relief, wondering who had called them, and how they'd managed to get there so quickly. They loaded the woman onto the stretcher and moved off at the double, vanishing behind a stall selling confections of exotic fruits.

He cast around, wondering which way next. Ahead was a large archway that, oh joy, looked as if it led outside. Barry headed for it without thought, just to breathe some clean air that wasn't infused with God knew what kind of substance.

He came out onto a beach. No shit, Barry thought. There really wasn't any limit, was there, to what you could do with enough money. The sand, the waves rhythmically beating and retreating in little foamy lines. Even the smell of Coppertone in the air, although no doubt that was fake, and being pumped out of little hidden nozzles. Despite knowing it was all fake, Barry felt his shoulders relax, and a smile wreathed unbidden onto his face. He'd always loved the beach. You just couldn't improve on nature, he thought rapturously.

Just when he was contemplating

sitting down right there to enjoy the artificial sunshine and the little artificial breeze that played gently about his face, he saw Tommo.

Tommo was one of a group of people clustered about one of the new genetically modified animals. This one was a dragon; about ten feet tall, sitting up as it was on its haunches, with leathery, bat-like wings flapping about. It couldn't possibly fly with those, Barry thought. The wingspan couldn't be more than twenty feet, tops, and the thing looked like it weighed as much as a cow. Its skin was a uniform pearlised lavender, and it had what looked like emeralds set about its forehead.

There were various other GM animals roaming freely about the beach, Barry now saw, but none was as spectacular as the dragon. There was a group of tallish, well he supposed they were dogs except that they had curly green fur, and some long, low things that might have been based on ferrets before they were grown three feet long and given feathers and little twisted horns. The dragon, though, that was the real deal. Barry couldn't even imagine what had gone into it.

Never mind the dragon, though, he thought. He'd found Tommo, that was the main thing, what he'd come in here to do all those hours ago.

'Tommo, you bastard! Been lookin everywhere for yez, mate.'

'Aw, Barry. Get a load of this dragon! Awesome, innit?'

'Listen, Tommo, we gotta get out of here. This is the Premium Enclosure, we're not supposed to be in here. We get caught, there'll be trouble. It's a bloody miracle we've got away with it this long.'

'Yeah, alright mate... lemme just... oh hey! Lookit that!' And he was away, running down the beach in pursuit of God knew what. Cursing, Barry slogged off after him, his runners filling with sand.

He didn't get far, though. The beach had looked like an ordinary beach from where he'd started, stretching out in a great curve for miles and miles, but this had of course been an illusion, and before he realised what was happening, Barry was jogging in under another (the same?) big arch. He'd lost sight of Tommo, he was dripping with sweat and half mad with thirst, and his shoes were full of sand.

Bugger this for a game, he thought, disgusted. Tommo could bloody well look after himself. Running off like that. He was going to take care of number one for a change. Get himself a drink at least, and then find his way back out to the main dome.

There was another of the padded-floor areas not far away, and Barry headed over to it to sit down and get the sand out of his shoes. There didn't seem to be anyone in occupation. Perhaps he could even take a short nap before heading out. He was feeling terribly sleepy all of a sudden. He flopped down on the nearest mat, which had a pleasantly springy feel and a soft covering, and started to tug at his laces. A warm breeze puffed at him from somewhere, wreathing him with a milky, vanilla scent, at once comforting and oddly familiar. He'd just close his eyes for a few minutes and get his breath back...

***

Barry drifted back into consciousness with a vague sensation of a long time having passed. He was no longer alone on the springy pallet. Surrounding him at very close quarters were the same group of fursuit-clad mimes he'd encountered earlier. Or perhaps different ones; one couldn't recognise anything behind the animal masks. They seemed to be giving him some kind of massage, and he felt as if they'd been doing that for quite some time. Every muscle in his body felt loose and quiescent. How had he not woken immediately, he wondered vaguely, not caring very much. Everything seemed remote, dreamy, as if he were still asleep, and dreaming these gentle, stroking touches...

Wait on, though, a small part of Barry's mind objected. That wasn't quite... that was going a bit too... he struggled to wake himself up. Somehow he'd nodded off again. There was a definite erotic purpose to the furries' actions now. Barry's mind revolted even as his body relaxed further into bliss. They shouldn't be – no, dammit, somehow when he wasn't looking they'd got his shorts off! Barry lurched upright, arms flailing, brain desperately snatching at consciousness. He shook his head, trying to clear away the fog. That bloody vanilla scent, that was what it was. Some kind of thing that sapped the will... He snatched up his discarded shorts and struggled into them, hopping on one leg, and fled incontinent before they could drag him down again. Perverts.

Barry paused to get his breathing under control. He had no idea how much time had passed since he'd come in here, but it felt late, very late. Barry was accustomed to get up at five for his work shift, and he felt as if he were up long past his bedtime. It had seemed to be early afternoon on the artificial beach, but of course that was all artificial, and it would go on being early afternoon right around the clock. He thought it must be long after midnight, though. He was, he now realised, swaying on his feet, and he had that drained, drifting sensation that comes from missing more than one meal. If he didn't get home soon, he'd never make it to work on time, and the boss would dock his pay, perhaps take his whole pay. The Workers' Fair Rights Act of 2018 allowed him to do that.

In a momentary gap in the swirling crowd, Barry caught a glimpse of a security man letting himself out through a glass panelled door. If he could slip out behind him, he'd be back in the concrete tunnel, and he could just go back out the way he came in. He dashed for the door, no longer caring about drawing the attention of security personnel. He'd take his beating if he had to, just to get free of this awful place. He skidded to a halt on the heels of the departing security man, who didn't look round, but as he snatched at the edge of the swinging door, it slammed closed with surprising speed. Barry just managed to snatch his fingers away in time, and watched in despair as the door faded out, not even a faint crack visible. It must have a chameleon circuit, he realised, and those bulky packs hanging off all the service staff's belts had the override. For a wild moment he envisaged clubbing a worker unconscious and stealing his utility belt. But after all, they were just workers like him. Privileged workers probably, Class Eight or even Seven, but workers all the same. Sighing, he turned away, considering his options.

He could find another security man, attempt to explain his predicament, and hope for mercy. Barry shivered. That could be a last resort. He could keep on truckin' and hope for a break. Surely somewhere there must be an exit. All these bosses wouldn't stay forever; there must be an exit somewhere, probably directly out onto the street or the train station. Yes, that would be best. If he kept looking, sticking to the walls, he was bound to come to it sooner or later. After all, the enclosure didn't go on for ever; they'd been right round the outside of this building before.

Yes, that was best, Barry decided, relieved to have a plan of action. He'd grab something to eat, freshen up in the washroom, there had to be one somewhere about, and follow the wall right around until he came to the exit. He couldn't imagine why he hadn't thought of it before. All those weird scents must have muddled his thoughts. Barry normally prided himself on his clear thinking, and was considered shamefully clever by his workmates.

Back in the food court, he looked about, weighing his options. Whatever he got it was bound to be way expensive. He might as well live it up, he decided. Protein was what he needed. Get something solid in his stomach, and he'd feel a lot brighter. He'd try that Premium Meat, whatever it was. Well, once he ate it, he'd know what it was, he supposed. He sidled up to the counter, uncomfortably conscious of his sweaty armpits and no doubt greasy, dishevelled hair.

'Help you, sir?'

'Um, yeah... what is Premium Meat, exactly? What kind of meat, I mean?'

A little ring of silence crystallised around Barry. What had he said? People were looking at him funny, and edging away, leaving a vacant ring around him. The server had backed away from the counter, and was muttering urgently into a communit. Shit. He'd given himself away somehow. Through the crowd he glimpsed a pair of dark blue uniforms heading purposefully his way. Oh shit, shit, double shit. Barry turned and ran.

By the time he staggered to a halt, drenched in sweat, dizzy, breathless and rubbery in the legs, Barry had no idea where he was in relation to where he'd come in. He seemed to have shaken off any pursuit, that was all he cared about. He sank down onto a bench, barely noticing the two women who got up and moved away, expressions of disgust twisting their painted faces, and put his head down between his knees, taking deep breaths and trying to force his whirling thoughts back into order. A faint memory of coming in here in search of Tommo brushed across the surface of his mind, but he shrugged it off. He was concerned with survival now.

As his breathing slowed and the erratic thumping of his heart settled back into a normal rhythm, Barry decided on a course of action. He'd accost the first service worker he saw and just ask the way to the nearest exit. He hoped he wouldn't have to reveal his unlawful entry here, but if forced to, he would confess the whole thing frankly. It no longer mattered to him what penalty he might incur; probably a beating from the SecPols at the very least, he thought, but never mind that. It wouldn't be the first time and no doubt it wouldn't be the last. He could stand a few bruises, if only they'd let him out of this terrible place. And then he'd go straight home, have a hot shower and a strong cup of tea, and hope he could make it into work on time for his shift. A wave of faintness swept over him, and he longed for his tiny, airless apartment with every particle of his soul.

*****

The plan was a good one, or it had seemed to be, but it was unaccountably difficult to put into operation. After what felt like about three hours, Barry, by hanging around the backs of the more complicated-looking exhibits, had spotted seven maintenance workers. But when he tried to get their attention, he seemed to have become invisible and inaudible. Even clutching at the last worker's sleeve hadn't succeeded in getting his attention. The man had just ignored him, looking straight ahead and forging on until Barry's fingers slipped from his sleeve.

The service workers weren't the only ones who seemed not to be able to see him, either. In desperation, Barry had tried to ask a few of the barkers who were calling people in to different attractions. They couldn't see or hear him either, it seemed. It was as if he no longer existed. He could smell himself alright, though, Barry reflected gloomily. If he could at least find a rest room he could clean himself up and get a drink of water. He pinched the back of his hand and watched the telltale slow crawling of the skin. Yes, he was quite badly dehydrated.

There, he'd spotted some more of those health workers in their white suits. They had some poor mug on a stretcher and were jogging towards the inner wall. They'd be going outside, to the sick bay or whatever. He put on as much speed as he could manage and caught up with them just before they reached the invisible door that he knew had to be there. He'd grab onto the edge of the stretcher, he thought, then even if they ignored him in the same weird way that the maintenance chaps had, he'd be able to go with them through the exit. Once he was back in those corridors he'd easily get out. And go home. He was so consumed by the thrill of desire that washed over him at the thought of his greasy little apartment that he almost failed to recognise Tommo.

Tommo, to be fair, Barry thought, was hardly recognisable. He lay still on the stretcher, his face a dirty white, lips faintly tinged with blue.

'Crikey!' Barry blurted out, clutching at the medic's sleeve. Is he gunna be alright? I'm his mate. Listen, I'll come with you. Where are ya taking him?'

But he was still invisible, and his hand fell from the white sleeve as he watched, hurt and shocked, as they carried Tommo away. At the last moment, he lurched forward, snatching at the tail end of the stretcher as it disappeared through the door, but the door whooshed shut in his fact, activating its chameleon circuit and disappearing from view, leaving Barry stranded once more.

At least he knew Tommo was safely out, he comforted himself. He looked bloody crook, but he was in good hands with the ambos, they'd see to him. All he had to worry about now was getting himself home.

This, however, seemed to be easier said than done. Barry tried half-heartedly to accost a couple more stray workers, but he was losing confidence, and it creeped him out the way they seemed not to see him. He didn't dare to try to speak to any of the bosses. Even in extremity, he was too strongly conditioned to keep his place to dare to interfere with one of the privileged.

One long-standing inhibition, though,

he did overcome. Barry made up his mind to ask a policeman.

Having made up his mind to go directly counter to every bit of wisdom he'd ever possessed, however, Barry found there didn't seem to be any SecPols around. He didn't seem to be able to see as well as usual, though. His vision kept blurring, and his heart was pounding like a jackhammer. He felt weak in the knees, almost as if his legs were collapsing, and then, with a dull, distant horror, he realised that they actually were, his knees were giving way and he was subsiding onto the floor in a crumpled heap, and he couldn't cry out in alarm or even care very much because everything was very far away and in fact was receding down a dark tunnel.

He roused as his shoulders were lifted, and opened his eyes to see an angel. Well, not an actual angel, with wings and that, he thought muzzily, but it might as well have been. As the white-uniformed workers surrounded him, he closed his eyes in bliss. It was all over, he was safe, he was going home, he'd been rescued. Tears of relief and gratitude formed in the corners of his eyes, and he let them spill over as the stretcher lifted and started to move.

He opened his eyes again as he heard the door whoosh closed. They were back in the wide concrete passage, moving at a fair clip back the way he'd come that morning. Or yesterday, or whenever. He recognised, with a surge of happiness more usually conferred on a long-lost lover, the big yellow doors (AUTHORISED STAFF ONLY. ELECTRICAL), then the green ones (AUTHORISED STAFF ONLY. ENVIRONMENT), the dark blue (AUTHORISED STAFF ONLY. SECURITY) and finally the lighter blue, the first ones he'd seen (AUTHORISED STAFF ONLY. MAINTENANCE).

The workers kept going in the same direction. Round a corner, down a longer, narrower corridor, at the end of which a single pair of white-painted doors filled the entire width of the end of the passage. Soon, Barry gloated, he'd be sucking up the rehydration fluids and energy pills, and then he'd be on his way, going home at last, forever grateful to these wonderful, wonderful men and women, who worked so tirelessly to save him and others like him, just as it said on the propaverts.

And then he registered the writing, starkly black against the white doors, and he tried to sit up but he couldn't, and he tried to roll off the stretcher but nothing seemed to be working, and he cried out then but nothing emerged from his parched throat except a strangled croak, and as the white-coated workers jogged silently through the double doors he saw the light shining off gleaming stainless steel surfaces.

AUTHORISED STAFF ONLY

KITCHEN

☙THE TROUBLE WITH KNICKERS☙

The trouble with knickers, Graeme thought, was that they were always getting in the way. Sexy underwear was all very well, but in the cramped back seat it was nothing but a liability, especially right now, when he was preparing to celebrate his tenth wedding anniversary in the time-honoured manner of loving couples everywhere.

Danni was not being much help. She was otherwise occupied, and he wouldn't have had it any other way. The tiny part of Graeme's brain not fully engaged in the moment chewed at the complex spatio-temporal problem. If he could just shift a little *that* way, he could – ahh! The offending garment came free, and was tossed over his shoulder and instantly forgotten. As he buried himself in his wife's perfumed warmth, just before the rational part of his mind shut down entirely, it occurred to him that his life was perfect; there was nothing, nothing at all, that he would change.

Graeme Parker was Living The Dream.

***

Of course, he mused as they lay entwined, sweat drying in post-coital bliss, there *was* the partnership. Being made a full partner in his firm, a goal towards which he had been working ever since he'd joined the firm eleven years ago, a wet-behind-the-ears articled clerk, would be the cherry on top of the rich sundae that was his life.

It was practically in the bag, though, he was sure of that. On Monday, he'd be picking up old Bartrop, the senior partner and the firm's CEO, to carpool to the office. Again he blessed the impulse decision that had led them to buy the shambolic old house on the Esplanade. It had been a struggle in the early years, but somehow they'd managed the payments, and now, not only did they own a prime piece of real estate in one of Melbourne's most livable suburbs, with ocean views and just three minutes' walk to the beach, but he was well placed to take advantage of old Bartrop's carpool invitation. If they'd bought the place in Carlton that he'd been so taken with, he'd have been unfeasibly far away from the Bartrops' residence in Caulfield. At the time, he'd acceded to Danni's preference just because she was Danni, and deserved, he felt, everything good in life, but like most of her suggestions, it had also turned out to his advantage; she had an instinct for things, he felt, a kind of sixth sense for exactly where to step on the blindfold path of life. More and more, as they settled into their life together, he had fallen into the habit of relying on her judgement more than he did on his own.

The carpool invitation, Graeme believed, was a sure indication that he was in line for the coveted partnership. No doubt old Bartrop would be sussing him out on their drives, checking out his politics and family background to see if they were sufficiently conservative and wealthy for a partner in one of Melbourne's oldest firms. He'd have to be careful not to reveal his own humble origins. Not that there was anything wrong with Dad, but a socialist plumber probably wasn't going to have Bartrop fainting with ecstasy. You could tell he was a major snob by the way he dropped names, and that he was far to the right of the political spectrum by the kind of names he dropped. He wouldn't lie, but he'd have to hedge a bit. Maybe say Dad had been in property development. That was safe enough, because there was a lot of money in property development, and it was a kind of development, wasn't it, when you installed a tap?

***

Graeme was on top of the world as he drew up outside the wrought-iron gates of Old Bartrop's pretentious house. He 'bipped' once on the horn, and sat, mindlessly watching some ibis in the formal front garden. It had rained during the night, and they were poking their beaks into the lawn, finding, he supposed, worms or insects. He sat, comfortably full of the English breakfast Danni had made, every muscle in his body relaxed from their pre-breakfast activities. What a woman, he congratulated himself. He allowed his mind to drift back to Saturday night. How she had surprised him! It had been their tenth anniversary, and when she'd told him, the week before, that she was planning a surprise, and that he should leave the arrangements to her, he'd been expecting something lavishly conventional, and her reconstruction of their first, teenaged date, lovingly perfect in every detail, had blown him away.

Here came Bartrop now. He glanced at his watch. He'd been waiting for twenty minutes. He suppressed a snort as Bartrop caught sight of the birds and rushed at them, brandishing his briefcase and shouting 'get off my lawn, you fuckers.' Mustn't be seen laughing. Should he leap out of the car to open the passenger door? No, he decided, buggered if he would. He wasn't going to act like some obedient flunky. He settled back in his seat and reached for the ignition, and then, as Bartrop bent to open the door, a flash of scarlet caught his eye. Danni's knickers from Saturday night, draped across the dashboard.

There was no time for anything fancy; Bartrop was even now opening the door and sliding into the car. He grabbed the knickers and stuffed them into his coat pocket, praying the old man hadn't seen anything.

****

Things weren't going as smoothly as he'd hoped. Graeme squirmed in his seat and surreptitiously crossed his fingers as he told yet another almost-lie. George Bartrop, Q.C., seemed to be trying to justify his silk as he conducted what felt like, what in fact was, a ruthless cross-examination. Now, he asked the unanswerable question: what clubs did Graeme's father belong to?

'Well,' said Graeme, breaking into a sweat, 'the MCC, of course.' No need to mention that the initials actually stood for Mordialloc Canine Club. 'And then…' it was no good. His imagination had gone on strike, had, in fact, done a runner, chased away from his mind by sheer panic.

He was saved by the traffic, which suddenly opened up, finally giving him a shot at turning onto St Kilda Road. There wasn't really time; the lights were already amber, but by planting his foot he just managed it before they turned red. This apparently triggered Bartrop's ever-present Car Boasting Syndrome, so that he held forth about his new Porsche for the remaining few blocks. By the time they got in the lift, which triggered another subject change in Bartrop's mind and turned the conversation to the current caseload, Graeme's breathing was almost normal again, and he managed to talk convincingly about his big litigation matter until they reached the eleventh floor, at which time Bartrop apparently lost all interest in a mere associate and swanned off to his corner office without bothering to say 'goodbye' or 'thank you', or to respond to the receptionist's cheerful 'Good morning, Mr Bartrop.'

His secretary, Deborah, was doing filing in his office. 'Morning, Deborah,' he said, carefully enunciating the name; the one time he'd called her 'Debbie' she'd chucked a hissy and sulked for a week. She was a large, big-boned woman, who dressed and styled her hair as if she were channelling Audrey fforbes-Hamilton, while failing to realise that there was any behavioural component to appearing upper-class.

Graeme flopped into his chair and pulled out his handkerchief to wipe his brow, which still felt unpleasantly clammy after his ride of interrogation. His shirt was sticking to him, too, and he wondered if he might be coming down with a fever; the handkerchief felt oddly scratchy against his forehead, and by the way Deborah was staring at him, he must be pale, flushed or both. Perhaps she'd be nicer to him because of it. He essayed a tentative cough, hoping for relays of hot Lemsip and a reduction in the volume of her braying voice. 'Think I'm coming down with something,' he said, wincing as she banged the file drawer.

'Huh!' she snorted. '*Going* down with something's more like it.' She stamped out of the office, banging the door as if offended. Graeme didn't see why she should be offended, but Deborah was perpetually taking offence at some imagined slight to her dignity; it was her favourite thing. Best not to get into it, or he'd get bogged down in some huffy, cross-purposes dialogue. Right, no Lemsip then. Sadly, he opened the filing cabinet and took out the Fraser file.

***

Deborah was enraged. After all the effort she'd put in on Graeme, now he was having an affair *with someone else*. It wasn't his infidelity that bothered her; that, to her, was a given. But it was supposed to be she, Deborah Wilson, to whom he would turn; she had had it all planned out, down to every detail. She *deserved* him; all the evenings she'd cheerfully stayed back to finish his correspondence, the patient way she'd accepted his constant corrections to her punctuation, redoing the letters without a word of complaint even though she *knew* double quotes were for emphasis. She had mined everything he said, every bit of casual conversation she could get from him or overhear, for clues to his interests, and had spent countless evenings looking up operas on Youtube, and googling for what the intelligent people were saying about them.

She knew, of course, that he was married, had even met Danni several times when she'd called in to the office, but that didn't matter; Danni, she felt, wasn't *real* in the way that she, Deborah, was real. She wasn't even *white*. Deborah thought all brown people should go back where they had come from, and should stop taking people's jobs and claiming social security benefits. Danni, therefore, was disposable, and would quietly disappear after the divorce, leaving her to walk triumphantly down the aisle with Bartrop and Winston's new Commercial Law partner.

And now, the ungrateful bastard was having it away with some other woman. After she'd gone to *all that trouble*. It just wasn't fair. She wanted to scream and punch someone. Instead, she picked up the phone. People should know what kind of sleazebag they were working with. Especially the girls. It was practically a *duty* to warn them.

***

'Bartrop and Winst– oh, hi, Deb.'
'Got time for a coffee? I've got some *amazing* news.'

***

'No way!'
'Yes, he is! He absolutely is!'
'But he's so nice! I can't believe it!

Did he *tell* you?'

'Not as such, but listen, Louise, he was looking frazzled when he got in this morning, and he took out his hanky to wipe his forehead, you know how he does, he can't bear perspiration, only it wasn't a hanky. Get this! It was a pair of *knickers*!'

'Get out! He couldn't have!'

'Well, he did, they were in his coat pocket, I suppose he thought he was grabbing his hanky.'

Louise shook her head. 'They must be his wife's ones.'

Deborah snorted. 'Oh sure, because men always carry around a pair of their wife's knickers. Besides, these weren't wife knickers. They were *mistress* knickers.'

'What d'you mean, mistress knickers? You're losing it, Deb. You're imagining things.'

'Look Graeme's thirty-four, right? I never forget because he's the same age as me,' said Deborah, mentally subtracting twelve years. 'And they just had their tenth wedding anniversary. He told me that on Friday, that it was their tenth and they were having a special night out.'

'Well there you go, then. They get hot and heavy on the dance floor, they go for a romantic walk in the moonlight, and Bob's your uncle.'

Deborah shook her head. 'I know him better than anyone. He confides in me, Louise. They've been having some problems. A *lot* of problems. They've been married for ten years and the gloss is off the cake.' She was not *lying*, she told herself. Not as such. She *knew* it to be the case; she just didn't have the concrete evidence. She seized on the one piece of evidence she did have. 'He had lunch with Steph on Friday.' Stephanie Miles was the head of the Family Law department.

'So what? They always go to lunch. At least once a month. They've been friends forever.'

Deborah shook her head, a pitying expression on her face. 'You're young, Louise. This time was *different*.'

***

Silly old cow, thought Louise as she scuttled back to Reception, uncomfortably aware that her ten minute break had stretched to fifteen. Got a bee in her bonnet as usual. As if nice Mr Parker would ever. Bet she wishes it was her. Here came Kylie, she'd get a laugh out of it.

'Hey Kylie!' She waved her friend over. 'You won't believe what that silly bitch Deborah is on about. Reckons Mr Parker's having an affair!'

'Yeah, like she'd know.'

'Get this – she reckons he had a pair of knickers in his pocket!'

'No way!'

'Yes way! She totally said that!'

Kylie shook her head. 'How does she know what's in his pockets? She copping a feel or what?'

'Yuk, gross! Don't be disgusting.'

'Come on, Lou, she's had the hots for him forever, the way she carries on, batting her eyelashes and spraying on scent whenever she's going into his office. You're lucky you're out here, it practically chokes me sometimes, reckon she must have no sense of smell. She's such a desperado.'

'Well anyway, she reckons he goes to get his hanky and out falls a pair of knickers.'

'Huh. He's probably one of those

cross dressing people, or a fetishist or something. Yeah, a fetishist, and he carries them round in his pocket and feels them all day. Sick fucker.'

***

'Hey, Jan!'

'What? Here, give me a hand with this box, will you?'

'God, that's heavy. What is all this crap?'

'Files for archiving. I have to go through them, copy all the original documents and send the originals back to the client, close the file and then it goes down to the vault. So boring.'

'Well listen to this. Mr Parker's a pervert!'

'What? What sort of pervert?'

'He steals girls' knickers and sniffs them. Dirty old perve.'

'Oh my God!'

***

'Lisa! Guess what?'

'I dunno, what?'

'You know Mr Parker, in Commercial Litigation?'

'Yeah, course.'

'He's a child molester.'

'What? No way.'

'Yep, he's got a record as long as your arm apparently.'

'But he's been working here forever.'

'Yeah well, I don't suppose he does it in business hours.'

'Holy shit!'

***

It was not until that evening that Graeme, emptying his pockets preparatory to hanging up his coat, came across Danni's knickers. The reminder of their wild night brought a glow of happiness, and he wandered back down to the kitchen, where Danni was preparing dinner.

'Look what I found, love,' he said.

'Oh!' Danni laughed. 'I wondered what happened to those. Where were they?'

'On the car dashboard. I nearly came a cropper because of them, too.'

'How's that, then?'

She handed him a glass of red wine, and he savoured his first sip, breathing in with pleasure the scent of garlic and onions gently browning in the pan.

'Well, they were right up behind the

steering wheel, and I didn't see them till right when old Bartrop was getting into the car. I shoved them in my pocket, he didn't see anything, but I reckon I lost a life.'

'Oh my God! Imagine if he'd seen them! You'd probably have missed out on the partnership, for Moral Turpitude.'

'Oh well,' laughed Graeme. 'I suppose every cloud has a silver lining. At least I'd have the turpitude to look forward to.'

***

Immersed in the Fraser matter, an immense litigation involving multiple apartment buildings and a quantum in excess of eighteen million dollars, Graeme did not notice anything amiss in his interactions with staff at Bartrop and Winston until Thursday afternoon, when Deborah entered his office.

'Mr Bartrop wants to see you.' Her pursed lips and cold glare didn't ring any alarm bells; she'd been in a mood all week. Probably menopause, he'd thought when he'd first noticed. She was about that age, wasn't she?

'Okay, well tell him I'll pop round in

half an hour, okay? Just in the middle of something. And if you could hold my calls.' He turned back to the file.

'He said now.'

Something in her tone sounded off, and he looked up, surprised. 'Did he say what it's about?'

'No.' She turned and marched out, her ample backside radiating hostility. Graeme allowed himself a moment to dream of a pleasant, cheerful secretary with a happy home life, who didn't have moods and knew what to do with an apostrophe and how to spell 'possession', before he wandered down the hall to see what old Bartrop wanted.

***

As soon as he got into Bartrop's office, he knew something was wrong. Bartrop didn't get up to greet him, hardly glanced up, in fact, from the papers in front of him.

'Sit down, Parker. Close the door.'

Graeme felt his stomach sink. Something was very wrong. Doors were only closed if someone was going to be told off. Also, Bartrop had his coat on. You put on your coat to see clients or lawyers from other firms; everyone wore shirtsleeves the rest of the time. He fought an impulse surreptitiously to fold down his cuffs. When you were caught wrong-footed, always best to brazen it out. Therefore, he closed the door, and with a light and jaunty step he trod the vast expanse of carpet to Bartrop's huge, antique desk, and arranged himself in one of the visitor's chairs in an attitude that he hoped suggested carefree, yet alert, repose.

A long silence ensued, during which Bartrop stared penetratingly at him while somehow managing not to meet his eyes. Graeme gazed blandly back. It was Negotiation 101 – if you couldn't handle a bit of a silence, you were dead in the water. Yet as the minutes wore on (seconds, it's only seconds, he reminded himself, it always seems much longer than it is), the pressure to speak, to ask what the trouble was, even to start babbling, mounted to an almost unbearable pitch. He could feel the first faint dampness of sweat on his forehead, and inwardly cursed his inability to control the process. Whatever you do, he urged himself, do not get out your hanky and wipe your forehead. He probably can't see anything, so don't draw his attention to it, or he'll know he's got you on the run. Should he shift into a more ostensibly relaxed position? No, don't move at all. Any movement in one of these silences looks like squirming. Above all, keep your hands and feet still. He allowed his eyes to unfocus; that helped the appearance of relaxation.

At last, Bartrop spoke, after clearing his throat in what was no doubt meant to be a portentous manner. A flash of irritation stabbed at Graeme. Could the man not just say what was on his mind, without all this posturing? Silly old fart.

'Some very disturbing information has come to my attention,' said Bartrop, in tones of the utmost gravity.

'Yes?' responded Graeme, raising his eyebrows and allowing himself a slight smile. He was conscious of nothing with which he could be reproached. The Fraser matter was progressing satisfactorily, as were all of his other matters, he had entered his timesheet information conscientiously at the end of every day this week, nothing out of the ordinary had come up. He'd even checked the recent

High Court judgements that morning, verifying that no startling development had eventuated that might derail any of his litigations.

'How long have you been working for this firm, Parker?' asked Bartrop.

'Not counting articles? Ten years next month, isn't it?' He knew it was; the subject had been raised by Bartrop quite recently, had in fact been mentioned in the very conversation in which he had started to hint about the possibility of a partnership.

'And in that time, Parker, has it never occurred to you that there was anything you should have disclosed?'

Graeme was at sea. Whatever it was obviously wasn't something recent. Disclosed? It wasn't a term that was ever used of anything good. His profession required him to disclose events that could bear on his fitness to practise: criminal convictions, mental illness and so on. He'd never had anything like that. Even when he'd applied for admission, where he had been required to disclose any such matter in his past, all he had had to declare had been a single traffic fine and a few parking tickets. Anyway, he knew he was on firm ground here; his life had been exemplary, without even any questionable sexual conduct, since he and Danni had started dating in high school and subsequently married. He was Mr Clean.

'No, it hasn't.'

Bartrop was now shaking his head sadly, as if in disappointment. What an old ham he was.

'Well, I must say I'm disappointed, Parker. I had hoped you'd own to it like a man.'

'What? Own to what? I have no idea what you're talking about.'

'I am referring to your conviction for paedophilia.'

Adrenaline slammed into Graeme's core, so hard that it felt like a physical impact. He was aware that his jaw had dropped, but for a moment he was blind, deaf, immobilised by shock, unable even to perform the simple action of closing his mouth. And in the ensuing moments, he watched helpless, from a small, dark, inner chamber of his mind, as the blood rose to his face, as he flushed, he knew from bitter experience, bright scarlet, and saw the smug satisfaction spread over the senior partner's face, saw him start nodding to himself as the blush confirmed whatever the hell he thought he knew.

It was all downhill from there. Nothing he said had any effect. In vain did he rant ('how fucking dare you!'), in vain suggest, demand, that they run the police check, which he knew would squash whatever vile story Bartrop had heard. In vain he demanded to be told who had accused him. Everything was met with the same closed face.

In the end, Bartrop heaved a deep sigh, and said, 'well, I don't know what we can do. You'd better take the rest of the week off. Go home and sort yourself out, and we'll talk on Monday.'

'Sort *what* out,' screamed Graeme, by this time making no attempt to control his rage. 'There's nothing to fucking *sort* out! I am not a fucking rock spider!' But Bartrop only shook his head, managing at the same time to convey both pity and distaste, and gestured towards the door.

The silence in the outer office was profound as he walked the Walk of Shame back to his office. It was a tableau, nothing moving, every face turned his way. His shouted protests must have been easily audible out here, perhaps even out in Reception. As he tidied away his work and shut down his computer, he noticed his pot plant was dead.

***

'Danni? Could you come home?'

'Graeme? What's wrong, what happened? Are you hurt? Are you sick?'

'Yes, no, I don't know. Please come home.'

***

He was hunched at the kitchen table, face in his hands, when she barrelled in the back door. At least there were no visible signs of injury, and the slight dizziness that always plagued her at times of stress faded a little.

'Graeme? What's wrong, what is it?' His shoulders, when she touched him, were like granite. She pulled a chair around the corner of the kitchen table and sat next to him, dropping her bag on the floor. 'Tell me, sweetheart. Did you get some bad news? What?' She pulled his hands away from his face, leaning over to get right in front of him. 'For God's sake, Graeme, what's wrong? I blew off a meeting with the Hedley people.

Whatever it is, we can fix it, but you have to *tell* me.'

She'd never seen him like this, such a picture of frozen misery. He wasn't meeting her eyes. Was it something he was ashamed of? That was silly. Her Graeme, her solid, dependable, upright Graeme, who never even parked in a permit space, couldn't have done anything to be ashamed of. Not on purpose, anyway.

'Did you screw up at work?' she offered, tentatively.

His face worked, and his voice, when it came, was a hoarse croak. 'Danni. Listen, you know me, right? You know I'm not a bad person, well I might be a bit of a jerk sometimes, but I'm not *evil*, right? I'd never hurt a child.'

It all started to make a horrible sense. Her stomach filled with ice. 'Graeme, did you have an accident in the car? Did you hit someone?'

His eyes met hers for the first time, in blank amazement. 'No, of course not. Why would you think that?'

'Well, you said, hurt a child... I don't know, I thought perhaps you'd hit a kid... if it ran out in front... look, can't you just tell me what's the matter?'

'It's not true, Danni, you have to believe me. Look, you can run a police check, I'll give you an authority…'

'Graeme!' She thought she might scream with frustration. 'You're not making sense. I'm your wife, why would I be getting a police check, for God's sake?'

He dropped his head back into his hands, mumbling something, and she pulled his hands away again, perhaps with a little more force than was necessary, and grabbed his head, forcing him to look at her.

'Just. Tell. Me.'

He heaved a great sigh. 'Promise you won't believe it?'

'Believe *what*, for Chrissake?'

He sat up and squared his shoulders, obviously fighting for composure. 'Bartrop called me to his office today.'

'Oh my God, did you lose your job? Sweetie, we'll manage, it'll be okay.' She was making enough now to support them both, if it came to that.

'I don't know. Probably, I suppose. He told me to take the rest of the week off while he "thinks about things." That's a pretty clear sign I'll be getting the boot, I guess.'

At last, she was getting somewhere. 'Did he say why?'

Another sigh. 'Yes, Danni, he did.'

'And?' She couldn't imagine what could make them want to get rid of solid, dependable Graeme.

'Danni, he thinks I'm a paedophile.'

She couldn't move, couldn't speak, could not even think, so great was the shock, so unexpected. She was conscious of time passing, of seconds ticking away as she sat, her mouth hanging open, trying to get her mind around the monstrousness of it. Poor, poor Graeme. Her inability to have children had been a great sorrow to him; the eldest of five children himself, he had grown up in a large, close family, had helped with the youngest ones. She felt sick; she might, she thought, throw up.

'How could he,' she got out. 'Why? Is he crazy?'

'Nah. Stupid, maybe. He's past it, really. He's well into his seventies, but he won't retire. Spends all day sucking up to the property group clients, going out to lunch, gossiping with the secretaries.

Believes anything. I mean, he spent ten grand on some ugly piece of shit done in automotive spray paint for the front office. The management consultant told him it would appreciate. Probably did it himself in his garage. Stuff like that, you know? Gullible, but I don't think he's actually insane. Never seen him eat bugs or anything like that.'

'Graeme, for heaven's sake. Mad people don't all go round eating insects. Anyway, you have to talk to him. Find out why he thinks that. What exactly did he say?'

'Well, he asked me how long I'd been with the firm, and I said ten years, and he said didn't I think there was anything I should have disclosed, and I said no, and he starts shaking his head and going I'm very disappointed in you, Parker, I hoped you'd own up like a man, and shit like that. When I asked him what the fuck he was on about, he said, your conviction for paedophilia.'

'Conviction! Well, then, that's easily sorted, isn't it? Those things are all public record, you know that better than me. You run a police check, it comes up clean, Bartrop apologises humbly, end of problem!'

'Danni. Don't you think I said all that? He wouldn't even listen. He's convinced he "knows." He wouldn't even listen when I told him to run a police check.'

'But that's not, not rational. I mean, someone tells you something like that, you want to check, don't you? And it's so easy to.'

'I know, right? It's not like I didn't try.'

'Graeme. What aren't you telling me?'

He looked away.

'Graeme? Did you lose your temper?'

'Course not. Well, maybe, a bit. You would too, something like that. Jesus, Danni.'

'What did you say?'

'Nothing bad, honest. Well, I might have said fuck a few times. And I might have called him a senile old buffoon. But that's pretty mild. In the circumstances.'

Yes, she thought. In the circumstances, it was.

'What am I gonna do, Danni?'

It hurt her to see him so helpless.

He'd always been a do-it-yourself kind of guy, confident and able to turn his hand to anything, brought up by his tradie dad with a 'Can we fix it? Yes we can!' kind of approach to life, especially in situations that called for tools. They'd saved a fortune on their renovations because of it.

'We'll think of something,' she said, wrapping him in a hug.

It was the first time she'd ever lied to him.

***

The seventh time Danni checked the time on her phone, it was after three, and she gave up on sleeping and slid quietly out of bed. Graeme was dead to the world, and the longer he stayed that way the better, she thought; the first sleep after something really bad gave you your first bit of distance from the event, and she believed that the length of it would influence how you bounced back.

In the kitchen, she closed the door before starting the coffee machine; it was noisy enough to wake the dead. She shivered in her plush dressing-gown and turned up the heat; although it was late spring, the mornings were still chilly. Outside, the world was still dark and silent.

All through the long, uncomfortable night, she had failed to come up with anything. The problem was, she thought as she hunted out her favourite mug, that she didn't really know *what* the problem was. Why the old man suddenly got such an idea into his head. Sure, he was probably senile – the lack of logic in his thinking that Graeme had described suggested that it was quite a strong probability – but there still had to have been something to trigger his delusion.

If she knew the basic *nature* of the problem, she thought, she might at least have a chance of solving it. Danni was, had always been, a Fixer; it was her basic nature, and her ability to turn things around and make them come out right had taken her from extreme popularity with other girls in her school days, through extreme popularity with both genders at university, and to a senior management role in the city's leading public relations firm. 'Feets, don't fail me now,' she muttered to herself as she settled herself at the kitchen table with a big mug of espresso.

She had already got all the information she could out of Graeme; there was no point questioning him any further; he'd already told her everything he knew, and returning to the subject would only distress him. She fished around in her handbag for the notebook and pen she always carried. 'Right,' she muttered to herself. 'Let's bring some order to the situation.' B thinks G is a pedo, she wrote. WHY?

Everything had been alright when he'd gone off to work on Monday, she was sure of that. He'd been laughing after work, what was it now, he'd come in while she was starting dinner… that was right, he'd found her knickers in the car. And he'd stuffed them in his pocket in the nick of time before Bartrop saw them. Or thought he had. What if Bartrop actually had seen them as he furtively shoved them in his pocket? But surely there wouldn't be any association between having some knickers in his car and being one of *those*? She huffed with frustration. She felt she was on the verge of something, but there was no way a normal person would jump to such a conclusion. Having a stray pair of knickers cluttering up your dashboard was just too far away from being a child molester. The two things had nothing in common.

No, wait, she murmured. They did both have to do with sexuality, however normal the one and perverse the other. That was a connection, however tenuous. She closed her eyes and let her mind drift in the free association that produced all her best solutions. People thought she was so clever, always coming up with a solution or the perfect spin to put on a thing, but it was more of a wild talent; she never really felt in control of the process.

Danni pillowed her head on her arms and let her thoughts drift away over a dark sea of memories. Scraps floated into her awareness, and she considered each one, turning it over for a connection, letting it go. Time passed, and she became dimly aware of the calls of early morning birds. There were six degrees of separation, she had once heard. Everyone was connected to everyone else in the world by only six removes. It was a comforting thought, if true, but then there was no way it could be tested. Still, the thought pleased her, although it wasn't quite right, not quite what she needed, not yet, and she tucked it into the side of her mind for later consideration. She felt a quickening, a mental warmth; she was on the right track now, she thought. Careful now, relax, don't strain… the memory of a childhood game floated to the surface. Chinese whispers. You whispered something into one person's ear, and they repeated it, and on and on, and presently the last person had to say it out loud. It was always wildly, ridiculously wrong. That thought had the glow that told her it was the key to what she sought.

She sat up, scrubbing at her face and raking a hand through the tangles of her long hair. She knew, now, how it might have happened, had almost certainly happened. Someone must have seen the knickers; he'd probably taken them out of his pocket by mistake for his hanky, not realising his error, anyway someone had seen them, and that someone had told someone else, the someone else had recounted it, perhaps with a little embellishment, and a dozen or so embroidered retellings later, there was her husband with a criminal record for the most hateful crime in the book. So terribly sad, she thought, so unnecessary. How many of the world's crimes had had their roots in gossip? Well, there was no use moaning over it. Now she had to find a way to fix it. She gave herself a little shake and prepared to face the day.

***

Google is your friend, thought Danni a few hours later. She had half an hour before she needed to prepare for her meeting with the advertising agency. She buzzed her secretary.

'Hold my calls for a bit, would you please, Martin?'

'Sure thing, D. Want me to bring you in a coffee?'

'That would be lovely, thanks.'

She started with the single name, Bartrop. She was looking for connections; anything that stuck out from the mass, anything she could catch hold of and build on. Danni worked this way, surfing the net without preconceptions or expectations as far as she was able, letting her highly-developed intuition have full reign. Later on, if needed, she could reverse-engineer a logical justification for her conclusions. This time, of course, that wouldn't be needed.

Bartrop came up on the first page of results, in a biography site. Good – she had his full name and his wife's name and maiden name too. An auspicious beginning, she told herself as she jotted it down. George Hamilton Bartrop, born 7th April, 1960. Jennifer Mary Bartrop, born 15th June, 1963.

Martin bustled in with her coffee. 'Here you go, and I got you a Danish to go with it. Apricot, your favourite. You look tired this morning.'

Bless the man! It was almost as if he could read minds. She took a huge bite and entered 'Jennifer Bartrop', hitting the Enter key with a flourish. Hello! Mrs Bartrop had a surprisingly large footprint. She clicked on the first result, and was rewarded with a photograph of a sharp-featured blonde in spectacles, standing with an enormous dog. The page seemed to be from some kind of dog organisation, and was chiefly concerned with a list of the dog's achievements. Mrs Bartrop was listed as the contact, and a link took her to the Member record. So, she was a dog breeder, then.

Danni knew almost nothing about dogs; they hadn't come much in her way. She was more of a cat person, herself, although working the long hours they both did, they'd never had an animal of any kind. It was obvious, though, that Mrs B was dead keen on it, and had been at it a long time too; the page said she had started breeding dogs in 1996. The Royal Melbourne and Royal Adelaide shows were both mentioned, as were the Sydney and Canberra Royal shows. She must travel all over the country showing her dogs. Danni wondered how she fitted them in the car.

By the time Martin buzzed her to say the advertising people had arrived, Danni had a rough plan of action. It was going to require some sacrifice, but it was Graeme, after all.

She left the office at lunchtime, after spending another hour on her research, and drove slowly back to St Kilda. She knew where the op shop was, because she always dropped off a couple of bags full after her twice-yearly wardrobe purges. This time, however, she was bent on acquisition.

She could, of course, have afforded

to buy what she wanted new, but the trouble with that was that new things always *looked* new. No, this was the best way to create the look she needed.

***

It was freezing, and the ground was a muddy morass. Danni shivered in her scratchy wool duffel coat. Perhaps the old-fashioned thing had been a bit over the top, but it was just like the one she'd seen a picture of Jennifer Bartrop wearing, and she was certainly glad of the warmth.

Despite the early hour, the ground was packed with little square tents. It made Danni think of mediaeval scenes, with knights in the lists. The dogs, when she found them, contributed to the general air, looking as if they had stepped out of an old tapestry. They were even larger than she had realised, seen in the flesh, and a small part of her quailed. 'Hell with that,' she muttered to herself. She was doing this for Graeme.

She spotted Jennifer Bartrop in a double-sized tent right at the edge of the ring, which despite its name was a square, marked out by painted lines on the grass.

Sauntering casually past, she glanced inside – and yes, there they were, in a wire corral sort of arrangement: the litter of puppies she'd seen on Mrs B's Facebook page. If they even *were* puppies; they looked to Danni to be as big as any normal dog should be. And here came Mrs Bartrop herself, flanked by two enormous dogs, the taller of which came up to Danni's chest.

'Hello!' the older woman greeted her cheerfully. Despite the early-morning chill and the thin drizzle of rain that had now started, she seemed in high spirits. 'Admiring my puppies?'

'Yes,' agreed Danni. 'It's my dream, you see. To have a Deerhound. Ever since I read The Talisman, as a child.' Her research had been extremely thorough, and she'd downloaded the book and skimmed it the previous night, enough to get all the bits about the dog, anyway.

'Really? Have you had hounds before?'

'Not *myself.* But my uncle, back in Sri Lanka, had a wolfhound.' *Careful*, she admonished herself. *Don't dig yourself into a hole.* 'That is, I'm not sure he was actually a purebred one.' There, that couldn't be checked. Danni didn't actually remember anything about Sri Lanka, since her family had left there when she had been a baby. 'But he was such a sweetheart. But it's a Deerhound,' she went on, 'that I really want. They're special.'

'Oh yes, they are indeed.'

There followed two hours of an interrogation that would have done credit to the Spanish Inquisition, covering Danni's lifestyle, her family situation, her experience with dogs, the layout of her house, her fences, and her position on desexing, interspersed from time to time with requests that Danni hold a dog, pass a grooming tool, or fill up the puppies' water bowl. Mrs Bartrop seemed to regard any person with idle hands as a ready-made assistant, and Danni was glad for the breaks from the questions.

By the time the call went out from the ring steward, as Danni now knew him to be – 'Can I have the Open Dogs please, Open Dogs to the collecting area,' Danni felt as wrung out as if she'd done a five kilometre run.

'Shit!' said Jenny.'Here, you hold Sapper while I find his show lead.' She disappeared to the back of the tent, where she could be heard rummaging about and quietly swearing. Danni looked at the dog. The dog looked back. His eyes bored into hers, and she felt a moment of extreme doubt. Could she really be contemplating sharing her living space with a creature that was going to grow to this size? But Graeme. Perhaps once everything was sorted, she could say she'd made a mistake and give the puppy back. Yes, that would be the thing. She could say her work had changed its policy and she could no longer work from home, as she had told Jenny she was able to do. It hadn't been a lie, exactly. All the company really cared about was results, and as long as she could go on getting the results they needed, she could pretty well do as she liked. Martin could take care of things at the office.

Her train of thought was abruptly derailed as Sapper lunged forward and covered her face with tiny, whiskery kisses. Danni jerked back and overbalanced on the folding stool, letting out a startled cry as she fell.

'Sapper! Get off her at once!' He had followed her down, and was continuing his ministrations, at the same time making a loud, singing kind of noise. 'You okay? He likes you,' said Jenny, satisfaction colouring her voice. She slipped a tiny lead, which didn't look as if it could restrain a gnat, over Sapper's head and removed his other one. 'Come on Sap, show time!'

She had a brief respite while Jenny was in the ring with Sapper. She watched, entranced, as the huge dog's stride lengthened into a long, floating gait that, she thought, could hardly be described as a trot. So smooth, so level was his movement that if she hadn't been able to see his feet, she might have thought him on wheels. There were three dogs in the ring, and as they came out, Jenny in the lead with Sapper, she saw with surprise that Jenny tucked the blue ribbon she'd won back into the box on the steward's table.

'Didn't you want your ribbon?' she asked, perplexed.

'Oh no! It's just a place ribbon, I've won thousands of them. Some people chuck them out, but it's best to give it back. Helps the club keep their expenses down, you know, they can keep reusing them.'

Danni was silent, wondering about the frame of mind that could work so hard to win a thing and then not want the thing itself.

'Anyway,' said Jenny, 'Sapper's obviously made up his mind in no uncertain terms. This lot's all spoken for, but if you'd like to put your name down for a pup, you can have one from my next litter.'

***

It was in some ways an ideal solution, Danni thought as she drove home. She'd made friends with the woman, and she could manufacture plenty of excuses, she was sure, to continue seeing her. She could just go to more dog shows, she supposed. They were mostly at the weekends. And this way she didn't need to get an actual puppy.

She found Graeme up a ladder, cleaning out the gutters. Although it felt as if the day had gone on forever, it was not yet four. Looking around at the tiny, manicured front lawn, the shining windows and his car in the driveway gleaming with fresh polish, she realised he'd resorted to his comfort activity, the handyman tasks he'd learned as a boy from his father.

'I'm home!' she called to him.

He descended the ladder in a rush, grabbing her in a hug. 'Where were you? You were gone when I woke up.'

'Looking for a solution,' she told him. 'I think we can fix this.'

He laughed ruefully, and shook his head. 'The old man rang this morning. I'm on indefinite leave without pay.' He spread his arms dramatically. 'Woman, behold your toy boy.'

'What – they can't just do that. Can they?'

'In theory, no. But what am I gunna do, Danni? I force the issue, they fire me. Then what? I've just got to, I dunno, ride it out somehow. Maybe when the old sod calms down a bit I can talk to him, reason with him, I mean a conviction that doesn't exist, that's so easy to confirm.'

'What about the Law Institute?' Danni had only the haziest notion of what the Institute was for, but it sounded powerful. 'Hey, what about the Fair Work Ombudsman?'

He sighed, a long, mournful sigh. 'I involve them, it's immediately an adversarial situation. Once that happens, I've got no future with the firm anyway.'

'Yeah. Yeah. Look, maybe it's for the best.'

'For the best? What the fuck d'you mean, for the best? Everything I've worked for, for the last ten years, is running down the drain, Danni. This'll be the end of me if I can't work it out. What other firm is going to want to hire me, if I get sacked for something like this?'

'But any other firm's going to be willing to run a police check, surely? Or you could get one yourself and give it to them. Without silly old Bartrop in the equation, it's a non-event, isn't it?'

'Danni. This is the legal profession we're talking about. It *runs* on gossip. The odd dark hint to a couple of people, that's all it would take. It'd be all round Melbourne before lunch. The only reason it probably isn't already is that I'm still working there. Nominally, at least. Bartrop's going to keep quiet as long as his firm's involved. The minute I left, you could forget that.'

Danni sighed and wrapped him in a

hug. She didn't like to tell him she had a fix underway. It could go wrong, it might not work out, and she felt, in a shadowy, unarticulated way, that if she said anything, she might jinx it.

***

They were having dinner when the phone rang, pushing spaghetti messily around plates, pretending to each other that they were eating, and at the harsh, intrusive sound they both froze, heads lifting, eyes meeting in panicked surmise.

'I'll get it,' said Graeme, shoving back his chair.

'No, let me,' said Danni. She couldn't bear the naked hope in his eyes, and turned quickly away. It wasn't going to be old Bartrop at this time of night; it was almost nine. 'It's probably just a telemarketer.' But she hurried out to the kitchen, anyway.

'Hello,' she said, already poised to hang up. It would be click click, and someone who could hardly speak English, but pretended to be called Patrick or John, asking for the owner of the house. Or perhaps it would be the ATO demanding an Itunes gift card. Either a beggar or a scammer, not that there was really any difference. If you lied to get something, it was a scam even if the asking was legitimate. She shied away from considering how this applied to her own actions today.

'Hello, is that Danni? It's Jenny Bartrop,' said a faint voice. Danni nearly dropped the phone, snatching it back to her ear.

'Jenny! How are you? Exhausted, I bet,' she said, going automatically into charm mode, while her brain spun its wheels trying to catch up. What on earth could the woman want at this time of night? They'd only parted at three o'clock.

'Exhausted? Oh, no – it was just a small show. I'm used to it. No bother. No, the reason I rang you, I just had a call from Denis Paterson, he was having a boy, you know, and he's broken his hip and going to be in rehab for God knows how long. So, thing is, there's one spare now.'

'One spare…' what on earth was she talking about? And then it dropped. 'Oh, my God – a puppy?'

'Yes, if you want him. You do want

him, don't you?'

Danni couldn't think, couldn't speak. The development was so shockingly unexpected. It had all seemed so safe, off in the future, and now here she was, well and truly on the spot.

'You mean right now?' she asked, knowing the question was a stupid one but buying herself a few seconds to think.

'Well, he's ready to go. The others are all going this week.'

Damn. 'I'll have to talk to my husband. Could I call you back?' There, that was safe – she'd have the option of making Graeme the bad guy if she decided to say no.

***

As she walked slowly back to the dining room, though, a horrible thought struck her. The whole point of the exercise, after all, was to use Jenny to influence her husband. To do that, Graeme, when mentioned, had to be a figure of shining goodness – not a wicked, puppy-denying sort of person. Spending the day with Jenny Bartrop had been enough to show her that the woman lived for her dogs, and like all people with a consuming interest, was quite, quite one-eyed about them. She was going to have to suck it up and get a puppy, and she was going to have to convince Graeme to accept it.

She crept up behind him and wrapped her arms around his neck. 'Graeme,' she murmured. 'I wanted to ask you something.'

'Anything for you, Danni, you know that.'

'Well…' she came around the table and sat facing him, leaning forward, elbows each side of her plate. 'You know how I couldn't have a baby, right?'

He took her hand across the table. 'Yeah, course I know.'

'See, I still have this… I want a child, so badly. I think about it all the time, so I wondered…'

'You want to have another go at adopting?'

'No, that was already a wash-out, remember? They won't consider you if you're both working full-time. No, but I was thinking – we could get a puppy. Wouldn't that be lovely?'

His face lit with the first smile she'd seen on him all evening. 'For sure!

Maybe a Heeler. They're a great little dog. Or a bull terrier.'

Tradies' dogs, she thought. Of course, he'd grown up with them. His father always took his dog in the ute with him.

'Well, I was thinking of something a bit more… Graeme, I want a Deerhound.'

'A what? What's that? Something like a Dachshund?'

'Well, sort of.' She crossed mental fingers. 'A bit bigger. Not so short in the legs.' It wasn't really a lie. Not as such.

'Do you want to go down the Lost Dogs tomorrow, see if they've got one? Or the Lort Smith?'

'Well, actually I know someone who's got a litter of puppies. And I can get one, a boy.'

'Who's that? Someone from work?'

'Sort of.' It was, really – Jenny Bartrop was, after all, connected with Graeme's work. Don't ask any more questions, she mentally begged him. Just say yes.

'So what's this puppy going to cost? It might not be the time for extra expenses, you know, Danni. What with me not working.'

Her heart ached to see his downcast expression. He actually seemed to shrink, his shoulders pulling in. She squeezed his hand. 'Don't be like that, Grae, that's not the way to think. We're going to sort this, it'll all be over and you'll look back and laugh. Just keep on living, that's the way. A puppy will give us something positive to focus on, it goes into the future, you know? And he'll be company for you while I'm at work.' She was starting to convince herself, she realised. Now she wanted the puppy, she realised, wanted it badly, just as she'd wanted a baby for so many years. 'So, are you okay with that? Can I ring her and tell her we'll take the puppy?'

'How much is it going to cost?'

'They're cheap, only a thousand dollars.'

'What? We could get one from a shelter for probably a couple of hundred, already desexed and everything.'

'It's a pure-bred pedigreed puppy, Graeme, a thousand isn't expensive. One of our clients was bragging about her new puppy the other day, she paid two and a half thousand and it's not even a breed, it's just a mongrel, she called it a shitzoodle, said it was a "designer dog". A thousand's dead cheap, really.'

'Well, okay, if you want it that badly, go ahead.' He shook his head fondly, humouring her.

***

Danni's stomach jumped with nerves as she pulled up outside the Bartrops' pretentious house on Monday morning. Look at that formal garden, she marvelled. How the hell do they stop the dogs from digging holes in it?

Her question was answered when Jenny Bartrop answered her pretentious doorbell (the opening bars of the 1812 overture, chimed out in Avon tones) and led her down a long passage to a massive enclosed verandah that ran all along the back of the house. The big room seemed full of dogs, heaving with them; everywhere you looked there was a dog, sprawled on sofas, trotting over to investigate the newcomer, and a rolling wave of puppies scampered about, competing for possession of a battered-looking stuffed toy.

'That's your one,' said Jenny, pointing. 'The one with the teddy.' She tried to imagine the puppy as hers, and could not. It was overwhelming, and when three huge dogs crowded round her and one stood on his hind legs to wrap his paws around her neck, it was all she could do to keep her feet.

'Get down, Sapper,' said Jenny. 'Go on, get down, you wicked thing.' Sapper complied, rather slowly, and leaned heavily against her hip, twisting his long neck to gaze up at her. 'He's really taken to you! Come on in the kitchen, I just made a pot of coffee.'

The kitchen was beautiful, an oasis of peace. Danni sat at a big, scrubbed pine table and looked about at the white woodwork, the granite counters, the copper-bottomed saucepans in a wall rack, the blue and white curtains. She was sure she'd seen a kitchen just like this in Home Beautiful. The mug Jenny set before her was large and yellow, the bright yellow of an egg yolk. It was all inexpressibly comfortable, and although everything was clearly expensive as hell, it reminded her of her mother's kitchen, and a hard lump rose in her throat. How wonderful it would have been to sit at her mother's table and just let it all go, let go of the burdens, the responsibilities, and be a cosseted child again. She was so tired, so very tired. And there was Graeme, in trouble and depending on her to make things right, even though he didn't know she was. And they might well lose their house; she wasn't really all that sure she could manage the mortgage on her own.

'Here, have a biscuit.' Jenny pushed a plate across the table. 'Just out of the oven, they're still warm.'

They were Anzacs, just like the ones Graeme's mother always made, and the last touch of homeliness undid her. She set the biscuit – it was indeed still warm, and smelled heavenly – on the table and started to cry. Stop it, stop it, part of her mind screamed, it's too soon, she hasn't even sold you the puppy yet, you're going to blow everything, but she couldn't stop.

'My dear, whatever is the matter?' Jenny sat down opposite her. 'What is it?'

The kindness in her voice was the last straw, and Danni watched in horror from the back of her mind as it all came tumbling out, Graeme's trouble, her worry about losing the house, everything. Thank God, she managed to refrain from mentioning the firm's name; her duplicity was not exposed, not yet, anyway. 'I thought – I thought the puppy would be a comfort. Someone to love… I can't have children, you see. But I don't know if we're going to be able to keep the house…' And, as she realised she might not be taking home the puppy after all, something in her broke, and she dropped her head to her arms and howled her grief at the loss, the children she would never bear, the comfortable life she would lose, and worst of all, the prospect of seeing Graeme lose everything he'd worked so hard for and slide into despair. And all of it was her fault. After all, they'd been her knickers. And it came to her that if she hadn't had that bright idea of recreating their first date, the situation would never even have arisen.

The room was very quiet, now. She lifted her head, finally cried out, to find an empty room. No doubt Mrs Bartrop was completely disgusted with her. She'd probably gone to phone the police to get the mad woman out of her house.

The woman who presently bustled back into the room, however, was bearing a box of tissues and a packet of aspirin. 'Here you go, dear. Have a good blow, and I'll get you an aspirin. Crying always gives me a headache, so I expect you've got one.' She didn't give Danni a chance to reply, but carried on talking as she drew chilled water from a gadget in the refrigerator door. 'That boss of your husband's sounds a complete tosser. What on earth kind of person carries on like that? Have you met him?'

Here it came. 'No, I haven't – all the firm's social things are staff only, they don't invite partners, not even for the Christmas party. So I haven't really met anyone except a couple of the lawyers that Graeme's friendly with.'

'Oh, it's a law firm? Well, if things don't work out, maybe he could go to Bartrop and Winston. That's my husband's firm, you know. He's the CEO, so I'm sure he could find a place for Graeme. What kind of law does he do?'

Danni could only stare at her. It was crunch time, and she was unprepared.

'Oh, my God,' she blurted. 'You're *that* Bartrop.' She knew all the horror she felt was written on her face. 'That's Graeme's firm.' There, it was out. Now she'd get thrown out.

'What, do you mean my George?'

Jenny's face had taken on a look of iron, of closed anger that made Danni's stomach lurch. She braced herself for the outburst. There was nothing so daunting to face as an angry woman defending her husband. 'We'll see about this!'

She had made a terrible mistake. She fumbled for some words of apology, but for once, Danni Parker was at a loss. The kindly, easy-going woman with whom she had established, she felt, a certain rapport was gone, replaced by this tiger of wrath. She gathered up her handbag and started to get out of her chair, but a hand on her shoulder pressed her firmly down.

'Don't you go anywhere! You can listen.' She reached for the telephone on the wall and punched in a single digit; speed dial, Danni thought numbly. She couldn't bear to listen; she had, she now saw, ruined everything, destroyed whatever chance there might have been for the old man to come to his senses.

'Yes, good morning, Louise. Jenny Bartrop here. I'd like to speak to my husband, please. She listened for a few seconds. 'Is he? Well, get him out.' Another brief pause. 'Now, Louise.' The iron tone admitted of no answer. 'Help yourself to more coffee, dear,' she went on in a normal tone, as though continuing the same conversation. 'You look as though you need it. Ah, George. You've been a Naughty Boy again, haven't you?' A brief pause. 'I am talking about that nice young Graeme Parker, George.' Another pause. 'Nonsense, George. What utter rubbish.'

Even from across the kitchen, Danni could hear the overly fast speech at the other end of the line. Someone was making excuses; she recognised the frantic sound.

'George…' It was almost a growl, and she heard the other end soften into what almost sounded like whining.

'George! I'm warning you!'

The other end was almost pleading, now. Danni marvelled at the effect of just a few words. Graeme had spoken of this man as fearsome, implacable, yet what she was hearing sounded like a child who'd been caught with his hand in the cookie jar.

'I don't care. You should have thought of that before. Now, what are you going to do?'

More frantic gabbling. Danni was on

the edge of her seat now, unabashedly enjoying the performance. She didn't know how, but somehow she'd managed to enlist this woman on her side, and it was very, very clear that it was the winning side.

'I should think so, and what else?'

Whining again.

'Nonsense, George. You are to apologise to him, and moreover, you are to address the gossip problem in your office. I can't think what those people are doing all day, to invent such rubbish. And get that partnership thing sorted immediately. And,' she added with a note of spite, as one who twisted the knife in the wound, 'you'd better give him a pay rise.'

A brief silence.

'Right now, George. As soon as I get off the phone. Or,' she finished, 'Else.'

And she hung up with a flourish. 'There, now,' she said, dusting off her hands. 'You won't have any more trouble. Now, come and see your new puppy.'

***

Graeme was on his back under his

car when they got home. She called to him, softly so as not to startle him; last time, he'd had a black eye for weeks.

'Graeme? Come and see what I've got!' She sat down on the driveway, arms full of warm, wriggly puppy. Even at nine weeks, he was big enough to overflow her lap.

'Hey! It's a bit bigger than I thought. Weren't you going to get a little puppy?'

'This *is* a little puppy, Graeme. I told you they were bigger than a Dachshund.'

'A lot bigger! Well, hello, little guy! Holy Dooley, look at the size of those feet! I hope to God we can afford to feed him.'

'Oh, I think we'll manage. Is that the phone? I expect it's for you.'

She carried the puppy to the gate, shutting it carefully before she set him down, and then she sat on the tiny lawn and watched him investigating their front yard, rushing busily about, his ridiculously long tail thrashing behind him. It was so long that it dragged on the ground when at rest. He'd grow into it, she supposed.

How tired she was! It was only eleven, yet she felt she'd lived a week already that morning. Here came Graeme now, walking slowly, but as he drew closer, she saw that he was smiling, a joyous, carefree smile that did her good to see.

'That was Old Bartrop on the phone,' he said, in tones of wonder. 'Danni, he *apologised*! I've never known him to apologise for anything before, he's an arrogant sod normally. And he wants me to come straight back tomorrow. And the time off's on full pay. And get this – he's having the papers drawn up and making me a partner! I just don't believe it!'

'Well, that's good, he's come to his senses,' said Danni. She didn't say anything else. Least said, soonest mended. 'I'm so pleased, darling.'

Graeme watched the puppy digging a hole in his lawn. He still couldn't quite take it in; the leap from despair to elation had been too fast to encompass all at once. Reinstated! The coveted partnership his! He slid an arm around his wife and sighed a sigh of vast content. He really was living the dream, he thought. Life didn't hold much else to wish for.

Of course, there were different kinds of partnership.

'Has he got a name?' he asked.

'Well, his kennel name's Greylord Majestica. But we get to give him his call name.'

'Let's call him Equity,' said Graeme.

The ball rolled right to Rory's feet and he picked it up. It was a bright, intense blue, the colour of Smurfs, and it stood out against the grey day as if highlighted. He held it out to the child, who came toddling up on his stumpy little legs, hands held out.

Just as the child was about to take his ball, his mother snatched him away, huffing with disgust. The ball fell to the ground and rolled under the bench, where it joined the smiles that simultaneously dropped from Rory and the little boy. The woman stormed off, dragging the wailing child by one arm and muttering audibly about 'disgusting alcoholics', and Rory sank back against the bench, his precious moment of human kindness revealed as fool's gold.

'I'm not an alcoholic,' he wanted to shout after her. 'I don't even drink.' It was, he knew, no use. *Keep your head down. Don't attract attention.* He got up, clutching his backpack, and shuffled off to find a new spot. Best not to stay in the same place after being noticed. You didn't want the police seeing you. He'd learned that the first week out.

It was after lunch, so he made his rounds of the park litter bins before settling down again. Today was a good day; he found a MacDonald's bag with half a Big Mac and even a few soggy fries. There were orange peels too, and he gathered every scrap with care, his mouth watering in anticipation of the tangy rind. The second bin yielded sandwich crusts and half a banana. Two fruits and a bit of meat, and the sun was coming out, too. He settled in the corner of a bench to enjoy his feast, as happy as he could remember being in a long time.

***

He was twenty-three, and in love. With Liz Turner, sweet smiling Liz who was always happy, always kind. He drifted through his days at the factory, smiling gently and humming to himself. His mates on the line ribbed him no end, but he didn't mind. Life was good.

He was twenty-four, and in love. With a scorching harridan who frizzled him with her angry glare and told him she didn't think it would work out, long term, and she thought it might be better if they saw other people. If he couldn't even be bothered to remember her birthday, she went on, rolling over the top of his silent, stammering distress, how could she ever trust him to remember more important things?

It seemed to Rory that if she was prepared to dump him over it, there couldn't be much that was more important to her than her birthday, but pain and shock choked his throat like sand, and he couldn't speak, couldn't beg her for another chance, couldn't even say he was sorry, although grief and sorrow burned him from the inside out. He watched her walk away down the street. She'd dumped him, right in public, right outside the factory at knocking-off time, with their mates still coming out around them.

***

Things just got worse after that. Rory was down in the dumps for a long time, and gradually slid into a dark place in his mind where everything was filtered through a soggy grey blanket of depression. His energy levels plummeted and his appetite became capricious. He stopped bothering to shower on weekends. He forgot to get his hair cut, and sometimes he forgot to shave. If he didn't have to go to work, he would spend all day slumped on the sofa, with the blinds drawn, staring at the television with the sound turned down. Then when he dragged himself off to bed, he would lie awake staring at the ceiling until he heard pre-dawn sounds: birds, the first tram of the day, the first flight from Essendon going over. He would then sink into a sodden sleep from which he awoke only with great pain and difficulty. Several times he missed work, and forgot to ring up to pull a sickie.

After several months of this, when Rory had exceeded his allotted days of leave, the foreman called him into the office and spoke to him. Things couldn't go on like this, he said. He'd been covering for Rory, who had always been a good worker, but he was out of options. Was something wrong? Did Rory need some kind of help? Tell me what the matter is, he kept saying.

Rory, who had been unable to muster words to speak in his own defence when Liz had dumped him, could not now find a way to articulate the thing that had him in thrall. He shook his head and muttered that he was okay, not meeting the foreman's eyes. Rory had not made eye contact with another human being for a long time now. He shuffled out of the office and took up his position on the line, shoulders drooping, not looking at anyone. No one greeted him. His lack of response had brought about in his co-workers a habit of looking past him, of failing to see him.

For a while he tried. He would set his alarm, take a shower and shave, clean his flat and do laundry, and get to work on time. But always the grey fog rose again in his mind, and he sank back into it, letting go of his grip on life almost with a kind of relief.

The day came when he was called into the foreman's office a final time, and given a pink slip. Rory went home as usual, slumped in front of the television as usual. Only the order of things changed: now, ironically, Rory would sink into sleep like a stone, waking early with the first rustling of birds outside, and remembering with a dull recognition that there was no reason to get up.

He tried, did Rory. He registered for the dole and spent several hours each day combing the paper for jobs. He applied for a number, but the lack of a good reference meant he was never hired. He told himself that, that it was the reference that was the problem. After a while, he stopped expecting to get hired. He bore his life with the dumb acceptance of an animal.

****

Gradually, life slipped away until Rory could hardly remember a time when it had been different, when he had not lived in the bleak, grey fog of depression. He went through his days mechanically, the depression its own anodyne, conferring a numbness that allowed him to drift through days, and weeks, and months without ever really adverting to its spoliation of the life he had once had.

He forgot things now with greater frequency, often not showering for days at a time, forgetting to eat sometimes, forgetting to go to bed and falling asleep in front of the television, whose muted sound was not enough to keep him awake, even as awake as he was when nominally awake. And, inevitably, one day he forgot to lodge his dole form.

The first he knew about it was when, driven by hunger and having run out of nearly everything, he attempted to draw cash from the autoteller. His transaction was declined; there were insufficient funds. He braved the bank, where a smirking teller informed him the regular deposits from Social Security had stopped the previous month.

The counter person at Social Security was no more sympathetic than the bank teller had been. Rory had failed to meet his obligations. He could reapply for the dole, and the usual twelve weeks' qualifying period would apply. In vain did he point out that that was three months, and that he needed the money for rent.

'Well,' said the smug clerk, 'you should have thought of that, shouldn't you?'

Except for the purgatory of unsuccessful job interviews, where he mumbled and looked down, Rory had hardly spoken to a living creature for months. He tried to talk to the clerk, to ask about ways and means, but the stone wall of the clerk's smug indifference defeated him and he crept miserably away, back to his dark flat where, blinds drawn against the day, he flopped in front of the television and stared blankly at the middle distance.

The next day, hunger drove him out into the streets, where he walked aimlessly until, in the early afternoon, he came upon the Salvation Army depot.

They were still serving lunch, and a smiling worker showed him into the large, high-roofed hall, where the steaming smells of hot food made him feel faint and a little ill. He sat down with a filled plate, at one end of a long table where there was a little gap. The presence of so many people all in one place was a burden to him; the buzz of conversation hurt his mind, and he ate quickly and left as unobtrusively as he could. After that his day took on the small focus of the daily walk to the citadel for the hot meal, sliding in and out in stealth mode, careful never to look directly at anyone. He could, he found with a little practice, remain as completely isolated in that company as if he were in his flat with the blinds drawn, as if the grey blanket of depression rendered him almost invisible. A few times a Salvation Army worker attempted to engage him in conversation, and then he would stammer something and leave quickly. Soon enough they learned to leave him alone.

On one such day, he returned to the safety of his flat to find the door locked against him; his key did not work, the shiny new lock did not accept it.

'We wrote to you three times,' said the real estate lady, her manner brisk and unsympathetic. Rory could not dispute this. He had stopped opening mail some time before.

'But what about my stuff,' he asked. 'Where's my stuff?'

The lady shrugged. 'They probably took it to the tip,' she said. 'Nothing I can do about it. You should have contacted us. Yes, sir, can I help you?' she chirped, looking past him to the next person.

Rory had ceased to exist.

***

Not existing was, he found, surprisingly easy. He roamed the streets aimlessly, taking turns at random, until the waning light and the chill on the air prompted him to seek shelter. He would need to find somewhere to sleep, he realised with numb horror. At no time did it occur to Rory to ask anyone for help. The months of isolation had nibbled away his sense of connection with the rest of humanity until it was all he could do to speak at all.

Rory spent that night huddled in a shop doorway, and woke in the grey light of dawn, chilled to the bone and aching in every muscle. Later, he realised how lucky he had been to pass that first night, his initiation into the not-world of the homeless, undisturbed. All too often he was roused from his uneasy sleep by police, sometimes with rough sympathy but more often with a boot, and ordered to move on. Then he would shuffle away, head down, shoulders hunched in unconscious submission, until he was out of sight, and would look for some other niche where he could hide until morning.

Hiding became more important to him than actual shelter from the elements.

After his first week on the streets, Rory stopped going to the Salvation Army for his meal. He smelt, he knew, and he was ashamed. He learned to comb through litter bins and haunt the back premises of restaurants for scraps of food. His social isolation had grown until it amounted to a phobia, so he did not beg, for to do so would have required speaking to people. He lost weight, and his gums began to bleed.

***

Rory's reverie was interrupted by a sharp poke in the shoulder. Two policemen stood over him. Startled, he dropped his food, the precious orange peels spilling over the ground. He started to get up, but was knocked back onto the bench by a blow to the face. The police spoke to each other over his head. Trying to get aggressive with us. Teach him to assault police. What's your reason for littering. What's your reason for assaulting police. And all the time, they rained blows on him, with some kind of sticks that they had. Rory could not sort out when they were talking to him or to each other. He raised his hands to shield his face, but this brought such a hail of blows that he fell off the bench entirely. He curled into as tight a ball as he could manage. They were kicking him now, their boots making dull, wet thuds against his ribs and back. One caught him in the kidneys, and a wave of pain rose and broke over his head, and he went under it.

They were gone when he came round, and it was nearly dark, the park silent and empty. A thin, soaking rain had started to fall, and his clothes were wet right through; even his underwear seemed to be damp. His feet were numb with cold, and with uncomprending horror he discovered his shoes were gone. His precious food was unrecognisable, trampled into the mud.

For Rory, the loss of his orange peels was the straw, the final straw. He sat in the mud and cried, a thin, hopeless wailing that didn't carry above the sound of the rain. He cried like a child, mouth open, nose running, face raised to the uncaring sky. He cried, and he went on crying. There was just no reason to stop. Eventually he fell asleep where he lay on the muddy ground, as the chill rain continued to fall, washing the blood from his face.

The rain had stopped when he woke again, and the sky was clear, sparkling with a million pinpoint stars even through the city's ambient light. He moved an experimental arm, cringing away from the pain in his ribs. Something was broken, he felt sure; there was a sharp, stabbing pain in his chest with every indrawn breath. His face felt hot, despite the shivers that shook his frame.

He was getting ill, he realised; he recognised the hot-cold feeling from a bout of 'flu a couple of years ago. A flare of panic shot through him, settling cold and crawly in the pit of his stomach. Things were bad enough already, sleeping rough, trusting to luck and rubbish bins for his food. How would he manage if he got sick?

Galvanised by fear, Rory sat up, his rain-soaked clothing squelching. A wave of faintness swept over him as he came upright. He hadn't had anything to eat since yesterday; now, perhaps, the day before yesterday. Those cops had happened before he'd had even one bite of the food he'd collected. And as he thought of that, thought of the little feast he'd been about to enjoy, and his quiet happiness in the sunshine, Rory became angry.

It wasn't a great, big rage, just a small, flickering flame of anger, but as flames will, it gave light and heat, dispelling a little of the grey fog of depression that had clouded his mind and suppressed his will for so long. In its light, Rory looked at his circumstances and found them wanting. It wasn't right, what they'd done. He hadn't been doing anything wrong. He never even begged, like some of the homeless people. He could never bring himself to speak to anyone, to brave the contempt in their eyes. He kept to himself and they had no right, no right to beat him and spoil his food. Fed with these twigs of acknowledged injustice, the flame grew a little stronger.

He was a taxpayer, Rory remembered, at least he had been. He had rights. He'd paid tax for, well, a long time. Years and years. And now, now that he was in trouble, he was by God going to get something for his money.

Rory sat up a little straighter. A small

flame of determination now started to blossom in him, fed by his growing commitment to it. He was going to get some help. There were places. He'd go back to the Salvos, that was what. He'd been stupid to stop going there in the first place. They had programs, they did. That was what the Red Shield appeal was for every year, wasn't it? He had always given to that. He had helped them, and now they would help him. There was nowhere to go but up.

In the light of his new resolve, Rory thought he'd been stupid to run off every time one of those Salvo guys had tried to talk to him. He'd been ashamed, but screw that, he thought. That was what they were *for*, wasn't it? To help people like him. They said so themselves. He'd go there right now, right this minute, and wait till they opened. Then he'd be able to get something to eat, get cleaned up a bit, perhaps even some dry clothes. And he'd listen, and they'd tell him what to do next, and then he'd have a plan. And a hot drink. The thought of a hot mug of tea, with sugar, sent a shiver of pleasure through him.

He was going to get his life back.

Nowhere to go but up.

He grasped the back of the bench and pulled himself to his feet, a bit wobbly, a bit swimmy in the head, and his heart was pounding, but that was partly excitement, he told himself. He took a step away from the bench, steeling himself against the not-quite-pain of the gravel path under his unprotected feet. Another step, and then another, and he almost crashed back to the ground as his left knee gave way. There was something badly wrong with it, he realised, something damaged, the pain was like nothing he'd ever experienced and it didn't take his weight well. He blinked away tears and set his mouth in a determined line. He'd just have to stand it. It wasn't that far to the Salvos, he lied to himself, shrinking away from the knowledge of how far it actually was.

He got almost to the edge of the park before he fell the first time. After that, it was sheer hell, an exercise in willpower as he stumbled on, arms flailing, letting out involuntary grunts and moans when the pain was especially bad. *Nowhere to go but up,* he reminded himself each time he faltered. He drove himself on, the pain feeding into his growing determination, and as he walked, the comforting phrase formed itself into a rhythmic chant that he muttered in time with his painful steps. Nowhere but *up*. Nowhere but *up*. Every step on the damaged knee seemed worse than the last, and by the time he had gone three blocks, Rory's vision was going away down a dark tunnel, and he sank down against a wall to rest.

He was forced to rest three more times before the Salvation Army building came into view, each time for longer. Once, he thought he must have lost consciousness for a time, because it seemed much lighter when he roused himself than when he'd sat down, and the last time he pulled himself up, clutching the wall, the street was quite busy, and passers-by sneered their sneers of disparagement and detoured on the pavement to give him a wide berth. Several times he caught the word 'drunk' from passing couples. The unfairness of it galvanised him to a final effort. All he had to do now was get across the street; he could see the door from here, the big double door standing open in welcome, the portal to warmth, to safety, to a *hot drink*. And to the assistance that would see him once again stand tall, on a production line or behind a counter, whatever, hell, he wouldn't mind even being a lollipop man, it wasn't like he was proud. He had nowhere to go but up.

He pushed himself away from the wall and lurched toward the kerb, his eyes fixed on his goal, his heart on fire with hope.

There was a sudden explosion of shouts from the pavement behind him, and with the ease of long practice he blanked them from his perception. You didn't look round, you didn't engage. That could get you noticed. He stepped out, eager to reach his haven.

He heard the sudden *dingdingding* of a tram's bell, impossibly loud, right in his ear it sounded, and there seemed then to be a slice cut out of the world, a moment of blackness and then it was all upside down, the Salvos' doorway, his goal, now horribly inverted, and there was a warm, spreading wetness and then he couldn't feel anything, and as the light faded he heard in the distance, faint and growing fainter, the sound of sirens.

DANSE MACABRE

Mrs Chan was late again. Terry watched with mounting rage as she sauntered across the floor and shoved herself into the centre of Antonio's carefully ordered Salsa class, throwing it into disarray. Bloody old bat. A couple of the more advanced students shot her slitty-eyed looks, but no one actually said anything. Antonio, of course, took it in his stride, although Terry knew he'd have to listen to him moaning and bitching later on.

He sighed and returned to his contemplation of the accounts. It was not a pleasant occupation. In the last few months, the Firebird School of Dance had seen a marked drop in the attendance of male students. It wasn't so much the diminished fees that worried him, although that was a problem in itself, but that Basic Salsa, his flagship class, was his number one source of new students. People came, enjoyed themselves, learned a bit, and signed on for private lessons. It had always been this way. If the numbers got too far skewed, people, or the ladies at least, didn't learn as quickly or enjoy it as much because they spent too long waiting to take a turn with a partner and not enough time actually dancing.

Tonight was the worst it had been yet, with only two men, *including* Antonio, to ten ladies. Terry groaned softly and pushed his hand through his hair, disordering his carefully oiled waves. He had to get more men in the class. But how? He'd already increased his advertising budget, which he could ill afford, and spent a dismal series of lunch hours handing out leaflets in the street. In an access of desperation, he'd even armed himself with a texta and graffitied the walls of men's lavatories in all the nearby hotels and railway stations. MEET HOT CHIX AT FIREBIRD SCHOOL OF DANCE. None of these measures had produced any discernible result. At the rate he was going, he wouldn't be able to afford Antonio's exorbitant salary for much longer, and that would be the beginning of the end. Antonio, with his cherubic Italian looks and natural curls, was a major asset, charming old and young ladies alike. He flirted indiscriminately with them all; Terry didn't think he even knew he was doing it. Like his long eyelashes, it was a part of his biological makeup, not subject to conscious control.

Class was finishing, he noted through the one-way glass that formed the front wall of his tiny office. There were no private lessons booked this evening; that in itself was cause for alarm. He might as well close early and go and have a beer.

***

Snatcher McGill was propping up the bar at the Imperial Oak, as always. Terry paused for a moment in the entrance, regarding him with affection. However much things changed in his life, however far he came from his grotty origins, there was always good old Snatch. They'd been mates since their boyhood at West Preston Primary, but whereas Terry had won himself a scholarship to the Werribee Academy of Music and Fine Arts, Snatcher had pursued the inclinations that had given him his boyhood nickname, graduating inexorably from petty shoplifting to more serious shoplifting and thence to burglary, and finally netting himself eighteen months inside. On his release, Terry recalled, he'd asked Snatcher if he planned to go straight, but Snatcher hadn't seemed to understand the question. In the same way that he, Terry, loved to dance, Snatcher loved to steal. It was in his blood, you might say.

Terry hitched himself onto a stool and gave Snatcher, who seemed to be lost in contemplation of the bottles on the top shelf, a not very gentle poke in the ribs.

'Oy, wake up!'

Snatcher roused from his reverie, a pleased grin lighting his pallid, weaselly face. They shook hands, pounded backs and did all the manly stuff, Terry being a bit more rough than necessary in unconscious compensation for his shiny polyester shirt and prissily oiled, jet-black hair.

The necessary formalities (mutual

insults and a cursory discussion of the football and, this being Melbourne, the weather) disposed of, Terry came straight to the point.

'Listen, mate. Got something for ya.'

'Yeah?'

'Yeah. How'd you like to have free dancing lessons?'

Snatcher snorted. 'Me dancing? Come on mate, you know I've got three left feet. Remember at school when we tried out for the footy team?'

Terry did remember, but forged ahead gamely. 'Well, that's the thing, mate, co-ordination's a learned skill, right? A couple of months of Salsa and you'll be a new man.'

Snatcher snorted. 'A new poofter.'

'Fuck off.' It was an old argument. Snatcher, like many Australian males of his class, regarded dancing with deep suspicion and cherished a secret fear that it would make his balls drop off.

'Listen, mate, I will bet you,' he paused for effect, and to calculate what he could afford, 'a case of VB that if you go to Salsa class every week for three months, you will be a total chick magnet by the end of that time.' He would have to pay up, he knew. Nothing could turn Snatcher, with his prison pallor and weedy, slightly bow-legged build, into a chick magnet of any degree.

'Nah. I can get a case of VB any time, mate.'

That was the trouble with trying to bribe a dedicated thief, Terry reflected a few hours later as he settled disconsolately in front of the telly. There was pretty well nothing Snatcher couldn't get for himself, at no cost.

It was too early to go to bed. Terry, accustomed by his job to late nights, never could get to sleep before two or three in the morning. Morosely, he flicked through the channels. Sport, sport, *Pot Black*, current events, meh. He perked up as a ballroom came on the screen. At least there was some dancing. Pretty ordinary waltz, but it was something he could watch. He poured a glass of cheap Scotch, rolled a careful joint from his diminishing stash and settled down to watch.

The film was pretty cheesy, he realised after a few scenes, as it became apparent that it was about vampires. All the same, Terry thought as the marijuana nibbled away at his mind, they did look suave. Nothing like white tie to make a man look his best, even if he was an undead monster. If only he could get a dozen or so vampires for the class, it would take off like anything. He drifted into a chemically-assisted dream in which tails-clad dead men spun deftly around the studio, the phone rang off the hook with hot chicks desperate to sign up for lessons, and he, Terry Scunthorpe (known to the public as Rodrigo Valentino), had his own television show.

He woke at the crack of eleven, still on the saggy sofa with the curtains drawn. Groaning, he rolled onto his stomach. His head was stuffed with anvils and a budgerigar seemed to have shat in his mouth. He needed to be at the studio by twelve to open up.

A long, hot shower revived him enough to remember that he hadn't been to the laundromat that weekend. As he stumbled around his bedroom, picking up discarded socks and sniffing them in a vain effort to find a pair that was still reasonably fresh, he remembered his dream. He sighed. Weed made everything look so hopeful. In real life, Terry knew, vampires bit people in the neck and killed them. Not so good for business. Oh, and there was the whole not existing thing, too.

As he neared the studio, five minutes late for opening time, he saw the couple standing outside the street door, and remembered, with a cold, sinking sensation, that it was Wednesday, his very least favourite day of the week. The couple waiting at the door were Mr and Mrs Stanton. She was okay, but Mr Stanton, to whom Terry privately referred as Shithead, was his least favourite student. A big, burly man, built like a Westinghouse, he'd obviously been some kind of football star or soldier or something in his glory days back in the 1960s, and had great difficulty in accepting that he wasn't good at anything physical, despite all evidence to the contrary. Any hint of correction to his technique was liable to send him into a tantrum, where he'd shout abuse at his wife and, on occasion, storm out of the studio. When this happened, Terry still charged him for a full lesson.

They were working on waltz. Mrs Stanton was not bad, and had obviously danced before, but Shithead was having a lot of trouble mastering the basic moves. Of course he would have done better with a female instructor, and Terry had tried a number of times to persuade him to book private lessons with one of the ladies, but Shithead insisted on being taught by the head of the school. He was the kind of man who ordered drinks he didn't like, just because they were more expensive. And he was incredibly resistant to instruction. He irritated Terry beyond belief; he'd insisted on having Terry as his instructor because he was the proprietor, but the least little bit of instruction Terry gave him, he had to argue with it. It wasn't natural to bend one's knees that much. The proper frame made his back hurt. It looked better to stand up straight. On and on. If Terry hadn't given him anything to work with, he'd find fault with the music, or with his wife. Anything and everything, rather than admit he was just a pathetic dancer. If only he would have faced up to the fact he had the grace of a dead pig, Terry could have worked with that. He prided himself on being able to teach absolutely anyone to dance. But the student had to come to the party.

It would be easier, Terry thought as he watched Shithead lumber round the floor dragging his tiny wife, stubbornly travelling on the third beat despite constant admonitions, to teach a corpse to dance.

***

The following Tuesday, there were only seven women in Basic Salsa. People were starting to drop out, Terry realised with a sinking feeling. It was just not a satisfactory class with such an imbalance of numbers. He'd offered free classes to just about every warm-bodied male he knew, with no success. The graffiti had produced no result except a few obscene messages on his voicemail. The bank had written a nasty letter about his overdraft. If he didn't come up with something soon he'd be in trouble. Hell, he *was* in trouble.

That night's cheesy film was about a zombie apocalypse. The zombie master, chuckling evilly (*bwahahahaha*) raised an army of slavishly obedient corpses. Terry watched blearily as they overran a shopping centre, slaying everyone in their path. Why the evil zombie master wanted to kill everyone in the shopping centre hadn't been explained; it was a B movie.

If only, thought Terry as he vainly tried to get one more drag out of his last roach, he had the power to raise the dead. He wouldn't waste them on some shitty old apocalypse. Oh, no. He'd raise up an army of expert Latin dancers and take the dancing scene by storm. He started to giggle. He'd fill up the Basic Salsa class with red-hot salsa dancers.

As the last hit of marijuana flooded Terry's already whisky-soaked brain, an idea was born.

***

Thank God he was an educated man, Terry smugged the next day as he fired up his computer. He knew all of the world's knowledge was just a Google away.

It wasn't as easy as it looked, though. At first, he'd thought he'd found his answer on the first page of results, but as he worked his way through the tutorial (How To Raise Zombies), jotting down a list of required items as he went, he found to his chagrin that it related to a computer game. The second likely-looking page (How To Raise The Dead) turned out to deal with a group of Christians praying to Jesus. Terry didn't think Jesus would help him raise zombies for his salsa class. In any case, he didn't want real people raised to proper human life, like the centurion's little girl in the bible story. They wouldn't be his obedient minions. They'd just be inconvenient and hard to explain. No, it had to be zombies. Terry kept digging.

On the third day, he found the voodoo site.

At first, he couldn't access the Advanced Practitioners' forum. But time passes quickly in Cyberspace, and by the end of the second week, by dint of copious posting, judicious copying of terminology and agreeing about everything with all the people who seemed to be in charge, Terry had succeeded in colouring himself as a trusted and knowledgeable Voudun Practitioner, and was granted admission to the inner circle's private forum. There he found more information than he rightly knew what to do with, but however much he hung about in the forum, he found no one who seemed ever to have succeeded in raising a single zombie.

It was time for Phase Two, he decided. Printing out all the recipes, he set himself to analyse them for common factors.

LIST
grave dirt
salt
black rooster
candles
dead body

Salt and candles could be had easily enough from the supermarket. The other items might be a little more problematical.

The grave dirt, surprisingly, turned out to be quite easy. Aunty Lou was always happy to see Terry, and received with pleasure his offer to take her elderly mongrel, Collingwood, for a walk. Armed with a roll of poo bags, Terry drove Collingwood to the old cemetery, and after a pleasant, rambling walk among the gravestones, checked that no one was near him, slipped a bag over his hand, and stooped to gather a generous handful from a recently filled grave. He repeated this manoeuvre several times, returning to the car with four bright blue bags full of grave dirt. Collingwood's actual droppings, he left where they fell.

The rooster was a little more problematical. The terms of Terry's lease did not allow him to keep any pets, and he was mortally afraid of his landlady, a fat, moustached woman who lived on the ground floor and had a way of popping out of her front door just when Terry would rather she didn't, as, for example, the time he'd run out of light bulbs and was balancing on the bannister, trying to nick the bulb out of the staircase light. Roosters, Terry knew, always crowed at daybreak. There was also the question of what had to be done with the rooster. Terry pretended to himself that he didn't know what it was for, but he did know, perfectly well.

Could something else be substituted for the rooster, Terry asked himself? Something a bit quieter? Something, his inner voice whispered, that wouldn't need its throat slit? What was the purpose of it, anyway? Presumably some kind of propitiation sacrifice to some demon or spirit. Were demons very intelligent?

Terry thought not. If they were, then why would they be at the beck and call of anyone with some grave dirt and a dead hen? They must be pretty stupid, he reasoned, and it ought therefore to be possible to fool them with a substitute.

The dead body was easiest of all, given that Terry, full of natural caution and perhaps, now that he was so close, a bit of a desire to procrastinate, felt it was vital to test his process before trying it out on an actual dead person. He opened the cupboard under the sink, sprayed in a goodly amount of Mortein, closed it again and went out to buy the salt and candles. On his return he opened the cupboard, moved a couple of things around and picked up the nearest dead cockroach.

Given the nature of his subject, Terry didn't see why he should make his magic circle of grave dirt and salt twelve feet across. It stood to reason it could be done to scale. He spread out a couple of sheets of newspaper on the kitchen table and proceeded with the ritual, of which no details are given here. Persons with an unnatural interest in the dark arts will not learn how to reanimate corpses from me. Suffice it to say that a cupful of chicken stock, warmed to more or less blood heat, proved an efficacious substitute for the blood of a black rooster.

Although he'd gone to quite a lot of trouble by this time, Terry was operating more or less on autopilot, following his plan one step at a time as much to avoid thinking about his business problems as because he expected it actually to bear fruit. He was, therefore, astonished when, as he commenced the fourth round of the chant, the cockroach twitched a couple of legs and struggled upright.

By the time he had to leave to open the studio, Terry had succeeded in making the cockroach walk in simple patterns on the table, fly to the light fixture, fly back down, and return to its inanimate state. He was now ready for Phase Three. His heart beat a rapid, uneasy tattoo as he locked his door. Time for a real corpse.

***

All through the afternoon and evening, Terry thought through the final phase of his plan. The fresher the corpse the better, he reasoned; it would look more natural, and bits were less likely to fall off it. That would be very difficult to explain. It would be best, he decided, to source his subject from a funeral parlour rather than digging up a grave. True, it would be missed, but then who would look at live dancing students? He could change its hair and so on, give it a bit of a makeover.

***

'You want me to what?'

'Come on, Snatcher, it'll be easy for a man of your talents.'

***

HUSBAND, FATHER MISSING IN SHOCK FUNERAL HOME ROBBERY

A grieving family was devastated today when the Le Fir funeral home called to say the funeral of Mr Gary Nguyen could not proceed as planned.

Early this morning, police were summoned to the East Ringwood funeral home to find a back window smashed and a corpse missing.

'We just don't understand it,' said a police spokesman.

Mr Nguyen was a respected member of Ringwood's Vietnamese community. His wife, Thi, was not available for comment.

Anyone with information about the crime is advised to call CrimeStoppers...

***

It took several weeks of late nights before Fred, as Terry had renamed the late Mr Nguyen, was ready to join Antonio's class. They were weeks in which Terry wondered if he'd ever have a whole night's sleep again. For hour after hour he drilled Fred, first in the basic steps and then in fancy combinations. In between this, he worked on Fred's appearance. Given that Fred had in life been Vietnamese, the obvious disguise of a hair colour change was not feasible. As he was dead, his hair didn't grow, either, so whatever was done had to be less rather than more. Finally, Terry settled on a cheap wig ordered online. The different style changed the overall look of Fred's face, and a carefully applied false moustache did the rest. Terry blessed his days at the Werribee Academy of Music and Fine Arts, where he had learned, among other things, the art of theatrical makeup. A visit to the Salvos completed Fred's transformation from dignified elderly gentleman to aging fashion victim.

***

FUNERAL HOME THEFTS NOT RACIALLY MOTIVATED, SAY POLICE

There is no reason to think that the recent spate of thefts from Melbourne's funeral homes are racially motivated, a police spokesman said today.

Corpses have been stolen from four suburban funeral homes. Citizens living near funeral homes are advised to take extra precautions. 'There's no knowing what these sick individuals are capable of,' Sergeant Williams of the Unusual Crimes Division told our reporter.

The Unusual Crimes Division has been formed to counter the increasing wave of unusual crimes sweeping Melbourne.

Anyone seeing suspicious activity connected with a funeral home is urged to call CrimeStoppers...

***

That evening, Terry remained at the front of the studio to watch Antonio's Salsa class. He had a lot invested in Fred's success. Another three dead men lay neatly stacked in the unused downstairs part of the building. Fortunately the weather remained cold, but they wouldn't keep forever. He hesitated to animate them, though, without some solid evidence of success.

Surprisingly, Fred seemed to make it through the class without incident. Presently the studio emptied out, the women clattering away down the stairs with cries of 'Night, Antonio! Night, Rodrigo!'.

Terry wandered into the back room and found Antonio changing his shoes.

'How did it go tonight, Antonio? I noticed we had a new chap.'

'Yeah, ok. He seems to be picking things up alright. Danced a bit before, I think.'

'Get on alright with the ladies?'

'Funny you should say that. They didn't seem all that taken with him, I didn't think. It's hard to watch one student, of course, with a class that size.'

'Well, if he comes back, just keep an

eye on him, okay? Let me know if anything seems off.'

Antonio shot him a sharp look. 'Why would it? Something you want to share about this guy?'

'Oh, no, no, not at all, just, you know, we don't get that many blokes. Just want to make sure he settles in alright. Might get him signed up with Julie.'

Antonio accepted this without comment. He laced up his runners and was off before Terry could think of anything else to ask him.

He found Fred waiting out of sight underneath the stairs, as instructed. Fred had to be made to change into the other one of the two shirts he'd bought him, and then de-animated and stowed in the downstairs. Get him ready for next week's class now, Terry had decided, then there wasn't so much to do in the early part of the evening, when there were people around. He trudged back upstairs to wait for his private student. Once she'd gone, he could shut up shop and get to work on animating the new recruits. Fred's success made it feasible. He heaved a weary sigh. It seemed like forever since he'd been able to relax in the pub, or just go home and watch telly.

***

By the following week, Terry was able to introduce Ted, Joe and Michael to Basic Salsa. They had all been kitted out in varying styles, and taught carefully differing levels of salsa. The last thing he needed was them acting like some kind of weird synchronised squad and making Antonio suspicious. He believed that Antonio, being Italian, was bound to be Catholic and therefore more in tune with the supernatural, and lived in fear of him blowing the whole operation.

The new subjects seemed to get through the class as well as could be expected, yet watching, Terry could see what Antonio had meant. There was a certain stiffness about the women when dancing with them; they held themselves a little farther away. These women were all regulars at Firebird, and were used to dancing with different partners, yet Terry, watching them, thought they looked more like novices at their first class: uncomfortable with physical contact with strangers. As the class ended, he slipped out and stood in the dark under the staircase, hoping to hear something that would give him a clue as to what was going on. Presently Fred, Ted, Joe and Michael came silently down the stairs and shuffled into the narrow, dark space around him. Terry repressed a shiver as their dead flesh pressed up against him. There was a wrongness about them, somehow.

Here they came, all in a bunch. Good.

'... yeah, creepy. I don't like that Ted, either.' That soft voice was Jodie.

'Shit, they're all the bloody same. It's like dancing with bloody zombies.' Those were Kirsten's strident tones.

Someone else said something in a low voice and the group exploded with laughter, the kind of female laughter that a man always knows he doesn't want to enquire about. They were mocking somebody. Shit, shit, shit. This was a hostile audience.

The following week, Jodie was absent from Salsa class. When she came for her private lesson on Thursday, Terry mentioned it. She hummed and ha'd, and finally came up with some lame excuse about having to work late. Since Jodie was a nurse and worked strictly defined shifts, Terry didn't believe it for a moment.

The week after that, she was back, but there was a strange vibe about the class, Terry thought uneasily, spying on it through his one-way glass. The women kept shooting each other looks, almost as if they were communicating with one another. He didn't like it. Even the unpopular Mrs Chan, who as usual had swanned in twenty minutes late, seemed one of the group tonight. Antonio was his usual jovial self, wisecracking and flirting outrageously with the older ladies, but there was a heavy, leaden feel to it all, as if battle lines were being drawn and tanks rumbling into position.

When the class ended and Antonio dismissed it, Terry watched with mounting dread as, instead of dispersing to practise, change shoes and leave, get drinks of water and so on, the women in the class gathered into a little knot on the other side of the studio. Presently Kirsten left them and marched forbiddingly towards his office.

Forewarned, Terry closed the louvres over his one-way glass and scattered some random papers about his desk to give the appearance of work. As Kirsten's forbidding, five-foot-ten frame loomed in the doorway, he looked up with what he hoped was a carefree smile.

'Ah, Kirsten, good evening. How's it going with Antonio?'

Kirsten slitted her eyes at him, stuck out her jaw and launched into her complaint without preamble. 'It's those guys. The weird ones. We don't like them.'

'Weird ones?'

'You know what I mean.' Kirsten's pale, Nordic eyes bored into him, daring him to deny. 'Those creepy guys that have been turning up the last few weeks. That old fucker with the bad wig, and the others.'

'Well, Kirsten, you know with dance, we can't always choose our partners. It's an important part of the learning process that you dance with a lot of different...'

'Yeah, yeah, I know all that. But these guys are different. They're creepy. There's something not right about them. Look, we all feel the same way. Me and Jodie and Melanie and Sue and Megan and Annette. Mrs Chan, too. I said I'd come and talk to you.' She folded her arms and sat back, with an air of having said all that needed to be said.

Terry reached for his air of professional calm, but it seemed to be hovering just out of reach. 'Have they done anything inappropriate? Said anything...' He almost sniggered at the idea of his corpses talking, and bit his tongue sharply.

Kirsten snorted. 'Said anything – yeah right. That's part of the problem. I don't think I've ever heard any of them speak. Normally when you dance with someone new you introduce yourself, but these characters just stare straight ahead and it's like they didn't even hear you.'

'Right, okay, and you want me to...' Terry let his sentence trail off as his brain raced in small, unproductive circles.

'And they smell funny, that's another thing. They're all like it, sort of rotten.'

'Well, of course personal–'

'They fucking stink. And they're weird. It's like dancing with a dead corpse. And we all feel the same way. We're just not happy, Rodrigo, none of us are. We thought you ought to know.'

'Right, right, well thank you for

coming to me with this, Kirsten, I'll have a word with Antonio, see if he can get everyone to loosen up a bit.' *Including you, you Viking cow*, he thought. *Oh, I am going to make you suffer so much in your next lesson.*

***

As soon as he'd seen all the women off the premises and shuttled the corpses back to their storage area in the downstairs, Terry rushed back up the stairs. He found Antonio still in the staffroom, arranging his perfect curls in front of the looking glass. He had changed into a black shirt, open almost to the waist, and black jeans so tight that Terry wondered if they had a hidden stretch panel. As soon as he saw Terry, his face underwent a transformation, morphing in an instant from angelic composure to shrewish dissatisfaction.

'Those bloody men, where did they come from? Those four guys, Rodrigo, they're ruining my class, no one can relax, the girls don't like them, and their footwork is shit.' He paused, shoving a can of deodorant into his shirt and angrily spraying his armpits. 'And another thing

– they smell bad. I tell you what, Rodrigo, I don't have to work in some shitty studio with crappy facilities. I had six offers already from the Australian Ballet. I had...'

***

By the time he had soothed Antonio with promises that he'd deal with the men, and a ten percent pay increase, Terry was knackered. He still had to change the dead guys' shirts for next week, but to hell with it. Let them stay in the same ones. It wasn't like they were sweating, after all. He needed a drink. And food. He went next door to Caesar's Pizza, where he knew the owner.

Over a Spicy Mexican and several imported lagers, Terry persuaded himself into a more optimistic frame of mind. None of the problems was insuperable. He'd give them all a good scrub with Dr Wright's Coal Tar Soap, that was what he'd do. It had worked wonders on Collingwood, that time when he'd taken him to the beach and he'd rolled in a dead fish. Resolutely he forced his mind away from what it would be like washing four naked corpses. As for the other stuff, a bit more training should take care of that. He was better at it now. He'd been practising with Rover in his spare moments, and Rover could even dance in time to music now. Absently he patted his shirt pocket, where the de-animated Rover rested in a matchbox. In fact, he could probably make them wash themselves. Or each other, or something. Feeling immensely cheered, Terry signalled the waitress for another lager.

He was quite optimistic by the time he saw Bruno threading his way through the tables. Good old Bruno, said the five lagers.

'Gidday mate! Excellent food, as always.'

Bruno pulled out a chair. 'Glad you like it. We aim to please. How's it going?'

'Yeah, not bad. You?'

Bruno sighed. 'Look, mate, actually we've got a bit of a problem. I wanted a word. Just between friends, right?'

'Sure, mate, anything I can do, of course...' Between friends, hell, Terry thought, his mind racing in circles of panic. Bruno was also his landlord.

'See, mate, it's difficult with a

restaurant. There are some things people just won't stand for.'

Terry nodded and tried to look as if he understood what the hell Bruno was on about.

'It's the smell, see? One thing customers won't stand, it's a bad smell.'

Terry nodded wisely. 'Too right, mate, nothing like a bad smell to put you off.'

'Well, it's coming from your place. Over there in the corner, see? Look, I don't know what you're using the downstairs for, and I don't particularly want to know, but mate, there's a terrible smell coming through the wall there.'

Terry craned his neck, realising with a sinking feeling that the back corner, where none of the tables in the busy restaurant was occupied, shared a wall with his downstairs space; shared, in fact, a wall with the very corner where he'd been storing Fred, Ted, Joe and Michael.

'Shit, mate,' he stammered, 'I dunno what that'd be. Maybe a rat got in and died there or something. It's just boxes of costumes and stuff.'

'Yeah, well, look, mate, I need you to deal with it, okay? I've got almost a third of my tables empty because of it, I'm losing business, see?'

Terry did see, with frightening clarity. His lease was up for renewal in three months' time.

'I'll deal with it right away, mate, not to worry. I'll have everything out and find whatever it is. Right away.' *Shit, shit, shit.*

***

'You friggin' what?'

'You heard me.'

'Geez, mate, that's stretching things a bit. I dunno...'

'Snatch, I've gotta get rid of them. Tonight if possible. Tomorrow night at the very latest.'

'I dunno, mate, I mean, why me? I mean, if you wanna get hold of something, sure, I'm your man, I mean I got you the stiffs, didn't I? Didn't know you were gonna keep them. What you want them for, anyway?'

'Never mind that. Just think of a way to get rid of them, okay?'

'Let me call a couple of mates, okay? I'll get back to you.'

***

Terry sweated through the next day. Countless times his finger was on the phone to call Snatcher, but each time he stopped himself. He allowed Shithead to get away with not bending his knees, due to sheer inattention, and even complimented him on the improvement in his frame. By five o'clock, when Snatcher called, he was ready to scream.

Snatcher, it transpired, had a friend in the building industry, from his time as a guest of the state. He was, therefore, in a position to know that a large concrete pour was scheduled in two days' time for the foundations of a block of luxury apartments in the Docklands. Snatcher's friend's boss, he went on, had a daughter, and in return for free private lessons for said daughter, presumably in perpetuity, the night watchman would look the other way. But it had to be tonight, because tomorrow there would be a different night watchman, one over whom Snatcher's friend's boss had no influence.

Terry recklessly agreed to everything. No doubt the daughter was a left-footed pig, but it had long been Terry's boast that he could teach absolutely anyone to dance.

***

Ted, Joe and Michael sat in a row in the back seat. Fred, being the eldest, had the dignity of the front passenger seat. They stared straight ahead, eyes unfocussed, a row of formally dressed corpses, slightly shopworn. He'd got them back into their original clothes, lest any trace clue lead back to the Firebird School of Dance. All wigs, false moustaches, and other modifiers had been removed. These, together with their dancing clothes, had been disposed of in the illegal incinerator at the back of Bruno's restaurant, long after the last kitchen hand had departed.

It was three o'clock when they arrived at the construction site. The night watchman, following a coded text message, was not in evidence, but a soft glow and the faint sound of Latin music from a little hut indicated his silent presence. The steel mesh gates were slightly open, their chain dangling loose. He switched off his lights, checked the overhead was in the 'off' position, and slid out of the car, leaving the door open.

It would have been easier with

Snatcher along, he thought as he strained to shift the heavy gate, but then they'd have had to carry each corpse down the long path into the foundation hole. The spiral path leading down and down around the square edges of the foundation pit was designed to carry heavy earthmoving machinery, but Terry wasn't confident enough to take his car down there, especially with the lights off. This whole exercise was already far enough outside his comfort zone without extreme Tough Mudder-style driving stunts. He parked as close as he dared to the edge. The four shovels were there as promised, their blades glinting in the uncertain light.

The early morning air crackled with stillness as the little procession marched down the ramp. At the bottom, Terry moved the men into position and started them digging their grave. It gave him an odd feeling; they'd been through a lot together in the past weeks. For the first time, he wondered uneasily whether any consciousness remained behind those vacant eyes. He pushed the thought aside and returned to calculating the time remaining before the concrete pour, and trying to figure out a way he could get them to fill in the hole themselves, while lying in it.

There was one thing to be said for the walking dead, Terry thought as the first softening of the darkness warned of approaching sunrise, and he worked frantically to fill in the hole. They didn't get tired. It had taken the four of them only half an hour to dig their grave. He was left to fill it in, though. He hadn't been able to devise a way around that. He'd tried with three of them in it and the biggest (Joe) filling in on one side of the hole, but after a short time the dirt had started to fill up the empty space left for Joe, and he'd had to abandon the attempt. Now he was sweaty, filthy and his hands were blistered. Although his life as a professional dancer kept him fit, it hadn't equipped him for the kind of upper-body effort that was required for wielding a shovel for hours on end, nor had it hardened his palms. If only he had thought to equip himself with some gardening gloves. As the first rays of sunlight broke over the edges of the pit, and he trudged back up the ramp, dragging his shovel to obliterate the footprints, he was as exhausted as he'd ever been in his life.

***

In the weeks that followed, Basic Salsa at the Firebird School of Dance returned to its pre-corpse levels of attendance. Bruno, appeased after Terry had spent a further four hour session scrubbing the downstairs area with bleach, renewed the lease. And Terry entered into a long-term arrangement with Snatcher for the supply of a keg of beer every Tuesday. This keg, delivered to the newly scrubbed downstairs area, ensured the regular attendance of eight Engineering students from the nearby university campus.

***

BUILDING HAUNTED, SAY RESIDENTS

Residents of the Leo Chatto building in the Docklands say their building is haunted.

Apparitions have been seen by a number of people

in the upscale residential development, and property prices have fallen dramatically as a result. Some residents report hearing Latin dance music at odd times in the night, and others have seen men in evening clothes prowling the corridors. Our special report on page eleven...

❧LAST LIGHT☙

It got more difficult every year. Nancy leaned far out, aiming her secateurs at an encroaching frond. It wasn't so much getting up the ladder, nor yet climbing the tree from the top of it; that was a long-established routine, and the ladder slotted firmly into the holes at the bottom and was held steady by blocks of wood nailed to the trunk at the top. They'd done it together, she and Fred, back when they'd first bought the house, forty-five years ago next June. Back then it had been Fred who had climbed the ladder and set up the nesting boxes, and every year they'd made a day of it, setting up the ladder and clipping away the new growth that would interfere with their view from the hide, Fred up the ladder, swinging about with Tarzan yells and occasionally pretending to fall, and Nancy supervising down below, and then when it was done she'd have lunch all ready on the picnic table, the sturdy outdoor table with benches, all of a piece, that had been their first major purchase after the house. The first fine Saturday in October, it had always been. And when Fred had died, she'd kept up the tradition, always on the first fine Saturday, setting up the ladder and climbing up to the lowest branch, and from there, through the massive old tree, clearing away the new growth, checking for any needed repairs to the nesting boxes, making sure it was all good and inviting and easily watched from the hide. Even that first, terrible year, she'd insisted on doing it by herself, rejecting Reg's repeated offers of help. He was a wonderful friend, but this day was hers and Fred's, theirs alone, and she clung to the tradition with all the jealous possessiveness of a young bride.

This was the sixth time she'd had to do it by herself, but she had not allowed herself to fall short of their tradition by a single iota. There was fresh baking for the picnic lunch, the cross-stitched tablecloth and napkin (singular now, but still just as carefully ironed), and everything just as it had always been. If Fred turned up, alive after all, he would not be able to say that she had let anything go.

There, that was the last of it. She'd have a good, clear view, whenever the birds turned up. That would not be until high summer, she knew, but the yearly arrival of the Greater Spotted Coots had always been the high point of her and Fred's year, and they'd always liked to get ready for it early. Since Fred had been gone, it had taken on for Nancy an almost religious significance. It was not just the beginning of summer that it signified to her now, but her ongoing link to her husband, her way of connecting with him, of reaching out across the dividing grave, here, my love, it's all as you left it, all nice for you.

Nancy's eyes misted, and she reached unthinking to wipe them with her sleeve, forgetting the secateurs in her hand. She stabbed herself in the forehead with the sharp point, flinched backwards, slipped on the branch, lost her grip on the other branch, and as she fell, the last thought that went through her mind was the memory of why Fred had always been the one to go up the tree.

***

The doctor was still rabbiting on. God save us, thought Nancy, he'd talk the hind leg off a brown dog. She had tuned him out some time ago; she didn't understand any of the medical terms he was using, and she knew he would sum it all up in plain English when he got tired of showing off. She stared out the window and thought about birds, instead. Birds and their freedom, their beauty and grace. It had been their shared love of birds that had first brought her and Fred together. That and the ballroom dancing. Now, with her knee so badly injured, she wondered if she would ever dance again.

She became aware that Doctor Sanders had stopped talking, and an expectant silence was beating at her ears. What was the last thing he had said? Oh, yes.

'But, Mrs Bellingham, I just don't understand. What were you *doing* up a tree? You're seventy-eight years old, you can't be climbing trees. What did you do it for?'

This kind of thing was what really

annoyed Nancy the most. Who did this young snot think he was? She raised her small nose higher in the air, looking down it in what she believed was a forbidding expression, like that of Lady Violet in Downton Abbey.

'Young man,' she said, 'it's my tree, and I shall climb it if I see fit.'

***

The argument had gone on for some time. Nancy very much resented the doctor's attitude. It was not for him to command, but to advise, and she'd had his advice and didn't like it. A total knee reconstruction would put her out of action for months. There were no bones actually broken, she'd been told, just extensive damage to ligaments and things, and she didn't see why it couldn't be allowed to heal naturally.

'It would mean total rest of the knee for at least two months,' said the doctor. 'With your active lifestyle, I should think you'd find that difficult. You wouldn't be able to stay at home; you'd be confined to a wheelchair for most of it.'

Two months seemed like a better deal than six to Nancy, although she quailed rather when the doctor started blathering about the Sunny Glades Nursing Home. Good grief, a nursing home. The very thing she'd always dreaded. Over my dead body, she was fond of saying. She and Fred had promised each other they would never let it happen. She wanted to die in her own bed, in her beautiful house by the lake. Better yet, on the dance floor, of a sudden heart attack. Although that would be rather hard on poor Reg. Still, she told herself, needs must. Needs must as the devil drives, as her grandmother had been used to say. Whatever that meant.

***

Six weeks later, Nancy gritted her teeth as the fat-bottomed nurse closed her window without asking. How many times? Now she would have to struggle to the window again to open it. Forbidden as she was to place any weight on her knee unless it was perfectly straight, even the two steps were fraught with difficulty. It was no use, she knew, telling them not to close the window, or asking them to open it. The staff ignored all requests and admonitions with a breezy unconcern. It was best not to speak to them at all. If you drew their notice, you were liable to get a pat on the cheek and be told you were a 'good girl'. She wondered how swiftly the crime rate might drop if offenders were sent somewhere like this instead of to maximum security prisons. The thought made her smile.

'Oh, it's good to see you smiling, Nancy. Good girl!' said the nurse in a squeaky little voice, patting her cheek.

'That's Mrs Bellingham,' said Nancy through gritted teeth, eliciting from the nurse an artificial little laugh.

A tap on the door heralded Reg, who edged in furtively and sideways, dodging the nurse with a sickly grin. Good old Reg. Where would she be without him, she sometimes wondered. Always a close friend of Fred's, he had come into his own after Fred's death, stepping up quietly to help her with the arrangements and later, unobtrusively taking over the things Fred had always done – cleaning out gutters, cutting the grass, weeding. He wouldn't be thanked for any of it. If she tried, he got all embarrassed, shuffled his feet and muttered that Fred would have done the same for him.

The nurse departed with another skittish little laugh, which she probably thought counteracted her middle-aged complexion and huge backside. Reg sighed and sat down on the edge of her bed. There was no second chair; the nursing home liked, it seemed, to discourage visitors.

'G'day, Nance. How you travelling?'

'Honestly? I'd bloody kill for a beer and a fag.'

Reg grinned and got up. Tiptoeing to the door, he peered out, looking both ways up and down the corridor before closing it softly and returning. He picked up his scruffy old messenger bag and extracted a six-pack.

'Aw, bless you, Reg!'

'Cascade Premium Light, your favourite, me dear. And…' he opened the window, 'we can have a fag with it an' all. Here, just stand up a second and I'll shift the chair over here.'

Nancy stood unsteadily on her right leg as the chair was moved, then took Reg's arm for the couple of steps and collapsed back into it with a sigh. She grabbed the proffered bottle and took a deep draught. 'Ahhh, that hits the spot. Right, let's have a fag, then.'

'What happened to the wheelchair,

Nance?'

'They took it away. Said they don't have enough for everyone, and since I 'wasn't using it'… I reckon they just like to keep you shut up in your room. When I had the chair, I could sit out in the courtyard. Watch the birds, the fresh air… it made a lot of difference. Now, if I want to go anywhere I have to ask them for it, and they just say they'll fetch it, but they don't. I tried complaining, but they just go "she's *confused*" in that bloody patronising way.'

'Fuckers.'

'Reg O'Donnell! Mind your language, *if* you please.'

'Sorry, mate.'

They smoked in companionable silence for a while, blowing the smoke out the window.

'So how much more time you got to serve?'

'Buggered if I know, Reg. The doctor reckons it's not healing as fast as we hoped. Said it's "only to be expected at my age." They do go on at you. It's not as if I'm a hundred.'

Reg sighed. 'We're none of us getting any younger. I wish you'd let me fix up the tree for you. You're not handy at ladders and such, and that's a fact.'

'I know, Reg. It's just… it was always something that Fred and I did together, you know?'

'Yeah, mate. I know.'

He stayed until he was shooed out by the nurse at five o'clock. Watching from the window as he stumped down the drive, Nancy felt a warm glow that was not all beer.

'He's still looking after me, Fred,' she murmured.

***

Six weeks later, Nancy sat by her window and watched as the first flight of the Greater Spotted Coots winged overhead, their distinctive cry ringing out, on their way to the lake.

All day she was cross and out of sorts, and when the fat-bottomed nurse patted her cheek, she snapped 'Young woman, kindly keep your hands to yourself.' When Reg arrived at three o'clock, he found her in tears.

'Aw, geez, Nance, what is it? This place getting you down? It won't be much longer, will it?' He bustled about, a kindly gnome, plying her with glasses of water, boxes of tissues and sundry random items that caught his eye. Like a bower bird, she thought, sniffling.

'Oh, Reg. They're here, and I'm going to miss it,' she sobbed.

'Who's here? You mean the birds? The midnight coots?'

She sobbed harder, while Reg, now out of options for small items to pile onto her tray, patted her shoulder and made what he seemed to think were soothing noises.

'The Greater Spotted Coots,' she finally choked out. 'Damn it, Reg, you never get that right.' She reached for a tissue and blew her nose. 'Forty-five years, Reg, forty-five years and we've never missed seeing their nesting dance once. And I'm stuck in here…'

Reg's brow furrowed. Then his face cleared, and seizing Nancy's call button, he rang for the nurse. 'We'll get you down to the lake,' he said. 'Don't you worry, Nance. Leave it to Reg.'

It was forty-five minutes before a nurse came, slamming the door open and barging in in the usual way, and peremptorily removing every useful item from Nancy's table to bang down a tray of food.

'Mrs Bellingham will require her wheelchair tomorrow,' said Reg in a lordly fashion. 'We will be going out for the day.'

'We'll have to see what Doctor says,' said the nurse, with an air of playing a winning hand at Bridge.

'No, dear,' said Nancy, goaded beyond endurance. '*We* will have to do no such thing. I believe I am not a prisoner in this establishment. Now I should like to have the use of a wheelchair for the day, which, I will remind you, was supposed to be included in the tariff on a daily, not an occasional, basis. Therefore, kindly have it here no later than eight o'clock in the morning.'

The nurse's stare was as blankly uncomprehending, or as smugly insolent, as that of a cow chewing the cud. Nancy could never quite decide which.

'You be a good girl and eat up your nice tea,' she said, 'and we'll see what Doctor says on Monday.' She departed without listening to anything else, leaving the door wide open.

Nancy sat back limply, her round face a picture of misery. It was, she knew, no good. Yes, she was entitled to the use of the chair. No, they could not legally confine her. She supposed that, with the law on her side, she could eventually prevail, although even that was by no means certain; they would smirk and whisper that she was 'confused', and deny everything, and she would be left still a prisoner and worse off than before.

Reg didn't stay long after that, excusing himself with mutters about having a lot to do. Nancy smiled weakly and let him go. She was not, she knew, much fun to be around today, and was conscious of not behaving very well; she was of a generation that believed in the Stiff Upper Lip, not crying and pouting and spoiling everyone's day when you didn't get what you wanted.

Her bad mood lasted through the night, through hours of fitful half-sleep, dozing and waking repeatedly, and missing Fred more than at any time since those first terrible weeks after his heart attack. If Fred were here, she knew, he'd jolly her out of the dumps in short order; they had always done that for each other, no matter how bad anything was.

As the sky lightened from indigo to

grey and finally flushed with pink, she lay in bed and stared at the window. Morning came, and a pair of nurses to chivvy her out of bed. For the first time since she'd been in this place, she didn't bother to get dressed, but sat in her dressing gown and slippers, brooding. The trouble was, she thought, it wasn't just the birds. It was Fred. The nesting dance of the Greater Spotted Coots had been one of the highlights of their year, and every year, she felt specially close to him as she watched it. It was almost as if she'd been permitted that one day a year to be with her husband, and now it had been taken away. She wondered if she'd live to see the dance again. She wasn't sure she even wanted to. Sunk in a morass of unhappiness, she waved away her breakfast tray, letting her tea grow cold untouched, ignoring the fussing and poking of the nurses, only flinching a little as her cheek was patted. What was this obsession they had with touching people's faces, she wondered, but without her usual irritation. It was just too much trouble. Let them paw her if they got some kind of perverted kick out of it.

When Reg arrived, she was still

slumped morosely, staring out the window, not really seeing. She greeted him with all the enthusiasm she could muster, which wasn't a lot.

'Hello, Reg.'

'Hello! What's this? You don't look your normal cheerful self.'

'Oh, Reg. I'm sorry. I'm just feeling a bit down.'

'Well, you can forget that – I don't want a misery guts keeping me company. Right, up you get. I suppose that wheelchair never materialised? Nah, didn't think so. Never mind! Uncle Reg has taken care of milady's transport arrangements, fear not.' He waved a long, flat bundle. 'Well come on, up you get! Time's wasting!'

He unwrapped his jacket from around a battered old skateboard. 'I've got it all worked out. See, you stand on it, and I'll pull you along. Come on, it's easy.'

Nancy stared at him. 'What – me ride a skateboard? You can't be serious, Reg.'

'Huh. You don't appear to have any problems scuttling up and down trees, I reckon you can manage to stand on a skateboard. I borrowed it off my nephew's boy. He'll never miss it. Come on, get up.'

Moving slowly, as if in a dream, Nancy stood up. She wondered briefly if she should take time to get dressed, but bugger it, she thought. Best to get out immediately. She didn't know if this would work, but she was by God going to give it her best shot. Lovely Reg.

'Righto, hop on!'

Giggling, Nancy stepped onto the skateboard, wobbling a little bit and clutching at Reg's arm.

'Right, now just you stand on that, take my hand, and I'll pull you along, see?' He demonstrated a few steps. 'It's just like with dancing, see? You take care of your own balance, and I'll take care of everything else.'

Put like that, Nancy could see it better. She straightened up from her crouched posture and lifted her head. Immediately she felt more secure. She shifted one foot forward and angled her back foot to give her a slightly triangular stance, and beamed. 'Rightio, then! Lay on, McDuff!'

They proceeded at a slow walking pace along the corridor, passing the open doors of the other inmates and occasioning several exclamations. Nancy was rather alarmed at this.

'Reg! Everyone can see us. What if someone calls a nurse?'

'So what? We'll be long gone by the time anyone comes. Look how long it took them to answer your buzzer yesterday.'

'Yeah, you've got a point.'

They had a stroke of luck passing the front desk; the place was deserted, the staff no doubt all on one of their many breaks. They made it to the drive without incident.

'It's raining.'

'Only a little bit. Anyway, I brought a brolly along, just in case.' He withdrew a folding umbrella from his jacket and pressed the button, handing it to her with a flourish.

'What about you? You'll get wet.'

'Doesn't matter. I left a change at your house, along with the picnic basket.'

Down the drive, along the street…
'Right!' said Reg. 'We're out of sight of the joint now. Want to try going a bit faster?'

'No. And, oh God, Reg, I'm still in

my nightie and dressing gown! Oh Lord, we'll have to go back.'

'Rubbish, woman. Where's your sense of adventure? You look lovely. And when we get to your house, you can get dressed there. I suppose you didn't take all your clothes with you to that place?'

'But Reg, we're in the public street. And I left my bag behind, with my keys.'

'No you didn't, you left your keys with me, remember, to look after things in case anything went wrong at the house. Just relax and enjoy the ride. It's going to be a day to remember.'

***

They nearly caused an accident crossing the main road, as several drivers jammed on their brakes to get a better look. By this time Nancy was thoroughly enjoying herself, despite the ache in her legs, for weeks now unaccustomed to standing for more than a few seconds at a time. When they reached her house, she was almost sorry the ride was over.

'Phew! Oh Reg, I did enjoy that. I don't know if I can manage going back, though. My legs are aching like anything.'

'Huh! I thought of that. I'll take you

back in the wheelbarrow. In fact, now we're here, you can hop into it to go down to the lake. I didn't like my chances getting in with it, see? We had to be in stealth mode for Phase One of the mission. The conveyance had to be capable of concealment.'

Indeed, Nancy saw, her wheelbarrow was standing ready on the front verandah. It bore several cushions and a crocheted rug that she recognised from the couch in her sunroom. He had, she realised, planned the whole thing like a military operation.

Inside, her house, although slightly dusty, was quiet and orderly. Nancy revelled in the clean smell of lavender polish, after so many weeks of the fusty, dead air of the nursing home. She had Reg assist her to her bedroom, where he stood outside the open door and chatted as she dressed, recklessly choosing her best frock and adding the amethyst necklace Fred had given her on their first anniversary. Before leaving the room she sat on the bed for a moment, and picked up the photograph from her bedside table.

'Here I am, love. Here for the birds. Reg is taking real good care of me.' She kissed the photograph and replaced it, sat for a moment while her eyes cleared, and called to Reg.

'Rightio, Reg, I'm decent. Can you give me a hand up off the bed?'

***

The hide had been newly swept, and, she now saw, the two wicker armchairs had been moved into it from the back verandah. Reg settled her into one of them, fussily placing cushions around her and draping a rug over her knees, the field glasses at hand on a small table at her elbow. Nancy recognised one of the matching set of carved rosewood occasional tables from her drawing room, but held her peace. Today was special, a day of sheer magic out of time, and she would not, she determined, complain about anything.

All through that long, hot summer day, Nancy and Reg watched the nesting dance of the Greater Spotted Coots as they settled into the nesting boxes in the great oak tree. As she ate chicken salad at the outdoor table, as she sipped tea brought on a tray from her own kitchen (in the best bone china, but she didn't say a word), as she was pushed up the path in the wheelbarrow to visit the bathroom, she was filled with a great, wide happiness, a happiness that spread until it could, she felt, encompass the whole world. She hadn't felt this good since Fred had gone. Now, in peace and joy, she felt him very near.

He was near her, she knew. As the sun sank lower to dip into the treetops, as the light turned golden, she felt his presence, just a breath away, felt she could almost reach out and push through the surface of the world as if punching through a paper screen, to take his hand.

She stayed until the last of the light was gone.

❧NORWEGIAN BLUE☙

It was the best of times. It was the worst of times.

The best, because this early in the morning, before he had to open up, the shop was dim and quiet and empty. The worst, because starting the day mucking out half a dozen animal cages was just naff. Especially if you'd been down the pub the night before.

At least there weren't too many birds at the moment. Bert hated birds worst of all. Not that there was anything personal about it – but it was the noise, the constant twittering, and if it was parrots, the sudden screeches they let out. What he really liked was kittens. They were quiet, and pretty, and good for business. Although they couldn't half shit. Nothing so off-putting to customers as a smelly shop, Dad had always said. That was why you had to come in early every day and clean right before opening. But yeah, kittens. They did bring in the customers. Trouble was, Bert grumbled to himself as he slid out the tray under the canaries, the bloody customers didn't bloody go away. Bert's idea of a good customer was a person who came in, found his own stuff, paid for it and left, preferably in cash and in silence. But when you had kittens, they'd hang about watching them for bloody hours. Specially the young girls. Laughing and screeching and taking pictures on their phones. And they weren't a good *type* of customer. Half of them never bought anything. He ought to charge admission, bloody fools using his shop like a bloody theatre. Puppies were almost as bad. He always took puppies, though, if he could get them. They were a long-term profit item. There was practically no limit, he'd found, to the amount of stuff a person would buy for a dog. Special food, special bowls, leads and collars, and all the toys… over and over again. With kittens, they'd buy the animal and a few toys and that was pretty well it, but dogs kept needing new stuff, and needing to be washed too. The do-it-yourself hydrobath was practically a money machine, especially since he'd started charging for the towels.

The mice had made a right old mess, as usual. Bert always left them till last, pretending to himself that they weren't there. He hated the smell of them, and the mindless way they ran in the wheel. Vermin, that was what they were. Thank God for the slide-out tray bottoms Dad had put in.

There, the cages were all done and everyone fed and watered. Now a quick flit round with the vacuum, set up the till and he'd have time to nip next door for a coffee before opening. He paused for a moment, savouring the quiet. This was how he liked the shop best, after it was made ready, but before opening. The small, contented presences of happy animals, the peace, the cool dim. At times like this, he could almost feel grateful that Dad had left him the shop.

***

Bert drew in a great, contented sigh and turned the page. It had been a quiet morning, and if every day were like that he'd be worried, but having the place to himself, without anyone breaking into his thoughts, wanting special kinds of birdseed or some arcane dog toy that no one had ever heard of, was a rare pleasure. It was almost, he sometimes thought, as good as it would have been, if Dad had had the taste to open a second-hand bookshop instead of a pet shop. He twitched in annoyance as the bell over the door tinkled.

The customer was a short, cheerful-looking man in a gabardine raincoat. He stalked across the floor and banged a parrot cage down on the counter.

'G'day. This is Harry. Sorry, but we can't keep him, so I'm bringing him back.'

The bird fluffed its feathers and crooned to itself. It was a medium-sized, blue bird, a member of the parrot family, standing about a foot tall.

Bugger that, thought Bert. 'Sorry, no refunds. Store policy.'

'Listen, it doesn't matter about a refund. Keep the money, I don't care, but you have to take him. My wife won't have him in the house.'

'But it didn't even come from here.

I've never seen a bird like that. We don't sell them, whatever it is. Just budgies and canaries, a few finches, occasionally some quail or a cockatoo.'

'Oh yes it did, I bought it here myself. From an older man.'

Bert frowned. 'How long ago?'

'About two years.'

'Yeah, okay. That'd be my dad. He passed away about a year ago. But listen, it's one thing if you bought it here and it's sick or something. You could bring it back within a reasonable time. But if you've had it for two years… that's your bird, mate. You can't just bring it back now. Sorry.'

'Look, please take him. I just don't know what else to do. My wife won't have him in the house. It's more than my life's worth to come home with him. It's me or the bird, she reckons. Honest to God.'

'But, if you've had him for two years… what's changed?'

The customer looked down and shuffled his feet. 'It's this kind of idea she's got. I can't talk her out of it. See, she reckons he's cursed.'

Bert shook his head. He couldn't

have heard correctly. 'What even is it?' he asked. 'It's not like any bird I've ever seen.'

'Oh, I can tell you that. He's a Norwegian Blue Parrot.'

'You what? Come off it, mate, you taking the piss?'

'No, why?'

'There's no such thing as a Norwegian Blue. It was a Monty Python sketch. It's not a real bird.'

'Ah, now that's where you're wrong. I looked it up on Google. Apparently there was Norwegian Blues, a long time ago. In Norway,' he concluded, as if that settled the matter.

'Hence the name, I suppose,' said Bert sourly. He could feel himself starting to get pissy. *Don't bite*, he cautioned himself. *That's exactly what got you sacked from your last three jobs. Keep calm, you're in retail now.*

'Yes, exactly!' said the customer, apparently failing to recognise sarcasm. 'Very rare they are. Very rare indeed. Rare and expensive. The old chap reckoned it was the first one he'd ever had.'

Blimey, thought Bert. *The old man*

really saw you coming. Wonder what it is really? Out loud he said, 'Looks more like a budgie to me, mate. Bloody great oversized budgie. Anyway, sorry, but I can't take him. We only sell new birds,' he went on, inspired. 'Not used ones.'

The bird punctuated his outrageous claim with a sudden squawk. 'Gimme a biscuit,' it said.

'It talks,' said Bert lamely.

'Oh yes, talks nineteen to the dozen, Harry does. Hardly shuts up.' The customer heaved a sigh. 'That was the problem.'

'What, says some bad language, does he?'

'Not so much the language… it's *what* he says.'

'Biscuit, biscuit, biscuit,' cried Harry, jigging up and down on his perch.

'Seems normal enough,' said Bert.

'Oh, he's normal enough *now*,' said the customer dolefully. 'It was only that one time, really. Usually, it's all give him a biscuit, or random things he's heard. But ever since…' he broke off. 'See, it was so weird… and then Marnie got it into her head that he's cursed. And she's determined to have him out of the house.'

'Out of my house!' said Harry, with a note of triumph. 'That bird's got to go! Biscuit!' He pecked at his little hanging mirror.

'There, you see?'

Bert shook his head. 'Not really.'

'Look, it was all fine until that night. Harry lived in the kitchen, Marnie loved him, we both did, but he was with her mostly, all day while I was at work, see, the kids loved him too… then that night.' His face crumpled. 'Marnie's parents came for dinner. And the kids insisted on bringing Harry into the dining room. And that was alright, except for a few rude things Harry said, but we were all used to that. And then all of a sudden while we were having coffee, he starts jumping up and down and screaming, "you're all going to die, you're all going to die." Over and over. It was pretty creepy, but we just thought it was something he'd heard on the telly. Marnie got him back in his cage and put his cloth on so he'd go to sleep.' He stopped, staring into space for a long moment.

'On the way home, Marnie's mum and dad had an accident. They were both killed.'

'Woah, that's rough,' said Bert. 'I'm sorry.'

'Yeah. See, ever since that, Marnie took against him. Says he's cursed.'

So he had heard correctly. Sheesh, what a wacko.

'Look, I'm very sorry for your loss,' he said, hoping his face didn't show anything, 'but really, I can't accept this bird. You'll have to take him to a shelter.'

'But… hey, I didn't tell you who I am, did I?' The wacko brightened up. 'I didn't tell you my name. Did I?'

'Mate, I don't care if you're fucking Melania Trump in drag, I am not accepting a second-hand...' He trailed off as he realised he was talking to empty air. The little bell tinkled cheerfully as the customer left the store.

The bird squawked again as he rushed to the door. 'Too late! He's gone! Biscuit biscuit biscuit!'

By the time he skidded to the door and wrenched it open, the customer was nowhere to be seen.

***

Several hours and much googling later, Bert had discovered that the Norwegian Blue parrot really was a thing

(Mopsitta Tanta). Of course, it had still been extinct for thousands of years, and therefore could not exist. 'Bloody oversized budgie,' Bert muttered to himself. 'Freak of nature.'

'Biscuit! Biscuit!' said Harry, jigging up and down on his perch. Bert poked another Iced Vo-Vo through the bars. He'd caved in after the bird's relentless nagging, and bought them on his lunch break. The cage was still sitting on the counter. That was another thing he had to do – find somewhere for it. He couldn't very well stay in the little round parrot cage; it was far too small, suitable only for travelling. Bert had a couple of fine, big birdcages in stock, but they retailed for $549, and he was reluctant to sacrifice the profits on one of them.

'Turn on the radio!' demanded Harry.

***

By Saturday morning, Bert had given up the idea of a cage. Instead, he'd set up a free-standing perch next to his counter. It stood in a litter box, which he had filled with cat litter; this made it easy to clean up Harry's droppings. As a result of this brainwave, the aviaries housing finches, canaries and budgerigars were also now floored with a shallow scattering of cat litter. It halved Bert's morning clean.

The shop door tinkled, and Harry screeched and flew to the top of the refrigerated unit. There was a rustling and a few muffled expletives as the customer fought his way through the heavy strip curtain Bert had installed as an added measure for Harry's safety.

The customer was the local MP, Bert saw with a sigh. Liberal, of course. *Don't say anything stupid*, he cautioned himself. *You're in retail now. The customer is always right.*

'Morning, Mr Royce,' he said cheerily. 'Lovely weather, ay. Straight outter the box.'

'Yairs,' replied Royce, making an obvious effort to broaden his accent. Tosser.

'What can we do for you today?' That was the way. Stick to the standard shopkeeper remarks and he'd be alright.

He reckoned without Harry, though.

'Raarrrk! Keep it in yer pants, you old whore!'

The smile dropped from Royce's face as if it had never been, leaving behind a pursed-mouthed expression of disapproval. Bert could feel his face turning red. Royce had recently been the subject of a media shitstorm involving a pregnant office worker and his (now ex) wife of thirty years.

'Sorry, mate. Bloody bird's always coming out with crap like that. Makes him hard to sell. Can't really let him go to a family with kids, right?'

'Hmmph,' grunted Royce. 'I need a collar for a cocker spaniel.'

'Right you are, mate, they're all down here.' Bert indicated the long display of collars, leads and harnesses. 'You probably want a Medium size. Did you measure the dog's neck?' He quailed at Royce's glare of scorn. 'Hm, right, yeah… well they're adjustable, I'd say this size should fit.' He eyed Harry nervously. *Come on mate,* he thought. *Pick one and bugger off before he does something awful.*

He almost made it, too. Royce actually had his hand on the strip curtain when Harry swooped down like an avenging angel and shat on his head.

***

Three months later, he couldn't

imagine the shop without Harry. He had turned out to be surprisingly good company, and Bert found himself enjoying his chatter, which was quite often relevant to something Bert had said. There had been one or two incidents like that with Royce, but the customers involved had all been ones Bert disliked, and none of them had returned, so he counted that as a win.

Harry himself had acquired a modest following. A number of the regular customers had taken to exchanging a few words with him while paying for their purchases, and Bert now kept a container of carrot sticks under the counter, to let them give him a treat. Harry almost never swore at these people. There had even been one or two offers to buy him, but after a little research, Bert had set Harry's price at $20,000, and no one wanted to pay that. It suited Bert – he'd got used to having him around, and he was a talking point. A lot of impulse purchases happened when people were talking to Harry, since he'd arranged a display of small but expensive items near his perch. And as long as he didn't sell him, he didn't have to worry about validating any claims about Harry's rare provenance.

The shop was busy today; he'd managed to get in a whole litter of kittens from the pound, and they were just the right age – old enough to be active and playful, while retaining their kitten sweetness. Two of them had really unusual markings, too – they were white, and spotted with black almost like Dalmations. They were going to walk out of the shop. He'd made up a big red sign for the window – GOT KITTENS! – and the flow of customers had been constant, although many just came to look.

The crowd of teenage girls was thinning now, and Bert spotted what he'd missed before – a woman with a little girl of about ten. These looked like a genuine prospect.

'Don't blow this for me,' he muttered to Harry. 'Best behaviour, okay?'

'Biscuit!' demanded Harry, as if negotiating.

'After I sell a kitten,' said Bert. 'Then you can have one. No sale, no biscuit.' He lifted the flap and walked out onto the shop floor. 'Help you with anything?'

The woman turned to him. 'I

promised my daughter a kitten. Our old dog died last month, they were very close. Lizzie hasn't been herself since.'

Lizzie, on closer inspection, did indeed look rather under the weather. The expression of happy excitement usual in these situations was conspicuous by its absence. The child dredged up a polite smile, but it didn't reach her eyes, and quickly slipped away.

'Well,' offered Bert, 'there's nothing to cheer up a house like a kitten. Does any of them appeal particularly?'

Just then, Harry let out a screech. 'I am Sailor Moon,' he cried, 'guardian of love and of justice!' The words meant nothing to Bert, but their effect on the child was immediate and profound. Her face lit up, her eyes seemed to sparkle, and she even stood a little taller, as she cast about and fixed her gaze on Harry. Kittens forgotten, she walked to the counter, treading softly as if afraid to wake from a dream. She reached out a hand and gently stroked the blue feathers. Harry hopped onto her arm, walked up to her shoulder and nibbled her ear.

'Help me, Obi-wan Kenobi,' he said. 'You're my only hope.'

When Lizzie turned around, she was a different child, her face shining with joy. 'Oh, Mum, please can I have him instead of a kitten? Please?'

'Oh, I don't know, sweetie. I don't know anything about birds. And exotic ones are expensive, I don't know…'

'Please! Please please please!'

The woman looked helplessly at Bert. 'I don't know… they're delicate, aren't they?'

Bert swallowed a sudden lump in his throat. 'Nah, Harry's tough as. And his feeding's too easy. Mostly fruit and raw veg, a bit of seed… he's no trouble at all. I could let you have him for…' he wrestled briefly with his financial self, and lost. 'One twenty.'

Shit! What had he said? He'd have charged more for the kitten.

'Discount!' cried Harry. 'A set of steak knives! Do not send any money!'

'Make it two hundred,' said Bert, 'and I'll throw in his perch and a travelling cage.'

***

Following Harry's departure, Bert found the shop oddly unsatisfying. It was once again cool and quiet, just as he liked it best, he told himself, but he kept glancing to his left and noticing the absence of Harry's perch. After wrestling with himself for several days, he chose the prettier of the spotted kittens, which he had been planning to sell for a hugely inflated price, to keep for himself.

The kitten, which he named Euro to remind himself not to be stupid about financial decisions, was a revelation. Bert had never been much of an animal person; he'd inherited the pet shop from his father, and had meant to sell it, but after six months without an offer he'd resigned himself to it. Now, softened up by living with Harry, he found himself absorbed in a developing relationship with the young cat. Because he spent long hours in the shop, opening seven days a week because weekends were prime time for the business, he carried Euro back and forth in a carrier, and his rather morose outlook on life took on a softness that brought a smile to his face more and more often. He often thought of Harry, sometimes regretting his quixotic decision to let him go for such a bargain price, but comforted himself that Harry had, after all, not cost anything in the first place.

Then, on a cold, blustery winter's day, when he was ensconced behind his counter with a fan heater under it, sharing a plate of buttered toast with Euro, the doorbell, quiet all day, rang loudly and Mrs Blakely entered the shop like a Valkyrie, bearing aloft the travelling cage he'd sold her, with a ruffled, disgruntled Harry. She strode across the floor and banged the cage onto the counter. Harry let out an outraged squawk, and Euro fluffed up all his fur and took off for his refuge atop the collar display.

Bert was lost for words, but Mrs Blakely was well able to supply the conversational deficit.

'I've brought him back,' she said. 'I just can't bear the sight of him, after what happened.'

Bert was at even more of a loss. 'What… happened?' he faltered.

'The fire. You'd have seen it on the news, the fire at the Old Vic. It was Lizzie's school play.'

A cold feeling settled in Bert's stomach. The theatre fire had been big news. Several children had died.

'Lizzie…'

'Oh, she's alive. For what that's worth. She won't be coming home for quite a while, but she's… well, she's alive.'

'Won't she want Harry, then? She loved him, I thought…'

Mrs Blakely heaved a sigh. She looked, Bert thought, as though she'd been sleeping rough. She was still well-dressed, but there was a crumpled look about her, somehow.

'It's not Lizzie. It's me. I just can't stand the sight of him. Look, I'm sorry, I know it's not your fault and I won't ask for a refund, but I just can't keep him.'

Bert didn't know what to say, so said nothing. If he knew one thing about upset women, it was that if you just kept your mouth shut, they'd tell you what the trouble was. He'd learned this the hard way.

'I'm sorry,' said Mrs Blakely. 'You must think I'm awful, storming in here like a mad woman. I've been so worried… and I'm not getting much sleep at the hospital.' She started to cry.

Oh, shit. 'Look, come around and sit down. Let me get you a cup of tea or something. You sit there and get warm for a second.' He left her huddled in front of the tiny heater, and escaped to the back room. Hopefully by the time he made tea, she'd have got a grip.

When he returned five minutes later, with a mug of strong tea into which he had stirred three heaped spoonfuls of sugar, she was sitting up and looking more controlled. He heaved a sigh of relief. One thing Bert really, really loved about the pet shop was that he never had to deal with any of that emo shit.

Mrs Blakely wrapped her hands around the mug. 'It was what he did, you see. After what happened… it just gives me a cold shiver every time I see him.'

Encouraged by silence, she went on. 'It was Lizzie's school play, you know? They rented the theatre for it. Her two best friends came round for the afternoon, they were going over their lines and we all had dinner together before going on to the theatre. They were so happy and excited. A real theatre, you know, not just the school auditorium…'

'Right…'

'Well, while we were having dinner, Harry suddenly started jumping up and down on his perch, you know how he does when he wants something…'

'Yeah,' said Bert.

'But it was what he was saying. He kept screeching, "you're all going to die, you're all going to die," and flapping his wings and jumping up and down…' we laughed at the time, but then… when the fire started the fire curtain collapsed, some of the kids were under it. Both Lizzie's friends were killed outright, and Lizzie… well, they say she'll walk again. Eventually.' She dissolved into a storm of weeping.

It was like a nightmare. Bert dithered, reaching to pat her shoulder, thinking better of it and drawing back his hand. He occupied himself by removing Harry's cage to the back room. Best to get him out of her sight. Presently the storm abated, and Mrs Blakely departed, still sniffling faintly.

***

A long, happy time ensued. After a couple of early tiffs, Harry and Euro got on well, and Harry resumed his wonted position on a perch to the left of the counter. Bert ran his shop, read his way through *In Search of Lost Time*, and did his own tax return for the first time. This necessitated a number of frantic calls to the Tax Office to correct his blunders, but all was eventually resolved, and for the first time Bert started to think of himself as a Real Businessman. He thought he might join the Chamber of Commerce.

He was immersed in his new book when she walked in, a novel whose translation from the French had shaken the literary world. It was strange, but beautifully written, and Bert was utterly captivated, so that he didn't hear the bell at the door, didn't see the flash of reflection as the plastic strips swung aside, and when a sudden stillness made him look up, she was standing at the counter as if carved from ivory, a small smile lifting the corners of her mouth, her head slightly cocked to one side.

Bert dropped his book, his bookmark flying out, forgotten, his place lost. As he scrambled to his feet (it didn't seem right to address Her from a seated position) he caught his foot on the leg of his chair and it clattered to the floor, the ladder back catching as it fell the corner of a display of dog treats. As the pattering of small rawhide shapes died away, Bert's stammered, incoherent phrases of his wish to be of service also scattered, stones dropped into a well of silence.

'I need a pet,' said the goddess.

It was an unusual choice of words, Bert thought, oddly reminiscent of the faintly foreign flavour that he always found clung to novels translated from another language. It was never anything wrong, as such, but there were hints of difference, like the faint accent that always remains to tint the speech of even the most fluent foreign speaker.

'Um,' said Bert, cleverly. 'Um. Any particular kind?' Interiorly, he howled and kicked himself. Could he have sounded any more moronic?

'Ohh... I don't know... what do you have?'

There were no kittens that week, nor puppies either. Bert rang the shelters several times a week, but had drawn a blank for some time. Kittens were rare in the Melbourne winter.

'How about a rat?' he heard himself ask, and wanted to die. What is wrong with you, chided his inner self. Rats were for school kids, and the occasional Goth.

He found himself raising the flap and emerging from behind the counter. Harry, most uncharacteristically, was fast asleep, his head jammed so far under his left wing that he seemed to have been decapitated.

The rats evidently did not meet the customer's requirements. Harry escorted her to the cage of finches, mentally cursing himself for not getting out a clean sweater when he'd spilled the spaghetti sauce last week. He raked his fingers through his hair (when had he last had it cut?) and cupped a surreptitious hand to smell his breath.

The customer remained motionless in front of the finches for some time, but Bert could tell there was no spark. He'd developed a sensitivity for the moment when a customer 'took' to an animal; there was a subtle change in the air, a warmth, a quickening, that you could detect if you were really paying attention.

The canaries and budgerigars likewise failed to excite her. That was it, really, unless she wanted some tropical fish. Tropical fish were a good prospect; when kept by the inexperienced, they were always dying and having to be replaced, and the equipment they needed was a major sale up front.

The customer spent longer in front of the tropical fish than anywhere else, but in the end she sighed and turned away. Bert wasn't surprised. A woman who looked like that, as if she'd stepped out of an ancient scroll, needed something exotic. A dragon, he thought, a happy Chinese dragon, or a phoenix; a creature of myth and legend, not the dull clay of this quotidian world.

'I might be getting some kittens next week,' he said, praying it would turn out to be true. He couldn't just let her walk out of his life. 'If you wanted to leave your number, I could let you know…'

He restrained himself from punching the air as she wrote her name and number in the order book, next to a strangely comatose Harry.

***

It was three weeks before he managed to source two half-grown kittens, and he whistled to himself as he set up the display cabinet for them, using all new items taken from stock. The kittens weren't the best for mercantile purposes, having already grown past the greeting-card stage; they were rangy, leggy creatures with squalling, raucous voices and long, thin tails. Everything about them seemed black and spiky, but perhaps that would appeal to Mei Ling; they might, he thought, be part Siamese. He put up a backing of red paper to show them off better, and hung a pair of tiny Chinese lanterns in the corner, that he'd got from the two dollar shop. He wouldn't lie about an animal, he told himself, but there was no harm in *suggesting*. It was fair to show his wares to their best advantage.

'Rawrrk!' said Harry, from his perch. 'Bloody hideous, mate!'

He put down the phone three times before he finally dialled Mei Ling's number. Each time, he thought of something he needed to do first. A lunchtime visit to the hairdresser for a long-overdue cut and style, a hurried trip home for a pressed shirt, a clean pullover and a liberal splash of aftershave, and the third time, a frenzied dash back to the two dollar shop for some more of the tiny paper lanterns to replace the ones the demon cats had shredded.

Harry ran up and down his perch as he arranged the new lanterns. 'Sexy boy! Sexy boy!' he cried. 'Who's a pretty boy then?' he demanded as Bert picked up the phone for the fourth time.

The phone was picked up on the fourth ring.

'Hello?' Some music played faintly in the background. With a thrill of pleasure Bert identified *The Ride of the Valkyries*.

'Bert Collins here, from World of Pets. We've got a couple of kittens in, that I thought you might like a look at.'

'Go on, mate,' cried Harry. 'Give her one for me! Woof!'

'What was that?' asked Mei Ling. 'It sounded like someone else on the line.'

'Um… yobbos out in the street,' lied Bert. He made frantic shushing motions at Harry, who bounced up and down, unrepentant. 'Is that *The Valkyries* you've got playing there?'

'Yes, you like Wagner?' She sounded faintly surprised, and Bert felt himself bristle a little. People assumed that just because you ran a shop, you couldn't appreciate anything decent. He'd encountered it before.

'I do, yes, he's my favourite composer, actually. Did you see the Australian Opera production last year?'

'Oh my God, yes! It was amazing!'

Please, Bert prayed to the God of the Arts. Please, don't let her be pretentious about it. Don't let her come out with something about the diminuendo of the male libido or some shit.

'Wasn't it incredible? What did you like best about it?' This was the acid test. Here was where she'd show feet of clay if she had them.

'Oh, just the whole – it was like they had a different approach, right? I mean, the music was sublime, but the whole production, it was like it was fun, you know? Siegfried and Mime – remember when he sniffed the milk?'

'I know, I nearly wet myself, and Siegfried with his bunks and his homework… and Brunhilde striding about in her military outfit – that was genius.'

'Oh and that rainbow bridge, to Valhalla – it was like they were referring back to Ziegfield. Like, they just didn't take themselves so seriously, and that just made the whole thing…'

She was perfect, thought Bert, settling back in his chair, a dreamy smile wreathing his face. She really was perfect.

'Attaboy!' said Harry. 'Get yer leg over! Gimme a biscuit!'

***

He spent the afternoon cleaning the shop, although he'd cleaned it as usual that morning. Twice more he stepped out, once to the chemist for some deodorant, once to the two dollar shop for yet more tiny lanterns. This time, he'd wait until she was nearly due before putting them up. He picked all the shredded red paper from the Devil Cats' case. He replaced the litter in the tray underneath Harry's perch with a fresh lot. Just before she was due to arrive (she'd said about six, but you never knew with the traffic, so he wanted to be ready by five-thirty) he gave Harry a corn cob, hung the lanterns in the cat enclosure, and arranged himself behind the counter with a book, trying to look casual and relaxed. When the bell above the door tinkled, he jumped a foot, and fell off his chair.

She was even more beautiful than before, now that he knew a bit about what she was like. Bert found himself hoping she wouldn't take to the cats. Then she'd have to come back again. Even more desperately, he hoped Harry wouldn't say anything embarrassing. That was what the corn cob had been for; they were Harry's favourites, and when he had one, he usually went at it with single-minded determination until he'd stripped the entire thing, which could take up to an hour.

The Devil Cats, as he'd hoped, did not meet with her approval. 'They're so spiky,' she said. 'No, I don't think – I love cats, but these ones, they're just not…'

'Not,' agreed Bert.

****

The second time he called her, he had some ferrets. They were beautiful creatures, he thought, if you could ignore the smell. He didn't really think Mei Ling would go for ferrets, but it would get her back to the shop, and perhaps this time he wouldn't panic, and would be able to ask her out. The words had frozen in his throat, last time, and she'd been out the door, and never heard the mumbled 'I was wondering if you'd like to…'

The shop was busy that day, and in the rush of customers, she was there before he had time for any of the preparations he'd planned. The sale displays near the door were picked-over and untidy, and Harry had been eating sunflower seeds, and had spat the husks in a six foot radius around his perch. Customers' feet crunched slightly as they paid for their purchases.

Mei Ling was enchanted by the ferrets. She hung over their cage, her eyes shining. 'Could I hold one?'

'Of course,' said Bert. He reached in and lifted out the prettiest of them, a sable hob. Mei Ling cried out in delight as the small creature ran up her chest and whiskered at her face. Then the smell hit her.

'You can get their scent glands removed when you get them desexed,' Bert told her. 'It's not so bad then.'

'Here, put it back,' said Mei Ling, handing back the ferret. He noticed that, despite her disgust, she still handled it gently. 'He's lovely, but I just couldn't have that smell. Oh God, it's all over me!' She sniffed at her hands. 'God, I think I'm going to be sick. Could I possibly…'

'Of course,' said Bert. 'It's this way.'

The following ten minutes were a

roller coaster for Bert. He was full of elation until he remembered that he hadn't cleaned the staff bathroom since Saturday before last. Granted, he was the only person who used it, but what if there was no paper? What if the towel was grotty?

Finally she emerged, sniffling slightly. 'I can still smell it. It's on my jumper. Oh no, and I got the tram here, I'll have to go on it smelling like this…'

'Don't worry,' said Bert, seizing his opportunity with both hands. I'll run you home if you like, I was about to close anyway.' Inside his head he danced a little jig of triumph. 'As a matter of fact, I was going to grab dinner at the new Korean place that just opened up down the road. Would you like to join me? And then I'll drive you home.'

'I'd love to – oh, but the way I smell. I couldn't go into a restaurant like this.'

'You can wear my jumper. It was clean on this morning.' He stripped it off, praying, and held it out.

'But you'll be cold. I couldn't.'

'I've got my jacket, don't worry, and it'll be warm in the restaurant. You can drop it back to me next time you're round this way.'

'Well, alright. Thanks!' She disappeared back into the bathroom. Bert did a little jig. It was a fine, fine day.

As they passed the counter, Harry burst into life. 'I believe in Malcolm!' he sang. 'Where you from, you sexy thing!' It was scratchy and off-key, but the tune was recognisable.

'Miracles, Harry, not Malcolm,' said Bert without thinking. But Mei Ling was transfixed.

'Ohhh,' she breathed. 'I didn't see you when I came in. Oh, you're beautiful!'

Harry preened a little.

'And he sings! Oh, Bert, I think this is what I've been looking for. Is he very expensive?'

'Um,' said Bert. 'We can talk about him over dinner.'

When they were settled at a window table, with what seemed like a thousand tiny dishes spread about them, she returned to the subject.

'I just love that bird. What kind is he? What's his name?'

'I'm not really sure what he is, to be honest.' He couldn't lie to her, he found.

'A customer brought him back after I took over the shop when Dad died. He said he'd bought him from Dad. Said he was a Norwegian Blue, but that's obviously not true.'

Mei Ling burst out laughing. 'No, seriously? Did he claim he was dead? Did you tell him Harry was pining for the fjords?'

Even as he laughed with her, Bert was thinking she'd just ramped her perfection up a notch. Beautiful, loves Wagner, and a Monty Python fan. Don't screw this up, he warned himself. Don't you dare screw this up.

Dinner was a lively affair, with much quoting from *Monty Python and the Holy Grail*. But later, when they'd both passed up the authentic Korean dessert in favour of banana fritters, she returned to the subject.

'Seriously, though, I would like to buy Harry. If he's for sale, that is. He is, isn't he?'

Bert sighed. 'To be honest, I wasn't planning to sell him again. That is, I was, but there's been some problems with him – I did sell him once and he came back. Woman said she wouldn't have him in the house. The first chap, too, he reckoned his wife had said the same thing.'

'What on earth for? Was it language? Coarse language? I've heard that's quite common, with parrots.'

'No, not that. It's kind of embarrassing… the first chap reckoned he was cursed.'

'Cursed? What on earth?'

'Well, as the bloke told it, they'd had the wife's parents over for dinner, and Harry suddenly started going, "you're all going to die." And then when they were driving home, both the parents were in an accident. They were both killed. And then after that, she was all, "it's me or the bird." That's what he said.'

Mei Ling's expression looked as if she'd stepped in dog poo. 'What about the other people? You said you'd sold him and he came back?'

This was not going anywhere good, Bert felt. The rapport that had grown between them over the meal now felt like a fragile, tattered thing.

'Well, I sold him to a lady for her little girl. The kid just fell in love with him, right? So off they went and I thought that would be the last I'd see of him.'

This elicited a grudging, narrow-eyed nod.

'Well he was back six months later. Same story, well almost – you remember that fire in the Old Vic theatre? The little girl was in the play, it was their school play or something, and the two kids that died were her friends and she's in the hospital and can't walk. They'd all been at dinner before the show, the lady said, and he started jumping up and down, going "you're all going to die you're all going to die." The two kids that died were there, see?   And Mrs Blakely couldn't stand having him in the house, so she brought him back here. Brought back his perch and everything, well her husband dropped it off the next day.'

Mei   Ling's   expression   was unreadable. It looked, thought Bert, like a cross between rage and nausea.

'That's superstitious nonsense,' she spat. 'Utter rubbish. I can't believe you'd even listen to such crap.'

'I'm only telling you what they said,' objected Bert. 'It's not like I'm believing it myself. Course not, it's rubbish. Just that's why I got him back. Both times. They didn't even want refunds, neither of them. I mean, I actually refused to take him back the first time, I didn't even know if the bloke really got him from Dad, and I told him no returns, and he just dumped the cage on the counter and ran off. Just legged it.

'Of course,' he went on, 'it's all rubbish. Just a coincidence. Harry says all kinds of stuff. Lines from movies and that. You heard him tonight, singing that song.' He continued to step back from the precipice, one careful foot at a time. 'And then the other lady, well she came in the shop and she was all crying and stuff, and I just couldn't say no, really. I felt sorry for her,' he finished, rather lamely.

'Well, I think he's just what I want,' said Mei Ling. 'Come on, how much do you want for him?'

'I dunno,' said Bert. 'He's kind of grown on me, I'm used to having him around. Don't know that I want to sell him at all, truth be told.'

***

She wore him down in the end, as he had known she would. Not that she ever nagged; Mei Ling was never crass. But there was a proprietory air in her dealings with him; he was conscious every time she spoke to Harry that she wanted him, more, that in some indefinable way she already thought of him as hers. It was implicit in the little sigh that sometimes escaped her after she'd fed him one of his favourite biscuits. A sigh, not of wistfulness, but of quiet satisfaction. There was a definiteness to Mei Ling, a kind of utter certainty; her personality was, he thought, a pen and ink sketch, every detail sharply defined; it cast his own watercolour nature into the background. It was part of what he found so attractive about her, he supposed. There was a rightness to her certainty, a kind of safety. Mei Ling could be relied on. Increasingly, as winter gave way to spring and their first tentative dinner gave way to a settled habit of concerts, of adventurous dinners in strange cuisines, of Sundays spent walking along the river or at the Gallery (he closed the shop on Sundays, now) he found himself thinking that Harry would be in good hands with her.

Finally, on a perfect evening in late October, he booked a table outdoors at their favourite Italian restaurant, and set out carrying Harry, in his travelling cage, with a pink ribbon tied around it.

It wasn't like really parting with Harry, he told himself as he negotiated the Friday night traffic. He and Mei Ling were a couple now, after all. Most weeks he spent several nights at her flat; it wasn't as if he was never going to see him again.

And yet, as he lifted the beribboned cage from the passenger seat, he was conscious of a faint stirring of something that was not quite unease, but a feeling of finality, as if somewhere an ending had been set in motion.

Lygon Street was busy, as always, and Bert's progress through the crowded pavement was marked with a wave of smiles and giggles at his unlikely cargo. Harry responded to the attention, jigging up and down on his perch, flapping his wings and screeching. The constant shifting of his weight made the cage awkward to carry, and by the time he reached the restaurant, Bert was having second thoughts about the wisdom of bringing him.

She was already there, settled at the corner table with a book and a bottle of wine, and he experienced again that subtle lightening of everything that always accompanied his first sight of her. Everything about her was perfect, and once again he marvelled at his good fortune.

'We're a couple of lucky blokes, eh, Harry? Now keep quiet, okay, we'll see if we can sneak up and surprise her.'

She was engrossed in her book, and he made it right up to the table; he could, he thought, have smelt her perfume, had they not been surrounded by the fragrances of Italian cooking. Carefully he lifted the cage until it would be level with her face when she turned. He could feel the other tables going quiet behind him, and hear the small murmurs of amused speculation. Morons. Hadn't they ever seen a parrot in a cage before?

Harry, of course, stole his moment. He launched into his Malcolm song. 'I believe in Malcolm,' he screeched. 'Where you from, you sexy thing!' The tune was just faintly discernible.

She was already laughing as she spun around, leaping up to throw her arms around his neck, her dark eyes shining with happiness.

'And you brought Harry! I'm so glad

he can be with me on my birthday!'

'Well, he can be with you always,' said Bert. 'He's your present.' A little stab of sorrow jabbed at him, but he pushed it away, revelling in her happiness.

'Gimme a biscuit,' said Harry.

***

Bert emptied the cash drawer into his banking bag and took a final look around. All was calm, all was quiet. He glanced to the left of the counter, but of course there was no standing perch. Harry hadn't been here for six months. It still seemed too quiet, sometimes.

He checked the ring box in his pocket. Tonight was going to be the night. He'd been planning it for days. Last week he'd finally received his tax refund, and instead of upgrading the refrigerated display case, as he'd planned, he'd spent the lot on the biggest diamond ring he could find.

Reservation at La Mirage, check. His one suit freshly cleaned and hanging on the shower rail at home, check. He'd taken it out of the plastic that morning, to air lest any hint of dry cleaning fumes mar his perfection on this night of nights.

His best silk tie, ditto. A new shirt hung on the wardrobe door, the creases carefully pressed out before he left for the shop. 'Thunderbirds are go,' he muttered to himself.

'Come on, Euro,' he called, dragging the carrier basket from under the counter. 'Home time, mate.'

***

He paused for a last look around before he switched off the light. His small apartment was uncharacteristically neat; he'd been up late the night before, vacuuming, scrubbing the bathroom, throwing out the piles of newspapers and miscellaneous clutter that had silted up every surface. Not that he expected to bring her back here; they'd go back to her place, he assumed, as they always did; it was far nicer than his, and of course Harry was there now. But it had seemed right, somehow, to have everything nice. He'd know it was; he would have nothing to be ashamed of.

Was his tie crooked? It felt crooked. He dashed back to the bedroom and adjusted it in the mirror. He ran the comb through his hair again. He checked his pocket for the breath spray he'd bought.

He'd use that right before he got out of the car. Everything had to be perfect tonight.

Euro was sprawled on the sofa, and looked at him upside down. 'Night, Euro,' said Bert. 'Next time you see me, I'll be an engaged man.' Ah, yes, that was something. The final perfect touch. He'd call her to let her know he was leaving and would pick her up in fifteen minutes. It was considerate, that was what. Let her know he was thinking of her.

She picked up on the fourth ring. He could hear music in the background; he thought it might be the Enigma Variations, but couldn't be sure; he couldn't quite focus on it, because he could also hear Harry screeching something.

'Hi, it's me. Just calling to let you know I'm leaving now, and I should be on your doorstep in about fifteen minutes.'

'Lovely, I'll see you soon – it'll be nice to get somewhere *quiet*.'

Harry could be heard going ballistic in the background. He couldn't quite make it out, but he seemed to be repeating some short phrase over and over.

'What's he saying, love?'

'Oh, it's so stupid – he's just being an idiot. He's been at it for twenty minutes. He keeps starting up again. "You're all going to die, you're all going to die." Over and over, it's driving me batty.'

Bert couldn't breathe, couldn't see. For a moment he was deaf, blind, paralysed. Time collapsed and the short, fat man in the gabardine raincoat was present to him, overlaid with the weeping Mrs Blakely. He had to get over there, stop whatever was going to happen from happening. His knees had started to shake.

'You just put your feet up, love, take it easy, I'll be there before you know it,' he choked out, trying to sound natural. 'Okay, love you too, bye.' His keys were in his hand and he was out the door, racing down the stairs (*calm down, don't rush too much, you can't afford a fall that will slow you down*) and through the small, dingy foyer.

He slammed through the front door, hardly registering the shock of pain on his shoulder, and raced around his car, fumbling and dropping the keys (*oh*

Christ oh Christ where did they go), groping frantically till his fingers encountered the jingling bunch. He almost dropped them again getting the door open, and again as he jammed them into the ignition.

The engine caught on the third try, and he roared off, grabbing the seatbelt one-handed and giving up on fastening it (*careful, don't give it too much juice, it's still cold, you'll stall it*), tyres screeching with the too-sudden acceleration.

He got his seatbelt fastened at the first red light, his shaking hands fumbling even that familiar task. *Now calm down*, he admonished himself. *You don't need a cop pulling you over.*

Every set of lights he encountered was red. 'Come on, come on, gimme a break,' he muttered as he waited interminably for the fourth set to change, watching the steady flow of cross traffic with bitter envy. Tears of panic prickled behind his eyes, and the car seemed hot and airless.

Gardenia Street was quiet and empty. *Good, that's good, no ambulance or anything.* He screeched to a halt in the empty space at the front, hardly registering that it was a bus stop. He left the car running, but had only got halfway across the footpath before he rethought it and raced back to snatch out the keys. He had a key to Mei Ling's apartment, in case of emergencies. He might need that. Please God, he would not need it.

On the first floor landing, the building was dark and silent, lit only by a soft glow from the landing window. Bloody typical. Of course the light was out. He jammed his thumb on the doorbell, praying inarticulately to a God in whom he had often denied any belief.

There was no response. *Oh God, oh dear Jesus*. He held up his keys to the light. Mei Ling's was marked with a dab of red paint. He slid it in, praying, and turned the knob.

He paused for a moment in the tiny hall, senses questing outward? 'Mei Ling?' he called. 'You there, love?' There was no answer, but he could hear something.

From behind the closed door to the living room, he could hear soft, hopeless weeping.

He wasn't sure what he was seeing, at first; there seemed to be two of her, in the middle of a room that was impossibly large. Then his overwrought mind made sense of the picture; the heavy curtains, usually closed in the evenings, were open to the night and the antiglare film had turned the window into a perfect mirror, extending the room into empty space, and in front of it, seeming to float in midair, he saw the reflected image of an empty standing perch, and at its foot Mei Ling, weeping over a small, blue corpse.

✷RYAN'S AFFAIR✷

He was crossing the road when she saw him, head bowed against the rain, walking briskly. Her heart turned over. Her Ryan, her husband. She still wasn't used enough to their marriage to take the word for granted, and she stood for a moment savouring it in her mind, watching him as he crossed to the pavement. A small, unexpected pleasure in her day. He stumbled slightly stepping up to the kerb. That was her Ryan, handsome as dammit and spastic as a retarded elephant. Her mind drifted back to the night they'd met; it had been at her regular Salsa club, and he'd been there with some friends on a buck's night. He'd asked her to dance and had been utterly, abjectly hopeless, but so good-natured about his clumsiness that she'd given him her number anyway. They'd been dancing many times over the following two years, but he'd never really got the hang of it, and even at their wedding he'd failed to manage the simple routine of their wedding dance, losing his balance and falling onto the cake, dragging her down on top of him. How they'd laughed, although there had been a tiny part of her that had mourned.

The office was jumping when she got back with her boss's dry cleaning, and in the flurry of clients arriving and lost files she forgot about seeing him.

***

Ryan was late home, and she was almost starting to worry when she heard his key in the door. She ran to greet him, laughing with relief, burrowing her nose into the special place in his neck.

'Sorry I'm late, Liz. Traffic was awful. It's the rain – everyone drives instead of getting transport.'

'I know, and half of them can't bloody drive. Never mind, you're here now.'

It wasn't until she was clearing the

table after dinner that she remembered.

'Hey, I saw you in town today. Down near Officeworks.'

'What? Nah, must've been someone else.'

'No, really, I'm sure it was you. Weren't you down that way about two o'clock?'

'Nuh-uh. Didn't even get out at lunchtime. I was flat out today.'

'Oh, well, guess you've got a double, then.' She turned the tap and a cloud of steam erased the moment.

***

Thursday was their shopping night, and they met after work to do the weekly grocery shop. They were just joining the checkout queue when a deep, throaty voice called out. 'Ryan! Hey, fancy meeting you here!'

The woman didn't look like anyone Liz could imagine Ryan knowing. Small but voluptuous, she was dressed – almost dressed, Liz muttered to herself – in skin-tight leggings and a top that left little to the imagination. Glossy, jet-black hair flowed free to her waist, and her eye makeup looked more like stage makeup than anything Liz had ever seen on the street before. She turned to Ryan, waiting for an introduction, and was startled to see that he was blushing scarlet, and seemed to be silently signalling the woman. At least, she couldn't imagine why else he'd be waggling his eyebrows up and down like that.

'Um, this is my wife, Liz,' he mumbled. 'Liz, this is Lola... mumble mumble client mumble mumble.'

Good grief, thought Liz. What was the matter with him? She supposed the woman must be one of his criminal clients, but he never normally minded running into a client. On the way home, she started to ask him about the mystery woman, but he was so obviously desperately uncomfortable that she let the subject drop.

***

Friday was her half day, and instead of going straight home, she decided to call into Ryan's office and see if he was free for lunch. They hadn't been out for lunch during the week for ages; since their marriage, the habit had fallen by the wayside. It would be a little trip down memory lane.

The reception area at Zimmerman Associates was quiet and stuffy. Even the artificial plants looked more dusty than usual, and Hayley, the receptionist, seemed to be in a coma. Liz had to clear her throat three times before she activated, reinforcing Liz's secret belief that she was actually a robot in drag, perhaps a reconditioned air hostess.

Hayley startled into life, animation spreading over the painted face like a Powerpoint transition. 'Oh, hello, Liz. Were you looking for Ryan? He already left, sorry.'

'Oh, no biggie. I was just hoping we could have lunch. Do you know where he went? I could join him if he's not with a client or anything.'

'It's Friday, Liz, he went to his –' Hayley broke off, uncharacteristically flustered. 'That is, sorry, no I don't know where. Or who, or anything.' A tide of crimson was creeping up her face, obscured but not hidden by the thick layers of makeup. It was the first sign Liz had ever seen that Hayley was actually alive and had blood circulating, and she was intrigued.

'His what? Went to his what?'

'Oh, I don't know, his lunch, I suppose.' Hayley shuffled papers on her desk.

Well, that was weird. Liz left the office feeling oddly upset. Stupid Hayley probably just had a short circuit, she told herself. Probably needed to go for a service, or a rebore or something. Bloody fembot. She walked slowly to the tram stop, and although it was a rare and perfect day, the sky felt dark to her.

At home, she embarked on a cleaning binge, scrubbing and vacuuming as if her life depended on it. She'd get it all done this afternoon, she told herself, not noticing that she was scrubbing the bath a second time, so they'd have the weekend free. She suppressed the urge to call Ryan's mobile. He didn't like her to call him if he was with clients, and he must have been with clients, she told herself, that or in court. Then she scrubbed the bath a third time.

***

Saturday passed uneventfully, the morning occupied by sleeping late and going out for brunch, and the afternoon by Ryan's mowing the grass while Liz relaxed on the sofa with cups of tea and the latest James Patterson. But on Sunday, something happened that shattered her calm.

They had been invited to a barbecue, and she was putting the final touches to her makeup while Ryan had his shower. The theme from *Pirates of the Caribbean* thundered out from Ryan's bedside table.

The shower had only just gone on, so he wouldn't be out for a while. She'd better see who it was, in case it was something urgent. Low man on the totem pole at his firm, Ryan sometimes got calls from criminal clients arrested over the weekend. She picked up the phone and swiped its fancy pattern to unlock it, but by the time she'd done it four times and finally succeeded in bringing up the screen, it had stopped ringing. She was about to bring up the 'missed calls' list when it vibrated sharply in her hand, and the double beep announced a text message.

'Sorry, can't make it Monday nite, can u pls call me, luv Lola', read the message.

Liz now knew what it meant in

books, when they described people feeling the blood drain out of their faces. She'd always scoffed at the idea – how could you possibly feel something like that? But there was no mistaking that cold, prickly sensation in her face for anything else. She sat abruptly on the edge of the bed just as her knees gave way.

Lola. That had been the name of that glammed-up person they'd seen in the supermarket. The one Ryan had been all weird and bothered about. And then Hayley had been all weird when she'd turned up at his office to surprise him for lunch. The scene replayed in her head. 'Gone to his…' and she'd asked, hadn't she, to his what, and Hayley had started messing around with stuff on her desk and refused to look at her.

The shower squeaked as the water was shut off. She had, she knew, six and a half minutes before Ryan came out. That was how long it took him to shave. Every single time. They'd laughed about it often enough, about his predictable, same-every-time ways of doing things, and her own slapdash approach. Now, she wondered bleakly if they'd ever share a laugh again.

Of more immediate importance was the question of what she would do, right now, or in – she glanced at the time display on Ryan's phone – three minutes. She whipped her head around, staring about the bedroom, but neither the wardrobe nor the dressing table provided any inspiration. She was vaguely surprised to find the pleasant, sunny room looking no different than it had a few minutes ago. Somehow, she felt, there ought to have been some visible sign of the tsunami that had rolled over her placid life. Outside the window, their street remained normal. Mrs Jacoby across the road was sweeping her front path, and the scratching of her broom whispered through the open window.

With a start, Liz realised that something else could not be heard. The buzzing of Ryan's shaver had stopped. Her few minutes' grace were over; even now she could hear a soft footfall outside the door. Her heart pounded in her chest, as if, she thought, she were the guilty one. She reacted instinctively, switching off the phone and shoving it back on the bedside table, and stood to fluff the pillows as her husband, that faithless, cheating arsehole, entered the room.

***

Having opted for secrecy on the impulse of panic, Liz found she was stuck. She couldn't, she felt, confront him out of the blue; there had to be some visible trigger. If only she hadn't panicked and concealed the fact she'd seen that text. All through the barbecue she was absent and distracted, and gave unwitting offence to several friends by failing to hear their greetings. She escaped to the loo as often as possible, each time staying in the bathroom with the door locked for as long as she felt she could get away with. By the time they left, a number of people were giving her long, considering looks, and their hostess, whose youngest child was in fourth grade, made a point of mentioning that they still had their old pram and cot stored in the garage.

***

Liz hunched nervously over her macchiato in the back booth of the Hollywood Palace. It had started to rain shortly before she'd come out, and the air was damp and steamy, the hissing of the espresso machine a comfortable counterpoint to the rumble of trams passing outside. Kathy was late, of course; she was always late. Here she was now, rushing in in a spatter of wet umbrella and raincoat, dripping all over the waxed linoleum and skidding to a halt in a tangle of wild orange curls and various scarves in clashing colours, all of which she dumped on the bench seat in an indiscriminate pile with her dripping leather coat.

'Long black, double shot, thanks, Rula! Now,' she went on, 'what's going on, Liz? I had to practically break my back grovelling to old Welly-drawers to get a long lunch.'

'It's Ryan.' Having got that much out, Liz was at a loss for how to proceed. Saying it out loud would make it true, somehow, more real than when it was just something she knew that no one else did.

'Oh my God! What happened? Was he in an accident? Is he going to be alright? Can I do anything?'

Liz gestured frantically, fighting back tears. She mustn't lose it now. Kathy would go right off if she started blubbering.

'What?'

'He's having an affair.' There, the dreadful words were said. There was a brief silence, during which a quote from her favourite childhood book floated across her mind. 'The fat is in the fire, the die is cast, the jig is up, the goose is cooked, and the cat is out of the bag.' Despite the awfulness of it all, she couldn't help a faint snigger as the familiar words, with their cargo of childhood pleasure, lifted her spirits.

Kathy sat back, blowing a hard stream of air to lift her fringe. 'Boy, you really had me going there for a minute. Nice one, bitch. So what was really so urgent?'

'No, he really is. I found out yesterday.'

'Crap, you were laughing, you wouldn't be laughing. Pull the other one, it plays "Jingle Bells."'

'Kathy, listen. I saw a text on his phone, it was while he was in the shower and it was from this woman, going that she couldn't make it tomorrow night, that's tonight, and she said "love, Lola." And we don't know anyone called Lola, or at least we didn't, but on Thursday we saw this woman in the supermarket and Ryan was all funny, like he was embarrassed or something, he didn't want me to meet her, that was obvious. He was all red in the face and stuff. And you know how Ryan is.'

'Yeah, it's not like him. But that doesn't mean he's having an affair, does it? She might be a doctor or something. Or some lawyer that got the better of him in court or something like that.'

Liz snorted. 'Lawyer schmawyer. You didn't see her. Tits out to here, sprayed-on pants, eye make-up like Cruella De Vil. Honest to God, she looked like she was on her lunch break from working her corner.'

'Well, maybe she *is* a prostitute. Maybe he defended her or something. He's got clients like that, hasn't he?'

'Yeah, yeah, he's got crim clients, but Kathy, that's not it. He's not embarrassed if he runs into them. Come on, you know Ryan. Likes everyone, always feels at home, and *never, ever gets embarrassed*. Remember at our wedding when he fell in the cake? Even then he just roared with laughter. And besides, her name was Lola and that was the name on the text, and she signed it "love." And when I went round on Friday to see if he was free for lunch, he'd already gone out and the receptionist was all furtive, she started to say something and stopped herself, it was weird. And the other day I saw him down the other end of Bridge Road, and when I mentioned it that night he denied being anywhere near there, but I *saw* him, Kathy. I mean, it's not like I'm not going to recognise my husband.'

They stared at each other in silence for a while.

'Have you confronted him?'

'No, that's why I wanted to talk to you. I've got no idea what to do now. I mean, suppose I confront him and he just denies it? Then I've made myself into the bad guy. And what if it isn't what it looks like? I mean, I know it is, but just on the off-chance.'

'Hmm. But if you don't, then what?'

'I don't *know*!' wailed Liz. 'We've only been married less than a year. I've never had to deal with anything like this.'

Kathy had drifted into thinking mode, elbows on the table, chin propped on her linked hands, faraway stare boring through the back wall of the café. Liz sipped her coffee, waiting. It was never any good disturbing her when she got like this, she'd take your head off. She waved at Rula for another round of coffee. She ought to order lunch, she supposed, but she felt too upset to eat.

Rula came bustling over with Kathy's strong black and her own Macchiato. 'Any food?'

'Um, I don't think so today, thanks, Rula.'

Rula shook her head disapprovingly. 'Nice Spanakopita. You eat. And for your friend I bring the lamb souvlaki like always. With extra chips.' She nodded firmly and departed, a small, round force of nature.

Kathy shook her head and awoke from her trance. 'Did you order lunch? I'm starving.'

'Well, sort of. You're getting lamb souvlaki with extra chips.'

'Good stuff.' Kathy rubbed her hands together. 'Now, what I reckon is this. We need more information, so we'll have to investigate him.'

'What, you mean like detectives?'

'Yep. We'll have to follow him, go

through his phone, his bank statements, all like that. Get the goods on the fucker. Then when you do confront him, you'll know what you're doing. Maybe even catch him in the act.'

'I can't do that, it's like spying.'

'Yeah, so?'

'Well, it's... it's a violation of trust. We don't do things like that.'

'Liz, screwing around when you're married is a violation of trust. You're just acting in self-defence.'

'Anyway, I don't know how to investigate anyone.'

'Yes, you do. You watch television. It's easy. You can start with his phone. Just go through the call history and the text messages, you can do it while he's in the shower or whatever. Write down everything that's with someone you don't recognise. And then you look at his credit card statements. See where he's spending money, there's bound to be flowers or motels or something if he's having an affair. A restaurant you didn't go to or something. Write everything down, and then we can examine it. See if there's a pattern and stuff. Like, maybe there's always a text to and from a particular person with a motel charge the same day, that kind of thing.'

'I don't know, Kathy, it all seems so, well, sneaky. Sleazy.'

'Well, but you need to know, don't you? After all, Liz, he's your husband. You've got a *right* to know.'

'I suppose. Alright, I'll do it!'

***

She started with Ryan's phone, that very night. Once she was sure he was soundly asleep, she slid out of bed and took his phone to the spare bedroom, where a notepad and pen lay ready on the dressing table. She'd set up for it before he got home, wanting to minimise the amount of moving around she'd have to do. She eased the door shut before turning on the light. Ryan slept like the dead, but there was no sense taking chances. She couldn't even face thinking about what she would say if he caught her going through his phone. A pity she couldn't have done it while he was at work, taken a sickie or even done it at the office, but he never went anywhere without it. Even if he was popping out for a litre of milk he took it with him. *Now you know why,* whispered a sour little voice at the back of her mind.

She started with the text messages, and scrolled down as far as the history went, making notes as she did so. Most of the texts were obviously work-related, but she hit pay dirt, too. There were several texts from Lola, not saying much but making appointments, times and dates, but a place was never mentioned. *They must have their special place*, muttered the voice. *Probably her flat. Better check his keyring, see if there's an extra key.* She froze for a moment, horrified at herself. Who was she turning into? She wasn't the sort of person who had ideas like that.

She shook it off and turned to the call history. Nearly all the calls showed names, most of which Liz recognised – they were either people Ryan worked with, or they were places like the County Court, or other law firms. There didn't seem to be any with clients, but that made sense – he'd be talking to clients on his office phone most of the time, she supposed.

Then she found it, or at least something suspicious. This call had no name associated with it. It was to a local number, very local in fact, as the prefix showed it to be in the same part of town as both her and Ryan's offices. The call duration had been short, only a minute and a half. She kept scrolling down. There were a few more calls to that number, all short, until one day last month, when he had been talking to whoever it was for twenty-six minutes. She made a note of it and kept going, but that seemed to have been his first call.

Fighting an urge to stay right there and sleep in the spare bed, Liz hid her notes in the dressing-table drawer and crept back to bed, to replace her husband's phone on its charger and lie staring at the ceiling until dawn.

***

It was not until Wednesday that she got the opportunity to look into Ryan's banking records. He had a rudimentary home office set up in their tiny third bedroom, but other than to dust, vacuum and empty the waste paper basket, she had no reason to go in there. Her opportunity came, or was manufactured, when she declared herself too tired to cook and sent him out to fetch a pizza. As soon as she saw his car turn the corner at the end of their street, she rushed to the office, yanked open the bottom drawer with its hanging files, and abstracted the pile of credit card statements from their folder. She raced into the spare room and sat down with her notebook and the kitchen timer, which she set for fifteen minutes to give herself a safety margin.

It didn't take long to scan the statements. He evidently only kept them for a year, so there were only twelve. A few restaurant entries tallied with her memory of nights they'd gone out. There were two charges to Ticketek, matching the two musicals they'd gone to. There were some entries for Henry Buck's, where Ryan bought most of his clothes, and one for a jeweller's. That was the necklace he'd given her for her birthday. Looking at what he'd paid for it made her feel like a lowlife. It was all normal, all in order. She tidied the statements into a neat stack and replaced them in their folder, with six minutes to spare before the timer would have gone off.

The next thing would have to be his bank account. There was no time now, though, she thought with relief. This spying business gave her the creeps. It was just another way that infidelity damaged people, she supposed. You never read about this in the magazines, but she was, she felt, turning into someone else, a prying, furtive, suspicious individual that she didn't even recognise, and certainly wouldn't like if she met. She slid the drawer shut, took a last look around Ryan's office to make sure nothing was out of place, and returned to the kitchen.

***

The bank account was, in some ways, easier to manage. All she had to do was log into his account. This could be done from work, so the next day she waited until her boss had gone to lunch and called up the bank's website.

With trembling fingers, she typed in the account number and password, hoping her reasoning had been correct. The website would, she knew, lock the account if there were three wrong attempts. She was relying on Ryan's trick for remembering his pin number when it changed; what you do, he had told her, is you write it into your cheque book as an amount of money. That morning, after he'd left for work, she'd found his seldom-used cheque book, and sure enough, there had been a note scribbled on the inside of the back cover: N.B. $42.07. Now, holding her breath, she entered 4207.

And she was in! She almost laughed with elation before she remembered what she was doing. She was *spying on her unfaithful husband*, and she had just *hacked into his bank account*. She could probably go to jail for it.

She had brought her little notebook to work with her, and she opened it to the timeline she'd made, comfortably aware that Mr Coniaris wouldn't be back for at least an hour and a half, longer if he ran into any of his many friends.

The transaction listing looked regular, structured as it was into segments by the regular salary deposits and automatic payments into their joint account, from which they paid the mortgage and household expenses. There were cash withdrawals of a few hundred dollars each week and transfers to pay Ryan's credit card, and that was pretty much it. Most of their purchases and so on were of course made through the joint account, with their personal accounts only for private expenditure. She scanned down the list, and then she saw it. There had been a large payment made at the beginning of the month, and a similar payment at the beginning of the previous month, right after that long phone call. Liz felt physically ill. Was he paying the woman's rent, had he set her up in some nasty little love nest? She'd thought things like that only happened in old books. Surely men nowadays didn't 'keep mistresses'? She envisaged Lola lying about on a sofa in a black lace négligée, eating chocolates all day. But much as she had already come to dislike the woman, she couldn't really see that confident person she'd met in the supermarket lying about at some man's beck and call. Still, it probably explained the lack of credit card charges. He was taking out big whacks of cash so he could go wining and dining without any inconvenient paper trail.

When was he doing it, though? It was true he'd called to say he was working back a few times lately, more than a few in fact, more often than usual. But when that happened, he still got home no later than eight, much too early to have been going out to flash nightspots, and also, she now recalled, he was always ravenously hungry too, which didn't fit with having gone out to dinner. So he wasn't spending all this money on going out. With a sick feeling, she realised he must be buying jewellery for the woman. That meant it wasn't just a casual fling, but a commitment of sorts.

At this point Liz bolted for the ladies' room, where she lost her breakfast and possibly last night's dinner.

***

No one ever mentioned, Liz thought as she sat in the café across the road from Ryan's office, how *tiring* the whole business was. In the magazine stories she had read, and the personal accounts she'd occasionally heard from her friends about unfaithful men, there was plenty about how betrayed one felt, plenty about shock, and grief, and the damage to one's self-esteem. But no one ever mentioned the sheer drudgery of it. The toll exacted by constant watchfulness, looking for more signs of it. The burden of always watching what one said, lest one betray suspicion. Liz now woke up tired every morning, and by five o'clock she nearly always had a headache. Gone were the pleasant, carefree evenings and weekends she had come to take for granted. She'd lost weight, too. Ryan had remarked on it, and had suggested she see her doctor for a checkup. 'You haven't been yourself lately,' he had said. 'You might need extra vitamins or something.'

Liz would not have been recognised even by a close acquaintance. Not even her mother, she thought, catching sight of her reflection in the café window, would know her now. Wrapped in a long, scarlet coat she'd bought at St Vincent's, her face obscured by oversized, round, op-art sunglasses and a slash of scarlet lipstick, and her straight, blonde hair completely replaced with a short brown wig she'd also found at Vinnie's, she looked like an entirely different kind of person: flamboyant, and much older. She was pleased with her disguise; none of it was fundamental, and the whole lot could go on and off in five minutes in a lavatory cubicle. She kept it all in a tote bag which went to work with her, and effected her transformation in the public lavatory in the little shopping mall on the way from her office to Ryan's.

This was her third attempt; twice already she had donned her mystery woman outfit and staked out his office, blessing the single entrance that guaranteed he would exit the building in plain sight. Each day after work, she had rushed to the mall, put on the disguise, and arrived at the café across from Ryan's firm by 5:15. Thank God their offices were close, or it wouldn't have been possible.

The first time she had done this, she had watched as Ryan came out of the building and got on the Number 48 tram, scuttling across the road and boarding the tram at the rear entrance just in the nick of time before the lights changed. She had watched him sit on the tram and ride home, and from the tram she had seen him start towards their house. Lacking a plan for reversing her transformation, she had been forced to remove the disguise on the tram, occasioning some very odd looks from her fellow passengers.

On the second day, she decided to

count getting on the tram as a given, and had gone back to the mall to reverse her disguise before getting the next tram home. Ryan had not been there, however, and on checking her phone she discovered a text informing her that he would be working late. This was annoying, as she now realised she had missed following him on the one day she would have struck gold. She had therefore determined to keep up the surveillance every day, no matter what. Today, despite pleas from Mr Coniaris to stay back just for half an hour to finish the correspondence, she had adamantly rushed out on the stroke of five, hardening her heart against the hurt, forlorn look on her boss's face as she left him in a welter of unanswered letters. He was a sweet old thing, and she hated to do it, but she'd make it up to him tomorrow. She'd bring him one of the sticky pastries he loved, which his wife had forbidden him, for his morning tea.

Here came Ryan now. Behind the big, ugly glasses, tears sprang to her eyes as she watched his tall, athletic form cross to the tram stop. Leaving her half-drunk coffee she rushed across the road just as the tram pulled up, belting around the back of it and in by the rear door just in time to see Ryan nearly fall flat on his face as he boarded the front steps. The klutz, she sniggered as she swiped her card. At least once a day he tripped over something.

She watched him like a hawk as they trundled along Bridge Road, craning back and forth to see between the crowd of standing passengers who'd piled on at the Town Hall. And finally her patient stalking was rewarded, when after only half a dozen stops he got up and pulled the cord. Flushed with elation at the success of her strategy, Liz congratulated herself for fully five seconds before she realised that the evidence she was about to collect so triumphantly would spell the death of her marriage.

She waited until the last possible moment before getting off the tram, and as it pulled away she saw him crossing the road, reaching the opposite pavement just as the lights changed and she was stuck watching the red man, listening to the slow, aggravating clicks that would warn a blind person not to cross. The traffic at this hour was much too heavy to risk crossing against the lights, and she stood helpless, her eyes fixed on her husband as he walked along the footpath and turned in at a narrow door.

Right, well she'd found where he was going, at least. As soon as the pedestrian sign turned green and the rapid clicks sounded, she dashed across to the door where he'd disappeared.

It wasn't an ordinary shop or business, that was evident – all she could see through the glass door was a flight of carpeted steps leading up to the next level. Other steps led down to a basement. Not knowing which way he'd gone, she plumped for up, as those stairs were lit and the down ones were not.

Heart pounding, she had set her foot on the first step before she thought of her disguise. If she was going to catch him and confront him, she didn't want to look like a clown. She glanced hurriedly about, saw no one, and ripped off the wig, sunglasses and coat, stuffing them all pell-mell into the tote bag. Then, with a last, unsteady deep breath, she climbed the stairs.

As she climbed, the sound of music from above filtered down, growing louder as she passed the halfway landing. It was Latin music, and a flood of nostalgia washed over her as she recalled the night they'd met, at that Salsa club where Ryan had so distinguished himself by the combination of his awful left-footedness and his unshakeable good humour about it that she'd been intrigued enough to give him her number. And now here they were.

Get a grip. Don't start crying now.

She had reached the top and stood amazed in the doorway, for a moment unable to process what she was seeing. The door opened into a single, enormous room, brightly lit and largely empty. One wall was mirrored for most of its length, and small groups of tables and chairs were clustered at each end, but most of the space was taken up by a huge dance floor. And there in the middle of it, large as life, were her husband and That Woman, doing a very creditable salsa.

It was the last thing she had expected to find, and her knees threatened to give way as she processed it. She sagged against the door frame as she watched Ryan execute a really nifty combination. So this was what they were up to. Coming here to dance, when he couldn't dance with her, his wife, but he could dance alright now with Bloody Lola, oh yes indeed. It almost seemed like a worse betrayal than the affair itself, that he would share something that had been so important to her with this other woman.

As she watched, though, it became clear that this was not merely an assignation; this was a *lesson*. Lola was instructing him, and not taking any crap, either. As she listened to Lola's strictures about his frame and footwork, Liz recalled the long-ago days of her own dance lessons, and her carefully-constructed theory flew apart into its components and circled dizzyingly around her head. She didn't know what to think now.

The lesson came to an end, and Ryan and Lola walked off the floor towards a small desk in the corner opposite the door. There was nothing affectionate in their appearance now; they didn't even walk particularly close together.

'So when is your anniversary?' asked Lola.

'Twenty-second of October,' said Ryan. He was talking about their wedding anniversary? To this woman?

'You'll be fine,' said Lola. 'There's still six weeks to go, you're going to knock her socks off.'

'I hope so. I screwed up so badly at our wedding. Did I tell you I actually fell over in the middle of our wedding dance? Landed on top of the cake. It was an absolute disaster. I've been wanting to make it up to her ever since. I've got it all planned. I'm going to take her to dinner at Fidelio's, and the salsa club where we met is just around the corner, it's still there, I checked, so we'll go straight round there after dinner.'

'That's so sweet,' said the femme fatale, looking soppy. 'She must love you a lot.'

They still hadn't seen her. Liz stepped back from the doorway and ghosted away, stepping quietly until she reached the street and then running, running hell for leather back along Bridge Road, running to avoid being seen, running to let out the rush of energy and the joy of living.

⁖UNCLE ZAN'S DOG⁎

'**H**old the lift!'

No please, of course. No thank-you, not even a smile as I stuck my hand between the closing doors, risking losing it. She shouldered into the packed lift, elbowing me in the ribs as she squeezed past.

The lift is rated for seventeen people according to the little sign above the control panel, but with the Senior Partner, the Junior Partner, three 'sekketries', the new associate, Zheng Fang, and my humble self, there already didn't seem to be room for even one more. That didn't deter Lana, the Office Bitch. Never go drinking with that woman. You're liable to find yourself on your arse in the gutter at three o'clock in the morning. She turned to face the doors, the sharp corners on her oversized handbag digging into various portions of my anatomy, and no doubt others'. Fang, of course, had got himself safely into the back corner. You can always rely on him to make himself comfortable, like a cat. He almost never says anything, but somehow he always seems to have the last word.

The lift groaned and started its slow descent to Ground Zero. Working on the fortieth floor has this disadvantage: apart from being utterly bloody terrifying every time you look out of the floor-to-ceiling windows, it takes forever to get up and down. Some people enjoy the view; myself, I've never got used to the fact the building sways in the wind. You can't feel it, but you can see it if you're looking out. Nasty, I call it.

Anyway, there we all were, diligently avoiding eye contact and watching the indicator as it inched downwards through the thirties. It's like a religious rite, as if we were somehow lending our life forces to the mechanism. Perhaps we are.

We'd reached twenty-four when it

happened. The lift lurched sickeningly and jolted to a halt. The sekketries let out little shrieks. They always act in unison, like the Three Little Maids. It's a female thing, I think. They all go to the lavatory together, too, if we're out anywhere. The Senior Partner groaned and muttered something under his breath, adding 'sorry, girls' to whatever filthy, depraved thing he'd said. He always does that; he'll come out with something breathtakingly obscene in front of young women, and follow it up with 'sorry, girls,' to bar anyone from complaining. The Junior Partner didn't say anything; he sighed in a patient way and set his briefcase on the floor. Fang didn't say anything either, but I thought I detected a slight wince in the corners of his eyes; Lana had grabbed onto him when the lift had lurched. She has this way of treating people as if they were furniture. I wondered if he'd have claw marks in his arm. That woman is a predator, pure and simple. I noticed she hadn't grabbed the elderly, married Junior Partner, although he had been a lot closer to her. Or me either, if it came to that. Evidently the only person capable of supporting her was Fang, even if she had to kick a few sekketries out of her way to get at him. He's a handsome devil, I'll give him that.

There were murmurs and mutterings about trains, and a few people got out their phones and sent texts. The Junior Partner, of course, was on the lift telephone expostulating in courteous and dignified tones with the maintenance people. It was hardly an unusual occurrence, after all – the lifts in that building go out with monotonous regularity; it's the standard excuse of the sekketries whenever they're late. Of course, five o'clock on a Friday isn't the most popular time for it to happen. We were all more or less disgruntled, and even the Junior Partner's modulated British voice was starting to take on a bit of an edge.

Then the lights flickered and went out.

Then, of course, it was on for old and young. The sekketries started screeching, and this wasn't helped by Lana remarking, in musing tones, that she believed the lift was held up by magnets, and wondering if they'd keep holding on with the power out. She was making it up, of course. That woman would do anything to cause trouble. She's only happy when she's ruining someone's day. The youngest sekketry started to cry.

'You know,' continued Lana, evidently thinking she was on a roll, 'now that it's dark, maybe we'll be lucky and get to see the ghost.'

'Ghost? What ghost?' I asked. I ought to have known better, really.

'Oh, don't you know, Pat?' As soon as I heard the amused little smirk in her voice, I knew she was making it up, but there's never any use calling Lana on her lies; she's careful never to say anything that can be checked. 'Back a few years ago, a woman jumped to her death from this building. They say she roams the corridors at night, weeping, and reaching out a ghostly hand to clutch at the living.'

At least two of the sekketries, and possibly all of them, were now in tears, snuffling and boo-hooing. I was glad to be on the other side of the lift from them. No doubt they were getting snot and makeup all over poor Fang. For once, I thought, you didn't get yourself the best position, did you, mate? Heh heh.

'Bullshit,' said the Senior Partner.

'There's no such things as ghosts. I'm surprised at you, Lana, believing such rubbish.' You could hear the undercurrent of 'hormonal female. I'll remember this at your next review,' and I couldn't help a small smile of satisfaction. We all dream of seeing Lana get her come-uppance.

A voice sounded out of the dark.

'It is not wise to discount the supernatural.'

The inscrutable Fang had entered the fray. I admired his courage; personally, I always find it prudent to remain silent when Lana gets going. But I could hear the sekketries ooh-ing and aah-ing. Did I mention that Fang's the office heartthrob? Well, he is. That's one reason I'm not so keen on him; I have to share a sekketry with him, and as Senior Associate I like to think my work should take precedence, but no such thing – the minute Fang bats one of his inscrutable Chinese eyes she drops my stuff like a hot potato. Be that as it may, I said nothing, content to wait while he dug his grave. I was, of course, expecting Lana to rise up and smite him. It would be doubly satisfying to see her demolish Fang and at the same time out herself as a hundred-megaton bitch in front of the Senior Partner. I was hoping she'd forgotten he was there.

'I am thinking,' said Fang, 'of my Uncle Zan's operation.' His accented words dropped into the dark like polished stones on velvet. 'You see, Uncle Zan had a serious bowel cancer. He must be operated or die. There was only a twenty percent chance of the operation succeeding, they told him.' He paused to wait for expressions of sympathy.

'Uncle Zan was my favourite uncle,' he went on, evidently feeling the sympathy expressed had been inadequate. 'All the children loved Uncle Zan. Well, he went into hospital and he left his dog, Shenshi, at our house. Shenshi was a huge dog, a rare breed from the provinces. He was the apple of my uncle's eye. They were inseparable. He had charged us children to take great care of Shenshi, and always to play with him and let him sleep on our beds. That was fine with us. We loved Shenshi too, and there was great competition as to whether he would sleep with the girls or the boys. Uncle Zan was going to have his operation the next day, and our mother had warned us that we might not see him again. We all knew he would probably die, because of what the doctor had said.'

There were murmurs of sympathy, and a general rustling.

'We cast lots for the honour of hosting Shenshi, and the boys won. I was the littlest boy, so I got to have him on my bed. We played with him all day, and at night he curled up on the end of my bed. He slept quietly until morning, or at least we thought so; he didn't disturb anyone.

'The next day, Uncle Zan had his surgery and the hospital said he had survived the operation and was in Intensive Care. We were still not really expecting him to live, because the doctor had said most people would die within a day after the surgery.

'That night, Shenshi was like a creature possessed by demons. He started to bark as soon as the sun went down, and he barked on and on. Nothing we could do would quieten him. Finally, our father came and took Shenshi away and locked him up in the shed at the back of our garden. Then, Shenshi started to howl. Even from all the way down at the back of the garden, we could hear his mournful howls. It went on all night; none of us got any sleep. We boys huddled together in one bed, and probably the girls did the same.

'Towards morning, about four o'clock I think, Shenshi exploded into a fury of barking. He sounded as if he was battling seventy demons! And then, suddenly, he was quiet. He didn't bark any more.

'In the morning, my father rang up the hospital and they told him Uncle Zan had unaccountably turned the corner at about four o'clock, and would certainly recover. We were so happy that for a while we forgot poor Shenshi, locked in the shed. But when my mother went to let him out, she found him lying dead.

'Because Shenshi was a valuable dog, and Uncle Zan set great store by him and would undoubtedly want to know how he died, my father took him to the vet to have an autopsy done. But the vet was not able to discover any cause of his sudden death. He told my father that Shenshi was a perfectly healthy dog, everything perfect – except that he was no longer alive.'

There were moans of sorrow from

the sekketries, who seemed to have appointed themselves as a kind of Greek chorus. The Senior Partner grunted and the Junior Partner murmured in polite sympathy. Lana sighed loudly, and I could almost hear her rolling her eyes.

Anything that annoyed Lana was alright with me, so I decided to help matters along. 'It's almost as if the dog gave up his life for his master,' I said. It went against the grain a bit to support Fang, but the enemy of my enemy is my friend.

'Yes, that was what we thought,' said Fang. 'The next year, my other uncle was also diagnosed with the same thing, and he didn't survive the surgery. Of course, he didn't have a dog.'

Just then the lights came back on, and the lift started to descend again. In the general relief, the subject of Uncle Zan died a natural death, and we all went on our ways, looking forward to the weekend and mostly glad to see the back of each other for a couple of days. It got me thinking, though. Several times over the next few days I found myself wondering about the kind of love that could cause someone to give up his life for another, and the depth of connection that could allow such an exchange.

I think this weekend I might drive out to the Lost Dogs' home. It won't hurt to have a look, right?

JOLAKOTTURIN

It was bean soup for supper again, as it had been every night that week. Lars knew he mustn't say anything; his grandparents worked so hard, and it wasn't Grandpa's fault the cows had all gone off their milk after that big storm. They had enough to get through the winter, Grandpa had said, although there wouldn't be anything over for frills. Frills seemed to mean everything, Lars thought, bowing his head for Grace. He had had no pocket money himself for months, and had had to resort to getting up early every morning and chopping extra wood for the stove as his Christmas gift to his grandparents.

He closed his eyes and thought about the dinner they'd had last Christmas Eve, and every other year he could remember. The roast goose, crisp and golden. The mashed swedes, rich with butter. The white rolls, fresh from the oven, soft and steaming inside. He could almost taste it…

He was recalled to the present by his grandfather's impatient 'harrumph'. Guiltily, he opened his eyes and crossed himself. *Gleðileg Jól*, they all told each other in the Old Language. *Gleðileg Jól.* Happy Christmas. Lars didn't really remember much of the Old Language, but certain things had to be said in it, or it just wasn't Proper.

'What is the news from the village, Husband?' asked Grandmother. She was old-fashioned, and always addressed Grandpa as 'Husband' in the traditional way.

'Oh, I've a fine tale to tell, indeed I have!' said Grandpa, rubbing his hands together and taking up his spoon. 'Young Alfar Strewelpfizer has just returned from a visit to the capital; he was visiting his uncle, who is the head dairyman at the castle, and he told me a most amazing tale about the King and his Winter Ball. Now what do you think they had at the supper table, Wife?'

'Oh, how could I possibly guess? Get along with you, Husband, now do tell us!'

'They had a life-sized dragon, all made out of butter. Now what do you think of that, young Lars?'

Lars didn't know what to think. 'How big is a life-sized dragon, Grandpa?'

'Hmmph!' said Grandmother. 'If it was only as big as a teacup, they had more butter than we do, for I've only so much left as would halfway fill a cup.'

Lars sighed. There was never butter for their bread, these days, just a scrape of dripping on Sundays.

'Now don't you be sad, my pet,' said Grandmother. 'I've a little of the best flour left, and that bit of butter, and a handful of currants. I'll make us a batch of sweet pastries for supper. It isn't what we're used to, but we'll have our Christmas treat.'

'And after supper,' said Grandpa, 'I'll tell you the tale of Jolakotturin. I've no gift for you either this year, so the telling will be my Christmas gift to you.'

***

The pastries were wonderful. Lars

took tiny bites, to make them last. When they were all settled on the bench that ran around the circumference of the big, round stove, Grandpa began his tale.

Lars had heard of Christmas Cat, of course; every child knew about the huge, fierce creature, who would jump out and devour you if you didn't have something new to wear at Christmas. Every man, woman and child in their village always had new clothes for Christmas; it was the custom. If you couldn't manage a whole new outfit, you always got something – a scarf, some mittens. In the months leading up to Christmas, children in rather too-small clothing were a common sight, as the poorer families saved up the new things for Christmas Eve.

He'd heard the traditional tale told many times, but tonight there was a new reality to it as Grandpa recited the familiar verses. He arched his back, he clawed his hands, he almost *became* the cat. Lars sat transfixed, eyes shining, as the tale unfolded, enjoying himself as much as if he'd been at a puppet show. Even Grandmother sat still, her work-worn hands folded in her lap, a smile of pure pleasure on her lined face.

When the tale closed with the familiar words, 'a happy day and a merry merry Christmas,' they sat in silence for a few moments. Lars heaved a great sigh of contentment.

'Well, my boy,' said Grandpa, his blue eyes twinkling. 'I hope that was not too much excitement for you to go to sleep?'

Lars jumped up and, forgetting his ten-year-old dignity, hugged his grandfather tightly, delivering a smacking kiss to the old man's cheek. 'It was wonderful, Grandpa. Thank you! It was better than anything! And Grandmother,' he hugged her, breathing in her unique scent, a compound of lavender, baking and clean linen, 'thank you for making the pastries. They were the best thing I've ever eaten. It's been a wonderful Christmas.'

'There now, you're a good boy, Lars. Don't think we haven't noticed all the work you've been doing, that woodpile will be taller than the house soon.'

Lars shuffled his feet. 'I didn't have any money, Grandmother. That's my

Christmas gift to you and Grandpa.'

'Well, off to bed with you, it's nearly ten. Go along now.'

Lars went, slinking and pouncing up the narrow stairs, being Christmas Cat. It was only when he reached his tiny room and started to change into his nightshirt that he realised.

He, himself, had no new clothes.

***

The small room was directly over the stove, for the warmth. Lars lay in comfort and listened to the faint sounds that drifted up from below. He liked to hear Grandpa and Grandmother talking as he fell asleep; it was a warm, comforting sound.

Tonight, though, the voices were louder than usual, and the words penetrated Lars' drowsy consciousness, stopping him on the threshold of sleep.

'...not one thing!' That was Grandmother. She sounded upset.

'Don't be silly, Marta. It's just a

children's story; do you really think the Christmas Cat is out there, waiting to gobble up our boy? For shame.'

'Oh, if only I had set aside one pair of the new socks I made him last autumn. Then he'd have something now.'

'Really, Marta. I thought you had more sense than to be worrying about a silly children's tale. You'd do better to worry about how to keep the rats down in the barn. They've got into three sacks of the flour already. If that keeps up, we won't make it through the winter, and we'll be having to beg food of our neighbours.'

'I shall pray to Mary, Queen of Heaven to send our boy something new to wear.'

'Oh, enough of your foolishness, woman. Why not ask her for a side of bacon while she's at it?' Grandpa evidently felt he'd had the last word, for presently Lars heard him stumping up the stairs and going into their bedroom. After a few minutes the bedsprings creaked, and soon Grandpa's quiet, even snoring sounded through the thin wall.

The murmured sound of Grandmother's prayers went on for a long time. Finally, Lars heard the familiar, faint rattle as she hung up her beads, and the swoosh, swoosh of her long woollen skirts brushing against the bannisters as she came slowly up to bed.

***

Lars lay thinking for a long time. He was afraid of the Christmas Cat. It would get him, he knew, for he had no new clothes. Grandpa had said it was just a children's story, but then if that were the case, how come everyone always made sure to have something new at Christmas, the grownups too? With a hot flush of shame it came to him that Grandpa and Grandmother didn't have anything new, either. He was a selfish beast, thinking only about himself. What if the Christmas Cat got Grandpa? Or Grandmother? That would be even worse. They were all he had, since the sickness two winters ago that had taken his parents and his little brother. He'd rather it got him than them, really.

Was there anything he could do? Anything that would protect his family? He had to think about it. Thinking was good; often it gave you a way to do something you'd thought you couldn't do. That was how he'd come up with the idea of chopping all that wood; he'd been in despair at how to get a Christmas present for Grandmother and Grandpa.

He ran over in his mind everything he knew about Christmas Cat. He was huge. He had glowing eyes and terrible claws. He hunted men, but didn't care for mice. He preyed on the poor, because they didn't have new clothes. That's us now, he thought, shivering. He forced his tired mind on, trying to remember every detail of the tale. He couldn't recite it, he didn't remember the exact words, but it was a familiar tale, always told around this time of the year, and he must have heard it a score of times.

Oh! It said something about him grabbing people's Christmas dinner and eating it himself. So he must not just eat people; their food, too, was his prey. A roast goose, like they always used to have, that would appease him, no doubt. Lars sighed. The very poverty that meant they hadn't any new clothes had also meant there was no fancy dinner. But it was *poor people's Christmas dinner* the cat stole, he remembered with mounting excitement. Stuff like bean soup. But they'd already eaten theirs.

Then he remembered the pastries. There had been six of the small pastries left over, and Grandmother had put them away, saying they'd have them for Christmas breakfast in the morning. His mouth watered at the thought of the rich pastry, stuffed with currants. Two for his share. Well, he could stand going without breakfast; missing one meal wouldn't kill him. Quietly, he slid out of bed and groped for his sheepskin slippers.

The moon was full, and by its light, Lars had no difficulty locating the pastries. He lifted the cloth and abstracted two, leaving the other four for Grandmother and Grandpa. His sheepskin coat, now tight under the arms, hung on its peg by the door. He slipped into it and fastened it close; you didn't go out in the snow in your nightshirt, not even for a minute. He drew back the wooden bar and pulled the heavy door open.

He'd go a little way from the house, he decided. If he put it about by the big lantern, he'd be able to see it from his bedroom window, and then he'd know if his plan had worked. That was, of course, if the Christmas Cat didn't jump out and devour him before he could get back into the house. He said a quick prayer for courage, and stepped out into the silver night.

One step. Two steps. Snow crunched under his slippers; there had been a fresh fall earlier in the night, so it coated the stone path. He must be careful not to slip.

Three steps. Four. Five. His heartbeat pounded in his ears, drowning out the shuffling of his feet. If it crept up behind, would he hear it? He risked a furtive glance over his shoulder. The open door was still comfortingly close.

Ten steps. That was far enough. He set the plate down on the path and bolted inside, slamming home the bar and racing upstairs, not even stopping to hang up his coat. He flung it in a heap on the floor and dived under his quilts, pulling them right up over his head. *If you can't see it, it can't see you.*

***

He couldn't stay under the covers forever; he was running out of air. Gradually, Lars was forced to emerge from his haven, first creating a tiny hole in front of his nose, then as he overheated under the pile of quilts, enlarging it, inch by inch, until his whole head was out. He lay, physically comfortable but in an agony of terror, wondering if he'd done the right thing, or if he'd just attracted the Christmas Cat to their house. Would the sun rise on a scene of carnage? He was confident enough that the door would hold against any attack, but might it get in through the windows?

After eons, the sky began to lighten. For the first time in all that long, weary night, Lars started to feel safe. Surely monsters did not come in the daylight?

It was then that he heard the sound.

It was not very much of a sound, not at all frightening in itself. It was the dreadful significance of that innocent sound that had him suddenly rigid with fear.

It was the scraping of the china plate on the path.

Lars could never say afterwards how, or why, he found the courage to get out of bed. Perhaps it was simple curiosity, or an instinctive need to inform himself about the movements of the enemy. Perhaps it was just that doing something, anything, no matter how pointless, was a small comfort in the agony of terror. Whatever the reason, he slid, quaking, out of bed, and stole as silently as he could manage to the window.

It was, after all, he told himself, why he'd gone those extra dreadful steps away from the house; he'd wanted to be able to see the plate from his window.

He reached the window and dropped to his knees. With infinite caution, he eased back a tiny fold of the curtain, just enough to fit one eye.

There in the cold, dawn light, a tiny, scrawny black kitten was devouring Grandmother's pastries.

***

When Grandmother came downstairs, Lars was settled on the bench, his back propped against the stove, the kitten draped purring about his neck. A wide, wide grin split his face.

'Look, Grandmother! I got something new to wear for Christmas! A fine fur scarf!'

❧DREAM WEAVER☙

Second Thinker Shey/'a/'tan grumbled to himself as he hauled his bulk along the passage. His research wasn't going well, his assistants were unruly and the Nest Council had again denied his petition to take a third mate. His contribution to the Nest Theory had, they said, not been sufficient during the last three spans to justify his further propagation. In addition to this, his own nest had developed a draught that whistled in his ears as he slept, causing him to awake cranky and out of sorts, in contrast to what he imagined was his usual mild humour, but which some low-caste persons had described as smug self-satisfaction.

The Senior Common Room was

hopping when he reached it, an horrendous din screaming out of the Tone Synthesiser. Muttering imprecations, Shey/a'/'tan pushed his way through the jumping, gyrating crowd – mostly the younger Thinkers, but several who ought to have had more dignity – to the far end, where First Thinker Ya/'a/'bhei had captured a small territory of sanity encompassing three lounges, an occasional table and a carafe of Vorn. He threw himself onto the nearest lounge, adjusting his robe, which had become untidy as he pushed through the throng.

'Shey!' cried Ya/'a/'bhei, slopping some Vorn into a beaker and shoving it across the small table. 'Isn't it marvellous?' His antennae bobbed up and down in an expression of pleased excitement.

'Evening, YaYa,' grunted Shey/'a/'tan. 'What is that awful noise, by all the Elders?'

'It's Nu/'a/'fat's new music. She captured it, you know, from space, with that amazing new device she's been working on.'

'Sounds different to the last lot.'

'She had the idea to play it at

different speeds. This is a factor of three, I think. Isn't it great? It's all the rage among the young people.'

Shey/'a/'tan listened for a moment. It sounded like 'shananashebopshebop' with an occasional burst of 'blooswaydshoos'.

'It's rubbish. So, YaYa, tell me – how's your project going?'

Ya/'a/'bhei looked despondently down, his antennae drooping. 'Not so well. I need something, I don't know, something...' He broke off helplessly, waving a claw in circles.

'That's no good,' said Shey/'a/'tan politely, secretly exulting. 'May your research never prosper,' he thought, delighting in the obscenity, which would get him thrown out by the proctors if spoken out loud in mixed company. He'd be First Thinker yet, see if he wouldn't.

***

The following revolution was rest time, and Shey/'a/'tan decided to leave the Nest. It was not customary to do so, as most Glorious Thinkers preferred to be surrounded by others at all times, but it was not forbidden, perhaps because the desire to do so was so unusual that no one on the Council had thought to rule on it.

This was not Shey/'a/'tan's first expedition outside the Nest, and he moved quickly past the familiar places; he had already explored these parts, and any secrets they had were known to him; he craved novelty, discoveries, something that might give him an edge. He ought to be First Thinker, he knew; his mind was more powerful than Ya/'a/'bhei's, his reasoning more incisive, his thinking more daring in its scope. He did not have his edge blunted by all the stupid enthusiasms to which Ya/'a/'bhei was prey. Nor was he constrained by the blind obedience to the Council of Wisdom that he had always felt held Ya/'a/'bhei back from true brilliance. It was a mystery to him why Ya/'a/'bhei, and not he, had been appointed First Thinker.

He moved briskly along the wide passage, his robe leaving a trail in the dust behind him. It didn't matter; no one ever came down here. He was looking, as he had often looked before, for some remnant from the Elder Race, that great and mighty people who had been the forebears of the Glorious Thinkers, who had, in fact, millenia ago, kept his own people as pets, the way the proctors and domestics sometimes kept Thurpods. He had never quite reconciled himself to the indignity of the fact, revealed to him, along with many other secrets, upon his assuming the robe of Second Thinker.

At the place where his previous explorations ended, marked by a chemical sign on the wall, the passage divided, branching off to left and right. He stared along the new passage. No special feature met his gaze in either direction; the luminary panels glowed softly, the floor was coated in dust, it was just the same as the passage he'd come down. He decided to go right, and after scratching a pointer on the wall, set off down the new passage.

The chambers opening off this passage were different; both larger and more cluttered, they had more an air of workplaces than of domestic residence. There was little furniture, and none of the big rectangular padded surfaces that nearly all of the previous nests had contained, and which he believed had been used by the Elder Race for sleeping. An uncomfortable business it must have been.

It was in the twentieth such chamber he examined that he found it. At first he took it for some kind of ornament, set as it was in the centre of the room, atop a column almost as high as his head. Its complex spiral design was pleasing to the sight, and the softly glowing crystal at its core gave off a sensation of warm pleasure. Despite his contempt for artistic matters, he felt oddly drawn to it. He lifted it from its platform and took it to a table, settling himself in front of it.

There were several smooth plates set around the outer curve of the spiral, and the protruding extensions by which he had lifted it, he now saw, were handles; the thing was meant to be picked up, and picked up often, which suggested that his first identification of it as a piece of artwork might not be accurate. Things made to be often picked up were made for use, and this was therefore a tool of some kind, although its position on the central column suggested it was important, perhaps special in some way. The worktables in the room, which he had thought to be haphazardly arranged, were, he now realised, placed about the perimeter in a circle, all at a good distance from the plinth, but focussing on it; people seated at these tables, looking straight ahead, would have been looking straight at the device. It was well known that the Elder Race had been of greater stature than the Glorious Thinkers.

Shey/'a/'tan stretched out a tentative claw to one of the smooth plates on the device's edge, and his world rippled and blinked out.

He was already recoiling, snatching back his claw in panic, even as he registered that he was still seeing, not blind as his first, panicked thought had been; that he was seeing, somehow, in a different way. He reached out to the device again, his claw barely making contact, ready to snatch away. Again, the strange disorientation, like a rippling not just of the physical world, but of everything; his own mind now one with the mere furniture, everything in the same way – not visible, as such, but perceived.

And it was not just surfaces he was perceiving, he realised – it was the totality, everything laid open to his examination, not limited by field or focus – he could, he realised, see down to the atomic level and in another way some ineffable vastness, all at the same time. He broke contact, chittering with stress, his antennae lashing helplessly.

He examined the newly acquired data, turning them over in his mind. He had not truly grasped, he knew, the meaning of what he had – well, 'seen', for want of a better term. He had thought he saw the atomic structure of the table on which the device rested, as well as its surface in exquisite detail, and some other aspect of it that he could neither name nor comprehend.

He rummaged in the bag he'd brought along and took out some grok rolls, three kwa fruit and a flask of zem. He'd eat and rest, and while he ate and rested, he'd rest his mind too. He bit into a roll and let his mind drift, freewheeling among his thoughts.

***

After stuffing himself with all the food in his bag, and making a mental note to chastise his second wife because the grok had been too dry and the zem insufficiently sweetened, he addressed himself again to the device, which sat, gleaming and perfect, its central crystal glowing, an enigma.

Touching the smooth plate had invoked that strange, alien experience. What if he touched another plate? He tried them all, but only the one on the right of the device had, or seemed to have, any effect. It was, he now saw, slightly larger than the others; in fact, they were all three of different sizes, the one in the centre distinctly small and surrounded by raised borders. Very well then, the right-hand one must be the main control, and the others must modify the device's operation in some way. Gingerly he reached out and touched the right and left plates at once.

Again the strange sense sprang up, replacing sight, but this time he had an odd conviction that it was not merely perception; that he could in some way interact with what he 'saw'. With a small part of his mind he reached out and *poked*. An area of what he believed was the table changed its state, and when he let go the device again, he saw that one corner of the table was smouldering.

Shey/'a/'tan's mind whirled. A thought had occurred to him, shocking in its implications, staggering in its possibilities. Was this the fabled Reality

Induction Coil?

The existence of the Reality Induction Coil was known only by inference, from interpretations of those fragments of the writings of the Elder Race that had survived. Several of the Council members had risen to their exalted positions by formulating theories about it, but of the devices themselves, none survived, at least none that was known.

Despite this, use of a Reality Induction Coil was utterly prohibited by the Council. The interdict was explained (to First and Second Thinkers only, of course – no one else knew about it at all) – on the basis that use of the device, which, it was believed, could actually create matter from nothing, had the potential to bring about disturbances in the space-time continuum that could be fatal, not only to the Glorious Thinkers, but to all life, everywhere. The general belief of the Council was that the Elders' indiscriminate use of the device, which was believed to be almost absolute in its capabilities, had resulted in their extinction.

Shey/'a/'tan did not himself believe

this. He thought it more likely that the Council wanted to ensure that a device of such power did not fall into other hands than their own.

But now, it had done – here it was in his hands.

***

It was some time before Shey/'a/'tan decided how best to use the Reality Induction Coil. His first thought had been to employ it to further his own research, but the consequences if he were discovered would be terrible, including, but not limited to, confiscation of all his property, annulment of his marriages to both his wives, a permanent ban on reproduction, and demotion to sanitation worker, third class.

Would it not be much, much better, he mused, if those things were to happen to Ya/'a/'bhei, leaving the coveted position of First Thinker open for him to step into? None of the other Second Thinkers, he thought, would give him a serious contest for it; he had been around for longer than any of them, and had, to boot, the advantage of having made several discoveries in the particular branch of knowledge currently most favoured by the Council.

Of course, there was Ya/'a/'bhei's habitual smarmy deference to authority. If he found a Reality Induction Coil, the risk was great that he might simply hand it over to the Council. Over against that, though, was his insatiable curiosity and contemptible frivolity. Could he, if subjected to the temptation, resist trying it out for himself? And once he had realised its potential, would he have the strength of character to hand it over, never to use it again?

Shey/'a/'tan rather thought not.

There was also, of course, the risk inherent in using the device at all. Perhaps Ya/'a/'bhei would manage to destroy himself, in which case it would be just as good from his, Shey/'a/'tan's point of view, although it would be best if the Coil itself survived, so that evidence would remain to discredit him, lest he be considered a martyred hero. Not that that would make any difference to the vacancy, but it would be annoying. He had spent his life playing second zaimen to Goody-goody Ya/'a/'bhei, and he wanted to see him brought low.

***

Shey/'a/'tan shifted restlessly in his lounge. The bickering of his two wives, although friendly, had irritated him to the point where he had sent them both off to the zul parlour to get their claws styled. Now alone, he thrashed about, unable to settle in comfort; the deep silence was somehow annoying, and he regretted sending his wives away.

He had, he realised, arrived at a decision over the last several revolutions. He would give the device to Ya/'a/'bhei.

It wasn't that simple, though. He could hardly just walk up and present him with the thing, gift-wrapped in karda leaves. There must be nothing to connect him with the device at all. Therefore, he must arrange for Ya/'a/'bhei to find it, as he had done. But where? The Nest was populous and always buzzing with activity; if he left the thing lying about, it was certain to be found by sanitation workers, or a domestic, or someone.

He toyed briefly with the idea of summoning Ya/'a/'bhei to a meeting at some unconventional hour, when the Nest was mostly asleep, and leaving the thing in a passage near his nest. But Ya/'a/'bhei would definitely remember the unusual request and connect it with him, and besides, a Second Thinker did not summon a First Thinker. It was not done.

Ya/'a/'bhei's own nest would be the ideal place for him to find the thing. There would be nothing to connect it to anyone else, and if it were concealed so that he didn't find it straight away, that would be even better. It would have to be somewhere safe from his wives, of course. Ya/'a/'bhei, in accordance with his status as First Thinker, had five wives. Have to get them all out, somehow.

Suppose he were to invite the whole pack of them to a celebration of some kind? He could make something up. But then, it would still be him, Shey/'a/'tan, issuing the invitation, and that was the kind of thing that tended to stick in the memory. People still talked about the gathering Nu/'a/'fat had hosted upon her elevation to Second Thinker. They dated things from it, for Wisdom's sake. No, it had to be something anonymous, with no connexion to him at all. Even then, he'd risk being seen by some sanitation worker or domestic. If he were seen entering Ya/'a/'bhei/s nest, that would be very bad indeed. Such a breach of courtesy would be bound to come to the attention of the Council, and he'd be in trouble even without the other matter.

His wives returned in a swirl of robes and chatter and a blast of sickly perfume, all amity now they'd been to the zul parlour together. If possible, they were even more irritating in this state.

***

Shey/'a/'tan leaned back in his lounge, sipping his vankra. His wives had not stopped talking for one moment since they'd returned from the zul parlour. First it had been gossip about Nu/'a/'fat, and when she would take a second husband, and why she had waited so long after her elevation to do so. Then it had been the new styles in claw embellishment. Then a long saga the claw-stylist had told Noori/'tan when Surai/'tan was for some reason absent. It concerned the plight of a sanitation worker in love with a cook. From there, they progressed to a thoughtful discussion of the sorrows and injustices arising from the caste system. Now they were going on and on about some rumour they'd heard. It was all piffle.

'What do you think, Honourable

Husband?' asked Noori/'tan.

'Think? About what?'

'About the Quake Drill, of course! We haven't had one for ever so long, have we, Suri?'

'No, indeed, I think the last one was before Bey/'grul laid her last batch. And those children are nearly grown now, I saw her the other day and she said they were almost ready to leave the Nursery. She was looking tired, I thought. It really is unfair of Zo/'a/'grul not to take a second wife. He's always been selfish. I remember when Bey first married him, he wouldn't even let her have a quondim.'

'Mean, that's what he is. I've always thought so.'

'Yes, and–'

'Enough!' roared Shey/'a/'tan, goaded beyond tolerance. 'WHAT quake drill?'

'Well,' began Noori'tan, obviously settling in for a long, long recitation, 'it seems that Rua/'beg's youngest, you know that boy who ate all the squa fruit that time at their renewal gathering and then sicked up over Retired First Speaker Soran/'a/'gul–'

'Oh, I remember that!' exclaimed

Surai/'tan. 'Wasn't he just cross!'

'Wasn't he! I should say so! Anyway, he's a Third Engineer now, and apparently he told Qualia/'dru's nest domestic, so she told Qualia, and she–'

'Yes, yes,' said Shey/'a/'tan, 'but WHAT did she tell her?'

Noori/'tan's antennae stood straight up and quivered in indignation. 'That is what I am trying to *tell* you, Honourable Husband, if you can, that is, spare a few moments from your *important research* to hear it. Of course, no doubt these trivial women's matters are of no interest to one of your excellence and wisdom. No doubt–'

'Alright, Noori, I'm sorry, I'm sorry. Please tell me about the Quake Drill, for I am deeply interested.'

She wasn't letting it go that easily, he saw with resignation.

'And may I say, dearest Noori, that the colour you have chosen for your claw embellishment is delightful. I have always particularly admired that shade of red, and it sets off your colouring perfectly.' There, down came the antennae, drooping backwards in pleasure and satisfaction. 'Please do go on telling me about the quake drill. I am always interested in your news, you know.'

For a moment he wondered if he was laying it on a bit too thickly, but there really was no limit to the woman's vanity. Presently it transpired that Third Engineer Korn/'ur/'beg, who probably was right at the bottom of his department and was unlikely to know much of anything, had said a surprise Quake Drill was to occur within the next cycle, probably some time around FactRev or EnquiryRev.

***

The Quake Drill took place in the early hours of FactRev, at a time when everyone except a few Sanitation Workers was sleeping. Startled into wakefulness by the raucous clangour of the alarm bells, Shey/'a/'tan fell off his hook and rolled blindly about in the dark, completely disoriented. By the time he recovered his wits, his two wives were already rushing about, shrieking.

It took some argument to get them to go ahead, leaving him to follow, but he eventually managed it by 'reminding' them that the famous musician, Grom/'oh/'Sim, would be performing in Central Plaza, where the residents of East

Nest were to assemble. This was not, in fact, the case, but the reminder had the desired effect, and soon Shey/'a/'tan was creeping from his deserted nest, the spiral device concealed in a fold of his robe.

He went cautiously; in order to get to Ya/'a/'bhei's residence he must travel in the direction away from the Plaza, and although anyone seeing him would hardly be likely to accost a Second Thinker, still the incongruity would stay in a person's mind. The short delay, however, had the desired effect; the passages were deserted, everyone having rushed to the Plaza at top speed. Grom/'oh/'Sim might not be performing, but Quake Drills were infrequent enough that they were regarded rather in the light of a festival. Shey/'a/'tan was quite sure that enough information would have leaked out that there would be stalls selling hot Vorn, plik rolls and other delicacies, and no doubt someone would have provided some kind of musical entertainment. Everyone would mill about until First Shift sounded, and next Rev half the workers would be absent on some spurious excuse.

He found Ya/'a/'bhei's residence

empty, just as he'd expected. After a precautionary jab at the visitor signal, he slid open the panel and entered the lavish quarters.

It had been some time since he had visited Ya/'a/'bhei at home, and there had been considerable enlargement of his residence. It looked as if the dwelling next door had been incorporated, probably to make room for the fourth and fifth wives he had acquired upon his elevation to First Thinker. Shey/'a/'tan ground his mandibles with envy. Ya/'a/'bhei was vulgar, he told himself. Downright vulgar. A sunken pool right in the middle of the Social Chamber. And tiled with Graidstone! Such ostentation, Shey/'a/'tan told himself, was unbecoming to a Thinker. He did not envy it. Not at all. Ostentatious, that was what it was. Common.

Ya/'a/'bhei's Thinking Chamber, though, was just as he remembered it from his last visit. Shabby, untidy, and comfortable. Ya/'a/'bhei didn't allow his wives in there, he recalled. It was just the place. Some of those piles of comrecs probably hadn't moved in ten Spans.

He slid open the storage units in the

desk. Just as he'd expected, the bottom one was full of miscellaneous junk, no doubt shoved in there to get it out of the way and then forgotten. Wasn't everyone's? Old calcmods, connector cables and bits of things that had probably been long rendered useless by obsolescence. He raked a hole at the back and shoved the device into it, and rammed the unit home. It might take cycles before Ya/'a/'bhei discovered it, but discover it he would. Eventually. If it took too long, he'd invent an excuse to ask him for some obsolete connector.

*

Ya/'a/'bhei was looking for his wife's quondim when he found the device. As usual, his scatter-brained third wife had lost the one possession without which she could not live another minute.

It had been his sensible second wife who had made the call.

'Yaya dearest, Shonti's lost her quondim again. She's having hysterics, could you come home? Please?'

Ya/'a/'bhei, First Thinker of the Glorious Thinkers, had sighed and closed his calcmod.

'Yes, dear.'

Now, in the sanctity of his luxurious nest, he looked upon a scene of chaos. Wives three through five were rushing about in circles in the main nest, throwing cushions from one lounge to the other and back again. Bel/'bhei, his first wife, had got a headache, and had retired to her private chamber. Ngoti/'bhei, his Second Wife, was nowhere to be found.

After hovering unnoticed for several quanta, Ya/'a/'bhei managed to catch Shonti/'bhei's eye.

'What is this about your quondim, my dear? Can you remember the last time you used it?'

'I can't stop, Yaya dear, I have to find it! I need it RIGHT NOW! Oh, oh, oh!'

He managed to catch hold of her as she rushed past with an armful of soft furnishings. 'Please, my dear, just stop rushing about and let's think about this.'

'Think? Think? What good is thinking? I must find my quondim!' With a despairing howl, she rushed into the hygiene chamber, whence presently emerged a crashing sound as various jars of unguents and those mysterious cosmetic preparations with which all of his wives seemed obsessed were apparently hurled to the floor.

'What good is thinking, indeed!' he muttered to himself. Had these women no respect? If not for his status as First Thinker, at least for common decency? She was a hussy, that was what she was. He retreated in a mild huff to his Thinking Chamber, which, in theory at least, was a sanctum inviolate.

He found he couldn't settle, though, to read or to think. Although the deliberately thick walls of his chamber blocked all sound from the outer nest, just knowing about the chaos and destruction that were taking place outside disturbed his peace. It was time, he decided, to take a Firm Hand.

Emerging, rather cautiously, from his chamber, he seized the robe of the first woman to rush past him. It was little Nerit/'bhei, his Fifth Wife. That was one stationary, at least.

'Stop! Stop it at once! All of you. Cease this mindless rushing about at once. I command it!'

There was a sudden stillness in the room. Nothing moved, except for a heaped pile of cushions, which swayed and toppled, plopping to the floor. The three women looked at him expectantly, and he realised he had no idea what to say next. He had never attempted this kind of masterly behaviour with his wives before, although he'd seen other people do it. It was rather gratifying, he found; they seemed to be looking at him with respect, even deference, as he had seen other men's wives do. Rather wonderful, really. He adjusted his robe, preening slightly. Directions, that was what they needed. These women were not Thinkers, after all.

'Nerit, go and fetch Bel. Tell her to come in here, I want to speak to her. Now, you two, where is Ngoti?'

'She went next door, Honourable Husband.' Great Wisdom, she was actually curtseying! 'She thought I might have left it at Popo/'von's house, when I visited her last FactRev.'

'Well, go and fetch her; it shouldn't be taking her this long to find that out.' Pleased with himself, Ya/'a/'bhei sat rather grandly in the biggest lounge, first moving some heaps of fabric out of his way.

Bel/'bhei wafted in from her

chamber, smelling strongly of quorn juice. Ya/'a/'bhei sometimes suspected her headaches had more to do with the intoxicant than with domestic stress.

'Ah, Bel, my dear, is your headache better? I was sorry to learn you were indisposed.'

Bel/'bhei waved her antennae amiably, swaying a little.

'Now,' Ya/'a/'bhei went on, wishing she would keep still, 'Shonti has lost her quondim. We will all help to search our nest for it, but we will do so in a rational manner.' He noticed he was swaying in time with Bel/'bhei, and paused to ground himself.

'Bel, you will search your personal nest and then the hygiene chamber. Ngoti, her personal nest and then the kitchen.' She was the most sensible of the lot of them; he hoped he could rely on her to search effectively and not break anything.

'Nerit, you can clear up in here, and go over this area again after you've finished with your personal chamber.'

Rula/'bhei and Shonti/'bhei now appeared with the missing Ngoti/'bhei.

'Ah, there you are, Ngoti. Was the quondim there?'

'No, Honourable Husband, it was not.' She shot Shonti a venomous look, her antennae vibrating with spite. 'I disturbed Popo/'von's meditation lesson for nothing.'

'You know what?' said Rula/'bhei. 'I think Popo/'von's carrying on with that meditation teacher. She never seems to get any further with her inner Ra, and she's been having those lessons for ever so long. And his robe was on back to front.'

'Do not engage in idle and salacious gossip, Rula. Now, we are assigning areas for a properly organised search. Your assigned area will be first your personal nest, and then Shonti's. Shonti, go with her. You are not calm enough to be rational and search effectively. Ngoti, please take care of your personal nest and then the kitchen. I myself shall search my Thinking Chamber.'

'How could the quondim be there, Yaya?' asked Rula. 'None of us are allowed in there.'

'When things are lost,' said Ya/'a/'bhei, 'we do not know where they may be. Now get on with your assigned tasks, all of you, and do not question my instructions.'

That showed them, he thought, closing the door to his Thinking Chamber, ignoring a burst of laughter that erupted behind him.

***

Once alone, Ya/'a/'bhei looked longingly at his desk. He could continue with his work on the second string of equations for his theory. But he had said he would look for the quondim, so he would. Thrice-blatted thing. Zo/'a/'grul had the right idea. Don't let them have quondims at all, then they wouldn't be losing them and disturbing the whole nest. He sighed and started on his desk units.

He had been through the two upper units, sorting, tidying and rearranging as he went, the steady, mindless task soothing his mind, and had just started on the lower unit when he found it.

It sat, glowing faintly, in the back corner of the unit, looking out of place among the jumble of memory cubes, spare cables, obsolete connectors and broken calcsticks. Ya/'a/'bhei had not the faintest recollection of having ever seen it before. In fact, he realised, he didn't even know what it was. Intrigued, he picked it up to examine it more closely. As he did so, his field of vision vanished and he found himself adrift in a maelstrom of knowledge.

***

Ya/'a/'bhei's pure, intellectual curiosity prevented him, for a long time, from facing the moral dilemma Shey/'a/'tan had encountered. It simply never occurred to him, since he had found it in his own desk unit, that it was not some forgotten piece of equipment of his own. The thought that he might be holding the fabled Reality Induction Coil never entered his mind, which was wholly consumed with discovering its function.

From the first day he found it, he spent the bulk of his leisure time closeted in his Thinking Chamber with it. After several spans of cautious experimentation, and much note-taking, he had achieved a basic familiarity with the conventions, if they could be called that, by which the perceptions offered by the device were ordered. This type of sensation was atomic structure, this was distance, and so on. After much careful experimentation, he was able to map the input from the device to many actual objects.

At this point, he realised that people were also objects, and that the device's field of operation was not stopped by other things being in the way, as vision was. It was thus that he was able to confirm Rula/'bhei's suspicions about their neighbour, Popo/'von, and the meditation instructor. After a brief battle with his conscience, he decided not to inform Jockta/'a/'von about it; he assuaged his sense of responsibility by reflecting that without the device, he would have known nothing, and that it was really not his business anyway. Besides, justice, he felt, must always be tempered with mercy. That was established Wisdom.

* * *

After several more cycles, Ya/'a/'bhei was a happy Thinker. With insight gained from his increasingly skilled use of the spiral device, he had sorted out the problems he was having with the troublesome second string of equations and had published his theory to universal acclaim. Retired First Speaker Soran/'a/'gul had given an entertainment in his honour, and when he was in the plaza, young women made their eyes big and riffled their antennae seductively at him. Although the Council had indicated its willingness to allow him to take a sixth wife, Ya/'a/'bhei did not respond to their flirtatious behaviour. Five wives, he felt, was already at least three too many. They had never found the missing quondim, and he had had to buy Shonti/'bhei a replacement.

By the end of the span, he had discovered the second plate, which he had hitherto overlooked. This opened up new and exciting paths for his research, and by the middle of the Cold Span, he was able to announce his cure for the terrible Thought Malaise which afflicted so many of the old and very young, blighting promising careers and spoiling golden retirements. He was acclaimed a Hero of the Glorious Thinkers and presented with the Order of the Lemniscate, First Class, and a parade was organised in his honour.

Shey/'a/'tan watched all this with mounting displeasure. He sent for a transcript of Ya/'a/'bhei's work on the Thought Malaise, but his rival seemed to have arrived at his cure by ordinary scientific means. Shey/'a/'tan knew he had to have used the Reality Induction Coil, otherwise why had he not come up with his cure at any time during the past ten spans, but there was no flaw in the work, nothing to suggest that it hadn't been all worked out in the usual way. Only a lack of recorded failures in the experimental program bolstered his suspicion.

It was not going the way he had planned, he fretted. Ya/'a/'bhei had been supposed to get all taken up with playing with the device and neglect his work, as he had done two spans ago when the new game, mar-fong, had been all the rage. At that time he had reminded Ya/'a/'bhei sternly of his obligations, because they had been working on a joint project and he had felt Ya/'a/'bhei was not pulling his weight. That had resulted in a fury of activity in Ya/'a/'bhei's laboratory, culminating in a stunning and unexpected discovery for which Shey/'a/'tan did not share the credit, as it had been achieved by an inferential leap and had not been part of the project's original scope. It had been that more than anything, Shey/'a/'tan reflected bitterly, that had influenced the council's choice, three cycles later, when First Thinker Ise/'a/'berg had suddenly died, of Ya/'a/'bhei as his replacement.

His antennae stiffened and quivered with rage at the memory, even after so long. Nothing had gone right for him since Ya/'a/'bhei had been elevated instead of him. Their long friendship, a friendship that went all the way back to the Nursery, was tainted by it. He had always been the dominant one, and now he must defer to that... that phony credit-grabber.

***

'You're looking tired, Yaya,' he said, the next time he encountered the First Thinker in the Senior Common Room. He had been haunting the common room every evening, waiting for an opportunity, but Ya/'a/'bhei had not shown himself there for eleven revolutions.

In fact, he was not lying. Ya/'a/'bhei did look tired; there was something about the way the ends of his antennae drooped ever so slightly, adding a tinge of weariness to all his expressions.

'You should take a rest cycle,' he went on. 'Spend some time playing with that dev–' he broke off, a flash of panic running through him as he realised how nearly he had betrayed his unexplainable knowledge. 'Er, with that devoted young Fifth Wife of yours, what's her name? Little Nerit. Charming young woman. You haven't taken a rest cycle for ages,' he continued, hitting his stride. 'All work and no play makes one a dull Thinker, you know!'

'Yes, I suppose so,' said Ya/'a/'bhei listlessly.

'The tools of work can become the toys of play, too, you know,' continued Shey/'a/'tan, wondering if he was going dangerously close to the edge. 'Last cycle, I discovered a completely new function on my calcmod, just by messing about aimlessly. It pulls out all the vrek functions, you know, and gives you an aggregated psoy vector. I think sometimes it's worth a bit of time just to play with stuff, try out new things. You never know what you'll discover.'

He left it there and turned the conversation to Nu/'a/'fat's latest musical venture, which was to harmonise the space music with vastly amplified recordings of the internal sounds of pupating grubs, a move which they both agreed was a mistake.

***

Ya/'a/'bhei was indeed feeling rather worn down, and as he made his way back to his home nest, later that evening, he wondered if there might not be something in what Shey/'a/'tan had said. Good old Shey, he thought mistily. They'd been best friends since they'd hatched side by side in the Nursery. He would follow his friend's advice, he decided. Good old Shey could always be relied upon to have his best interests at heart.

Accordingly, the following day, after sleeping late, to the amazement of his wives, he dressed in his favourite, tatty old robe, which Bel/'bhei did not allow him to wear outside the nest, and settled himself on a comfortable lounge in the warmest corner of his Thinking Chamber. On the small table beside him he placed the device, and a pot of hot zem. He would spend the day playing, as Shey/'a/'tan had suggested, and see what came of it; at the very least, he'd return to work refreshed, and at best, he'd fall upon some interesting new line to take in his work.

The first several periods did not produce anything, as Ya/'a/'bhei, soothed by the softness of his lounge, by the warmth of his corner, and by the unaccustomed idleness, drifted into a happy little doze. Well, that was all good, he told himself as he shouted for someone to heat up his now-cool zem. That was the rest part of it. After lunch he'd tackle the recreational, creative part.

Lunch was a protracted affair, his five wives treating the occasion as a sort of holiday. As Ya/'a/'bhei never took any of his rest entitlement, they were unused to having him home during designated work periods. Ngoti/'bhei, he found, had exerted herself to prepare several exotic dishes, and they had all dressed in their best robes, with lashings of perfume. As Ya/'a/'bhei was accustomed to eat a spartan lunch in the workers' canteen with whomever he knew who happened to be there at the same time as he was, this caused him to feel very happy, to relax even more, and to eat three times as much as he usually did. This resulted in lunch being followed by another little nap, rather longer than the first.

He woke in high spirits. This day-off

thing was rather a lark. He felt energised and full of pizazz, ready for anything. Now, he told himself, was the bit where he'd play around with the device and have an amazing idea. He was confident that that would be the result; after all, he'd conceived the stunningly simple and elegant solution to the Thought Malaise while fiddling with the device to see how it worked. He was no closer to a real understanding of its operation, but he had a pretty fair idea now of what he could do with it. He did not ask himself why he had carefully duplicated his results with old-fashioned empirical testing, and left all mention of the device out of his published treatise.

He picked up the device and examined it, turning it over, trying to see it as if for the first time. It was a technique he'd often employed to good effect when checking his own work. Familiarity, he had found, blunted his perceptions and allowed assumptions to creep in. And so it was that, for the first time, he noticed the third control plate.

Like the second plate, this one did nothing when it alone was touched. Nor did it appear to modify in any way the function of the first plate when the two of them were held. But when he made contact with all three plates at once, then his world was forever changed.

It wasn't so much that he could see anything new; the sensory data he was receiving still all came from the first plate. But, as with the second plate he had known, with a certainty that could not be denied, that he could *affect* what he perceived, modify its state, he now knew, with a terrible, lonely knowledge, that he could *create*. And with that knowledge came the realisation that what he held, the identity of the device, from consideration of which he had so carefully steered his mind away, was, could not be other than, a Reality Induction Coil.

***

Ya/'a/'bhei knew perfectly well what his duty was. It behoved him to contact the Council immediately, disclosing his possession of the device, and moreover revealing its involvement in his recent discovery of the Thought Malaise cure. And yet, he hesitated. Would the Council respond by suppressing his discovery? And what would that mean to the many current and future sufferers from the terrible condition?

If he alerted the Council to the fact he was in possession of the Coil, Ya/'a/'bhei told himself, he could be responsible for untold suffering, and death, too, since people infected by Thought Malaise often took their own lives.

The Council's rulings did not, on their face, absolutely oblige him to give up the device. There had been no explicit provision for possession, as no such device had ever been found. The device was only known at all through interpretation of the ancient writings of the Elder Race, and as none had ever been found, the prohibition on using it had been made solely as a precaution. Therefore, if he did not use it, he would be quite within the law, he tried to convince himself. His previous use of it had been before he knew the nature of what he had, so that could be defended on the grounds of accident.

Ya/'a/'bhei pulled his robe closer. His Thinking Chamber did not seem as warm as it had done earlier. He returned the device to the bottom unit of his desk, where he had found it, and placed a spare set of Tanka tables atop it, hiding it from view. Then he returned to his lounge, and huddled miserably over his zem, which had gone cold again, until Nerit/'bhei came to summon him to dinner.

***

He sat up long past his usual time to retire, turning it over and over in his mind and reaching no conclusion. When the gong sounded First Call, he was no nearer a solution. He stayed home from the laboratory again, feeling ill and out of sorts. His wives flitted in and out of his chamber, and conversed in low tones outside his door. This irritated him so much that he finally emerged, calling for hot soup and toasted frems. In the ensuing bustle, he slipped away to his Thinking Chamber, where he took out the device and sat staring blankly at it until a timid scratch at his door announced the food was ready.

***

Ya/'a/'bhei returned to the laboratory, and the second string of equations that he had neglected for so long, but his spirit was not in the work. He continued to worry at the problem. If only he had not discovered that his wonderful device, with which he'd done so much good, was a Reality Induction Coil. He could have gone on using it, with no one ever the wiser. But stay; *did* he actually know that? After all, it was not *labelled* in any way. What if it was something else entirely? Something else capable of creation, jeered his inner voice. Right.

That night, when everyone in the nest was sleeping, Ya/'a/'bhei left his sleeping hook and crept into his Thinking Chamber.

It was only fair, he told himself as he lifted the device from the bottom unit, that he get to try it out, just once. Only fair and reasonable. No Thinker could be expected to resist such an opportunity. Besides, no one would know, if he was careful. Trembling, he engaged the three plates in their proper order, and then, before he had time to think about what he was doing, he *pushed* with his mind.

It was a very small push, and the resultant thing, whatever it was, was also very small. It was shapeless and undefined, but he could tell something was there; something had come into being, at some unspecified location, that had not existed before. He peered at it with the augmented sense the device conferred; of course it was not really peering, as vision was not involved, but he could, he found, sharpen and strengthen his perception with regard to a selected object or area.

It really was *very* shapeless. He couldn't quite make it out.

'Let there be light,' he said.

***

Shey/'a/'tan's elevation to First Thinker, following First Thinker Ya/'a/'bhei's early retirement, was an event celebrated for many revolutions. Some ungenerous people muttered that the retirement had been *forced*, a thing unthinkable, but nevertheless provided for in the vast complex of regulations that was administered and constantly embellished by the Council of Wisdom. Most, though, revered the deposed scientist for his many contributions to the Combined Knowledge, and mothers and wives of the recovered victims of Thought Malaise, now happy and productive, blessed his name. A monument was erected in his honour in Central Plaza, commemorating the cure he had developed.

As for Ya/'a/'bhei, he seemed quite happy, according to his wives, although he was rarely seen outside his nest. He spent his days shut in his Thinking Chamber, and whenever he emerged to eat or sleep, was vague and distracted, but quite happy. He was no doubt working on something very grand and important, they said.

JUST LIKE CHRISTMAS

The cereal had run out yesterday, but that was the least of Ciara's worries. She huddled on the damp mattress, wrapped around the pain. The light was starting to go, the colour leaching out of the little bit of sky she could see through the grimed window. In the evenings, everything was grey. Then Ciara, lying on her back on the mattress she'd dragged with such effort from someone's hard waste collection, would stare at the diminishing return in her window, her mind as grey and blank as the concrete walls that surrounded her.

There had been a time when Ciara had laughed and played with other girls. She could still remember it, down the long tunnel of pain and weariness and cold and fear and the endless struggle to survive, to find food, to find shelter, to find a toilet, but most of all, to find a safe and secret place to sleep, where she wouldn't risk being attacked in the night by pawing, groping hands, or wake in the morning to find her meagre belongings ransacked.

The abandoned factory, dimly remembered as the site of daring adventures in childhood, had been a godsend. Situated in an industrial wasteland a good mile from the nearest shops, it was seldom visited by anyone except roving groups of children intent on exploration, or looking for an unregulated venue for complicated skateboard contests. She occasionally saw them in the distance, but the kids were more interested in the ranks of rusted, disused machinery, or in the parking lots. She was just the crazy lady. She had heard them talking about her once. 'That's the crazy lady,' a little boy had said. 'She lives here, and she only comes out at night.' Ciara had laughed, but only a little bit. She wasn't a lady. She wasn't even fifteen yet.

It had been less than a year since It

happened. Ciara's mind shied away from giving the event a name, that terrible hot afternoon when They had surrounded her in the alley, pushing, laughing, their hard, hurting hands all over her, (*you like that, don't you, coon bitch*) and when she had come to herself later, bleeding and confused and in terrible pain, and later that night, when her mum and dad had pushed her out of the door, no time to grab anything, not really even then understanding how her life had changed (*you dirty little slut*) and the door slammed in her face and the outside light blinking off and she'd cried and begged for them to open the door and finally crept away, shamed in her blood-soaked rags, still not really understanding.

She shuddered as another pain ripped through her, laying waste to her with its intensity. They were getting worse. And she thought they were coming more often, too. Dimly she realised she should time them. Because when they got to be three minutes apart, then... another pain shook her.

She'd lost her watch, along with her Hello Kitty charm bracelet, that first night sleeping under the bridge. She had no way to tell time or count seconds, unless she switched on her mobile phone, its battery charge carefully husbanded by plugging it into the hand dryer outlet in the McDonald's loo. Sometimes she could keep it plugged in for twenty minutes before one of the ladies came to kick her out (*bloody street kids, filthy little bastards*). She'd had to nick the charger cord from a servo, the first time in her life she'd ever stolen. Well, fruit off the next door's apricot tree didn't count. You were allowed to if it hung over the fence.

The phone battery was too precious to waste. Since they'd banned her from McDonald's, it had become more and more difficult to find anywhere to charge up. Sometimes she could sneak into the library if it was busy, but you couldn't rely on that.

Ciara started counting. She counted three times before the terrifying fact registered.

The pains were two and a half minutes apart.

TEXT SENT AT 1932: mum the babys comeing plees help

***

The best thing about Roselli's Café, thought Jasper, was the way the bouncers kept the pavement clear outside, so you had a good view of the street. It was hilarious watching the nobodies and wannabes being turned away. The affront and disappointment on their little faces – priceless!

He turned from the window, back to the heaving, shouting mass of his friends. The end of exam week was always a cause for a huge bash, but Jasper and his cronies had an added edge this time; it was the end of *final* exams. In just five short months Jasper would be graduating, the proud possessor of a Juris Doctor degree. He could still hardly believe it was over. He'd had to work, and work, and work. His eyesight would never be the same again. He'd actually had to *read books*. Huge books, with tiny print that hurt his eyes. He'd had to get glasses in the end, and he'd had to turn down so many parties that he didn't think his social life would ever be the same again. Worst of all, someone – he knew, just knew it was Mitch – had started a rumour that he was turning down invitations due to a lack of funds, and his mates had been taunting him about it ever since.

'Hey, Jas,' yelled Mitch. 'We're gunna go down to Julio's, get some dinner, 'kay?'

'Hey, I just got a fresh martini,' objected Jasper.

'Aww, poor widdle Jasper, what's the matter, Jas, you on a fucking *budget* or something? You gotta make that fuckin' drink *last?*'

The crowd exploded in laughter. Jasper cursed his fair skin as he felt the blood rise to his face. The only possible response was to empty the martini over Mitch's head. Chants of 'Fight! Fight! Fight!' surged up around them, and several older couples at nearby tables looked anxiously around and started to gather their belongings.

The sky was just darkening into twilight when the group roiled out onto the pavement. It was narrow here, and the two bouncers pushed several passers-by into the gutter to make room for them. A homeless man tottering by on crutches shouted admonitions to them to 'have some respect, don't be so rough'.

As they left, Mitch kicked the homeless guy's crutches out from under him, and he went down in a screaming tangle. It was hilarious.

***

Jasper's phone dinged while he was choking the serpent. The text was from an unknown number *mum the babys comeing plees help* and he was all 'WTF, dude?' until he realised it had to be some kind of windup.

'Okay, you arseholes,' he shouted as he rejoined the three tables that had been pushed together to accommodate his group. 'Who's the joker?' He was met with blank faces, and brandished his phone. 'Come on, guys, who's the one that sent this message?'

The phone was seized and passed around the table, to cries of 'fucked if I know, dude', 'who the hell cares', 'bloody telemarketers', and one 'whoop! Treasure hunt!' There was much laughter and raillery, the general theme of which was that Jasper was a hell of a lad and it was too bad for some bitch. The tone of the conversation edged into law-student territory, centring on more and more creative defences against the maintenance application Jasper was, they said, about to face.

Jasper himself expected to specialise in commercial litigation, which was not unreasonable given his father's partnership in one of Melbourne's leading firms. Because of this expectation, which he regarded in the same light as a birthright, he had not taken the elective Family Law subject, and much of the present discussion was over his head. He avoided acknowledging this by agreeing with every third thing that was said and remaining silent the rest of the time, a technique that had never failed him.

By the time the main course arrived, he was fed up. Jasper didn't like any conversation that excluded him; such talk was elitist bullshit. He felt less in sympathy with his friends than he had ever been before, and the arrival of the food did nothing to ameliorate this. Everyone else had ordered lobster. Jasper, who was allergic to seafood and would break out in hives if he took so much as one bite of garlic prawns, had ordered Scallopini Alla Romana, the house specialty. This was greeted with hilarity by Mitch, who held forth at some length about Jasper's supposed budget, and the economy measures Mitch said he was taking, which became more creative and more vulgar with every glass of Grange Mitch downed. Jasper looked about him, reflexively ducking as a crusty roll whizzed past his head. *Pack of losers.*

Under cover of his napkin, he sneaked another look at the text.

mum the babys comeing plees help

A new thought occurred to him. Why not respond, string her along, there might be some fun in that.

who are you? he texted back. The response came swiftly.

mum its me ciara plees help im not kidding plees the babys comeing i dont kno what to do

I'm not your mother, he replied.

This time, there was no response.

***

By eleven o'clock, the restaurant was starting to empty, and the general consensus of the group was that everyone should head on down to Entitlement, the new nightclub in King Street. There were rumours that the Aga Khan had been seen there, as had Donald Trump, Malcolm Turnbull and Rupert Murdoch. The cover charge was $500, which automatically limited the clientele to those individuals with whom Jasper's friends felt comfortable. Jasper had already been there, on the club's opening night, and hadn't thought it was anything special, but he didn't dare say so with Mitch on this 'budget' kick.

Everyone was parked in different places, so the group dispersed, and as he reached the parking lot and unlocked his car, Jasper decided he'd had enough for one night. He didn't feel like spending another three or four hours drinking and shouting to be heard over deafening music. He didn't give a toss if the Aga Khan was there, not even if Elvis was his date.

What he wanted, he realised, was a change. Something different. Not another polo match, not another wild night of wasting expensive liquor, not another meaningless round of casual (but carefully safe) sex. He wanted excitement, he wanted adventure. Above all, he wanted novelty, and so too did the vodka martini and the three glasses of Grange he had consumed. As he drove out into the gaiety of Chinatown, the dark sky seemed to beckon him to things unknown. *Points North,* sounded a dimly remembered phrase from his childhood, carrying with it the romance of snow-covered peaks in moonlight, and the Northern Lights.

His phone dinged again, and he pulled it out and held it up in front of the wheel.

mum i know you kicked me out but the babys comeing i dont kno who else to call plees help

Jasper's lips quirked upward and his eyes sparked with excitement. Hunting horns sounded in his head. He'd find the Mystery Woman, that's what he'd do. What a lark! 'Tally-ho!' he shouted, and turned left.

He was into the Docklands before the early-evening martini abruptly deserted him, and he realised he didn't know if he was heading in the right direction. He pulled over.

where are you?

im in the old bonds factory plees hurry i hurt so bad

where is it?

mum you know where it is you know the old factory

we used to go past there to the shops when we lived in howard st

There was a knock on the window. Jasper looked up to see a policeman. He lowered the window.

'Sorry, mate, you're in a No Standing.'

Jasper's sense of entitlement, never very far from the surface, rose up in outrage. 'Piss off, can't you see I'm busy?'

***

Three quarters of an hour later, a chastened Jasper started his car, buckled his seatbelt and drove slowly and quietly away. He had been fined for parking in a No Standing Area, for failing to indicate a right hand turn, and had been given a notice to repair his offside mirror, which Jasper didn't think had had anything wrong with it before the second policeman had gone around that side. He had been breathalysed three times, each time registering, so they said, 0.04. He had been treated to a long, slow lecture about many things, including but not limited to politeness, compliance with traffic signs, his bad attitude and the almost unlimited *de facto* scope of police powers. Every time he had said anything, it had started again, even more slowly, and in the end he had subsided, nodding respectfully and waiting until it finished.

He drove for a few blocks, making sure he was well away before pulling over to check his phone again. There had been two more texts.

mum are you comeing

and then, twenty minutes later

mum theres a lot of blood i think somthings wrong

That one had been sent more than a quarter of an hour ago. There had been no further texts.

For the first time, Jasper experienced a moment of anxiety. The mention of blood made him feel queasy. Blood didn't happen. It was just in the movies, blood was. He had a sensation of slippage, as if he were losing his grip on the world he inhabited, sliding out into a dark territory where things like blood were really a thing.

Are you still there? he texted back, and waited in the dark for the answering ding. It was a long time coming, and with every minute, with every second that passed, he slipped farther from the comfortable cradle of his Jasper-centric world. The response, when it came, did nothing to reassure him.

mum

Then, nothing.

Stay calm, Jasper told himself. He scrolled back through the previous texts. She'd mentioned a street... yes, Howard Street.

we used to go past there to the shops when we lived in howard st

So it must be within a short distance of Howard Street. He called up Google Maps on his phone. There were four Howard Streets in Melbourne. Three were in inner-city suburbs, and he discounted them, as land values were too high in those areas to allow old factories to remain. He texted again.

Is it the one in Reservoir?

No response. It had to be, though. He set his GPS and pulled out. The app said it would be twenty-seven minutes to Howard Street, and then if she didn't answer he'd just have to drive round until he found the factory.

Mindful of the police, Jasper drove carefully and did not exceed the speed limit. The few minutes he might gain were not worth the risk of another three-quarter-hour delay. He was in Preston before the phone dinged again, twice in quick succession.

yes in resi

MITCH McKENZIE: *Hey Jas where the fuck are you mate the place is hopping get your arse here unless you can't afford the cover hehe*

Jasper tutted in irritation and deleted the message. At least he knew he'd picked the right Howard Street, but he still had to find the actual place.

How are you doing? Still okay? he sent.

im not ok it hurts so bad and theres blood everywhere mum im scard

Right there with you, Jasper wanted to say. He was scared now, too. The reality of the situation had finally penetrated. If he didn't find her in time... it was life or death. 'Life or death,' he muttered to himself. Jesus. For the first time, he wondered if he was equal to the demands of the situation. It had all been such a lark, but now, it wasn't funny any more.

stay with me, he texted. *I need you to tell me the name of the street you're in.*

sloan st

Sloan Street, Sloan Street... Google

Maps didn't seem to think there was any such street. Where the hell was that old Melways? Not in the glovebox... not under the seat... damn, damn, damn. He shifted into neutral and pulled on the handbrake, and leapt out to run to the back of the car and rummage in the boot.

The tattered old Melways eventually came to light, half under the spare wheel. Jasper's hands were filthy by the time he got it out. He wiped them down his sides, remembering, too late, his pale blue cashmere sweater.

Never mind that now. It would either clean or it would not. Switching on the ceiling light, he flipped to the index. Sloan Street did not exist, but there was a Sloane Street. Jasper cursed himself. He'd had plenty of evidence the woman couldn't spell.

It was faster, now that he had the Melways out, to turn to the map and find it the old-fashioned way. He was, he realised, only three blocks from his destination. He tossed the directory onto the passenger street, switched off the ceiling light and pulled out.

The factory was not difficult to find; it loomed above the surrounding houses like a dinosaur among grazing sheep, a vast bulk of blackness. The street lights didn't penetrate past the first few rows of the huge, empty parking lot. Jasper drove in through the open gateway and parked right outside the main entrance, in defiance of the faded signs of admonition. The double glass doors were securely locked. He resorted to his phone again.

where in the factory are you

A long minute passed, and another. There was no reply.

how do I get in?

Again, no answering text. Shit. Was she unconscious? Dead? Jasper shuddered. She couldn't be dead, she was having a baby for fuck's sake, not open heart bloody surgery. He racked his brain for everything he knew about childbirth, which didn't take long, as he knew, he realised, basically nothing. He texted again.

are you okay?

Stupid, he chided himself, stupid. Of course she isn't bloody okay.

A small part of Jasper's mind screamed in horror as he opened the boot and took out his tyre iron.

It wasn't as easy to smash the glass

doors as he'd expected. It took three blows of the iron, swinging with all his strength, before a spiderweb of cracks appeared.

So far Jasper, impending law graduate, had committed, he realised, both Trespass and Criminal Damage, and he was now in the process of committing Burglary. As he stepped through the ruined door, he wondered with part of his mind whether he wasn't even committing Aggravated Burglary, since he knew, or believed, that there was someone in the building. A thing like that could prevent you being admitted as a lawyer.

A few feet from the door, the darkness became absolute, and Jasper blessed God and Mr Gates for the flashlight function on his phone. He found a light switch, but nothing happened when he flicked it. Well, it stood to reason they'd cut off the power.

From the reception area, a corridor stretched out in both directions.

'Hello?' he called. 'It's me, Jasper. Where are you?'

There was no answering shout, but very faintly, Jasper thought he could hear a faint crying sound, like a child sobbing.

'Hello?'

There was nothing but the faint crying, and even that he wasn't sure of. It could be the wind, or a loose bit of something, or plumbing. Plumbing could, Jasper thought, make sounds, although he had no idea why or how. He switched off his light and turned slowly in the dark, his whole mind funnelled into his hearing, trying to get a fix on the source of the sound. It was, he thought, slightly louder to the left. He set out down the corridor, moving cautiously, but as quickly as he could manage in the dark.

He'd have done better to use more caution and less speed, he realised a few moments later as something slammed him in the face. Dear God, the pain. Was his nose broken? Belatedly he fumbled for his phone and switched the light back on. He had come to a T intersection in the corridor, he saw, and had discovered it the hard way.

He was listening again, turning blindly, when he realised he held the answer in his hand. Cursing himself for nine kinds of idiot, he called the number, and heard, far off down the dark tunnel to his right, the strains of Waltzing Matilda.

He hit 'redial' at the end of the long corridor, and heard again the tinny little tune. The crying sound was louder now, and he was quite sure it wasn't plumbing. He called again, his words swallowed by the dark, and followed the new direction, which took him through a heavy door and down a long, cavernous room where clerestory windows cast a faint, ghostly light on silent ranks of machinery. He paused at the end, his ears straining, but the crying had stopped. A final call, and the tune sounded behind a door he hadn't seen, so close that he jumped in startled recognition. A turn of the handle and he found her, his nose raising a baffled question as he came through the last door (what *was* that smell?) and then the frightening sight, seen only dimly and a bit at a time in the torchbeam, *so much blood* and the tiny, frail body *dear God she's only a kid* with its grossly swollen belly. At first he thought he was too late, after all his effort and the last frantic run down that endless corridor, but he saw her chest move and *yes she's alive oh please please* he gathered her up, careless of the blood getting all over him and backed out, slowing only the minimum to avoid crashing into anything.

He hesitated as he reached the car, wondering should he prop her in the front seat and buckle her in, but in the end he laid her on the back seat. That was a minute or two saved, and he turned the car in a wide, screeching turn and roared back towards town, and light, and safety because he didn't know what there was out here but he knew where the Royal Women's Hospital was.

***

They gave him some grief when he pulled into the emergency entrance, but he powered on through, lifting his precious burden from the back seat and rushing in through the automatic doors, bellowing for a nurse until they came with a stretcher and rushed her away through another pair of doors, an oxygen mask already covering the small, parchment-coloured face.

They wanted a lot of forms filled in then, buzzing around him like mosquitoes, but his platinum Mastercard seemed to satisfy them, confirming his belief in the essential primacy of the dollar, and the single nurse that remained grabbed his elbow and rushed him like a whirlwind through a labyrinth of corridors that, in their pristine shiny whiteness, seemed the negative of those where he had so lately been.

He tried to explain, to ask, but no one was listening, they were like automata, able to perform only their programmed functions as they stuffed him into a surgical gown and mask and frog-marched him through another set of doors, where he almost fainted when he saw what was confronting him. No, he tried to tell them, I shouldn't be here, it's private, but they urged him on (*look, you can see the top of his head*) and it was only when he buckled at the knees, retching, that the nurse let go her iron grip and they allowed him to retreat to the top end, to hold the girl's hand and smooth the hair from her sweated face.

She was half-conscious now, groggy from whatever they'd given her, but her eyes tracked him, she knew he was there.

'Hi there,' he said awkwardly. 'Hell of a thing, eh? I'm the person you've been texting. See, I told you I wasn't your mum.'

Her voice, when she spoke, was a cracked little whisper, like dead leaves skittering over concrete.

'Mum... I thought... when you said you weren't my mum, I thought she was just... you know.' Tears sprang up in the brown eyes. 'They kicked me out when...'

'Hey, none of that. You can't be crying when you're having a baby, you know. It's against the rules.'

'Rules?'

'Yep! Demarcation dispute. Crying's the baby's job, see? You start, you'll have the union after your guts.' He was losing her, he saw, the joke going right over her head. God, she was just a kid. Keep it light.

'So, my name's Jasper. What's your name?'

'Ciara.' The cracked little whisper again.

'Ciara. Pretty name, it means 'light', did you know that?'

'Ohhhhh...' she cried, stiffening.

'That's right, love,' came from the foot of the bed. 'Bear down now, lovey. Push, push...'

Jesus, thought Jasper wildly, I have to get out of here. This is... I can't do this. But she was clutching his hand, almost cutting off the circulation. He supposed he couldn't just do a runner now, he was in it up to his neck and the nurses seemed to think he was the kid's husband, or her father or something. With his free hand he managed to get out his handkerchief and wipe the sweat from his forehead, and then, as an afterthought, from Ciara's.

'Want a sip of water, mate? Hey, nurse, can we get some water, please?'

'She's getting fluids from the I.V., don't worry. She can have some cracked ice if she's feeling dry. You want some ice to suck, sweetie?' The nurse left the room. That left only three clustered around the bottom end of the bed.

Shit, Jasper wanted to say, what about me? I'm not getting any fluids from the fucking I.V. But he held his peace. This wasn't about him. He'd get a drink as soon as this was over. Surely it couldn't be much longer?

The nurse returned, bearing a paper cup of ice. 'Hey, how much longer?'

'Not long now. Your first, is it? Don't worry. You'll be a proud dad in no time.' Jasper wanted to punch the smug look off his face. He opened his mouth to deny having anything to do with the baby, but stopped himself – they'd chuck him out if they realised he was a total stranger, and then the poor kid would be left all on her own. It didn't sound like her mum and dad were likely to be supportive, even if they were there. For the first time, he wondered what would happen to her now. He'd got only a glimpse of the room where he'd found her, of the dismal nest with the bare, blood-soaked mattress and the dingy blanket, but she obviously couldn't go back there, not with a baby. She couldn't go back there anyway.

He'd talk to the staff as soon as this was over. There must be a social worker, or a chaplain, or something. They'd figure something out. There was a sudden flurry of activity at the other end of the bed. Jasper cringed and turned his shoulder even farther round, trying to shut out the voices.

Ciara stiffened, her back arching, tears spilling and rolling down her face. Cries of 'push! push!' came from behind him. He felt his own muscles stiffening in sympathy. God, he'd never look down on anyone with a kid again, if this was what they went through. First thing when he got out of here, he was going to buy his mother some flowers. He gritted his teeth against the smaller pain as she crushed the bones in his hand.

'Right, I've got him... Okay, relax now. You've done great.' There was a bustle behind him and an appalling-looking object was thrust into his view. God, it was horrible. Was there something wrong with it? It was wizened, like a monkey.

'Congratulations, you have a beautiful daughter!' said the nurse. Jasper thought she was overstating it somewhat. As Ciara reached weary arms to hold the child, he recoiled from the slimy thing. What's that stuff all over it, he wanted to ask. Can't you clean it up first? And then it moved its hand, and his heart turned over and his world remade itself.

He felt hot tears start to his eyes, and his nose was beginning to run. He started to ask the nurse for a tissue, but Ciara was smiling, a smile of such sweetness, such joy, that his words died in his throat. It was the first time, he realised, that he'd seen her smile.

'Thank you,' came the raspy little whisper.

***

The sun was rising as Jasper came

down the steps, the first rays slanting oblique and golden through the surrounding buildings. His car was not where he'd left it. They'd had it towed, he supposed, or perhaps someone had driven it away; it occurred to him that he had left the keys in it and the engine running. It didn't matter. He'd find out later. For now, all he wanted was a hot shower, clean clothes and a huge breakfast.

The day stretched ahead, empty. He could go home and sleep now, sleep till evening and then catch up with the gang. But then he thought of all the things he wanted to do. There was the chaplain and the social worker to be found, and some kind of arrangements made for Ciara and baby Jaspah. He grinned hugely. Who'd have thought he'd get a baby named after him? He had promised to be its godfather. Her godfather, he corrected himself. Yeah, he'd better go and buy the baby a present. There was shopping to be done for Ciara too, he realised. She had come to the hospital with nothing. He'd get himself cleaned up, and by that time it would be after nine and he'd organise an appointment with the social worker or whoever, and then he'd go shopping, and

then there would be visiting hours...
It was just like Christmas.

Also by Tabitha Ormiston-Smith

NOVELS

Dance of Chaos (Fiona MacDougall Book 1): Lazy, frivolous, conceited and totally self centred, Fiona MacDougall is not an asset to the workforce. When she applies for a transfer to the Infotech department of her company, she does so only in order to get an afternoon off work.

Can she succeed in her challenging new job?

Can she save her little brother from the consequences of his evil deeds?

Will Moses do something embarrassing to the vicar's leg again?

Laugh till you drop as you watch the hapless Fiona at work and in the bosom of her dysfunctional family.

Gift of Continence (Fiona MacDougall Book 2): With the perfect wedding dress, what can go wrong? A great deal, as Fiona McDougall rapidly discovers. From the wedding from hell onwards, Fiona successively discovers that her new husband is stingy, bad-tempered and an adulterer.

Where The Heart Is: Widowed, broke and unemployed, Fiona moves to the country to save money. But she is not prepared for the realities of country life… or for whom she will meet.

The Secret Summer of Peter Fotheringay: Left at boarding school over the Christmas holidays, Peter expects to have a boring time. But when he goes exploring in the school's disused attic, he finds something that will change his world forever.

Bloodsucking Bogans: Dingo Flats hasn't been the same since the Murphy family moved back to town. The boys are delinquents, the daughter's a disgrace, and old Granny Murphy is constantly causing trouble. Even the dogs are delinquents. The crime rate's doubled since they arrived.

And what's with all the dead rats that have started appearing on the doorsteps of local businesses? The tabloid thinks it's a plague, but Sam's dad is convinced it's warnings from the Mafia.

Meanwhile, Sam's friends are determined to make her over and marry her off, and she's staring down the barrel of having to give up her police dog pup. What's a cop to do?

Reality Ever After: Rosalie can't remember much about her life before she was ill. Her life in the Gorgon Hotel is the same every day. But lately, Rosalie has started to dream, and the things she sees in her dreams are starting to make her think there is something very wrong at the Gorgon Hotel.

COLLECTION

Once Upon A Dragon: Collected short fiction. A non-themed, cross-genre collection of short fiction, including fantasy, science fiction and horror as well as general fiction.

NOVELLAS

No Such Thing: Twelve-year-old Callie has taken on the responsibility of running the house and looking after her father, following her parents' divorce. When the bank threatens to foreclose on their home, Callie is forced to admit that this is a problem even she can't solve, until help comes from an unexpected quarter. But Callie learns that all actions have consequences, and sometimes the price for getting what you want can be too high...

Melanie's Diary: Melanie's life is out of control. Her status-hungry parents have forced her grandmother into a home, and she's under siege from the school bully. But things are going to get a lot worse before they get better...

Dancing Feet: Ashley is devastated when her widowed father returns from his business trip with a new wife and her two daughters in tow. Pushed to one side by the interlopers, can she make a new life for herself?

A modern-day Cinderella

interpretation.

Operation Tomcat (Operation Tomcat Book 1): Left almost penniless after divorcing her cheating husband, Tammy moves to the country to reinvent her life. But life in a country town isn't as simple as it looks...

Operation Camilla (Operation Tomcat Book 2): A sleazy solicitor hacks into a dating website in order to boost his failing family law practice. But he doesn't count on Tom...

Operation Badger (Operation Tomcat Book 3): Detective Senior Constable Ben Jackson is handsome, kind, diligent, dedicated and a total mensch. He's also as thick as two planks.

His girlfriend, Tammy, is clever as anything, but sillier than a wet hen.

And then there is Tom. Tom is a cat.

NON-FICTION

Grammar Without Tears: Historical and fictional characters explain common grammatical errors in a funny-as-hell book that will forever change the way you see grammar.

Fifty Shades of Grammar: Everyone, it's said, has one book inside him, but getting it out can be problematical. Perhaps you can't English very well, or you work long hours and just don't have time, or you started writing and then got stuck? Fear not, for help is at hand.

Packed with friendly, no-nonsense advice, Fifty Shades of Grammar will answer all those questions you were too afraid to ask. From sentence structure to punctuation, from setting up your workspace to support your efforts to overcoming the dreaded 'writer's block', from traps and pitfalls to avoid to editing, the problems faced by the novice writer are clearly addressed – and with LOLCATS!

With this book at your side, the only variables will be your talent and your commitment.

ABOUT THE AUTHOR

Tabitha Ormiston-Smith was born and continues to age. Dividing her time between her houses in Melbourne and in the country, she is ably assisted in her editing business and her other endeavours by Ferret, the three-legged bandit.

CONTACT

Facebook:
http://www.facebook.com/Tabitha.OrmistonSmith

Email:
tabitha.ormiston.smith@gmail.com

Amazon:
https://www.amazon.com/Tabitha-Ormiston-Smith/e/B004TE35RS